LOVERS OF THE DAMNED

DEMON'S *Desire*

COLETTE RIVERA

Frustration shouldn't
feel this good.

Edited by Hummingbird Editing

Proofreading by CJ Editing

Cover design by We Got You Covered Book Design

People depicted in the cover image are models and should not be associated with the book.

Interior Illustrations by Angelika Süto, Angki.s_

ISBN

Print: 978-1-991284-10-5

Kindle: 978-1-991284-11-2

AUTHOR'S NOTE

Dear reader,

This book deals with adult themes and is intended for mature audiences. You may wish to note that there are some Dom/Sub elements in this couple's relationship—mostly in the bedroom, but they do not adhere to a strict Dom/Sub dynamic —and that this book features two people who are non-monogamous. Specifically, the couple ends up in an exclusive romantic relationship where, together, they are open to sexual relationships with others in the future. This aspect of their relationship is discussed between the characters, but does not occur on-page. They discuss their boundaries and expectations, and there is no drama around this aspect of their relationship.

If you wish to view a list of possible triggers, they can be found in the final paragraph of this note. Please take care and use your discretion.

Demon's Desire is part of a series with an overarching plot. If you haven't started the *Lovers of the Damned* series, it's recommended to begin with *Demon's Mate*, though each book features a different couple. The romance in *Demon's Desire* stands alone and ends in a happily ever after, but every question you have about the external story and the world won't be answered by the end. You can expect a minor, series-related cliffhanger.

Content Guidance & Trigger Warnings: (may contain spoilers) Magical and physical violence. Blood-drinking demons—similar to vampires. Mention of witches who worship Satan. Mention of antagonists involved in human trafficking. Mentions of a side character who escaped an abusive relationship in the past. Sexual content: intended for mature audiences. Spanking and bondage. Please note the characters in this book possess magic & supernatural healing abilities. Therefore, this is not meant to be a realistic representation of spanking, bondage, or aftercare in the real world.

LOVERS OF THE DAMNED

DEMON'S Desire

COLETTE RIVERA

1

———

ONYX

"THIS IS AN ART GALLERY, not a coffee shop." Onyx pushed past Ash and Dante, who stood in his foyer as if they were welcome to stroll in any time they liked.

They were not.

Ollie had come in with them today, and Onyx tried to reserve his contempt for his demon brothers, smiling apologetically at the human.

Ash glared, his hulking presence nowhere near as intimidating as he tried to make it. "Why are you yelling? No one could ever confuse this with a coffee shop."

"I'm not yelling." Onyx clenched his teeth, his voice barely raised.

Gallery Four was his space. His work. A legacy he was proud of. Why did his brothers have to barge in? Ash had no respect for anything. It was only a matter of time before he knocked over a sculpture. Damn oversized brute.

"We're sorry to bother you." Ollie eyed his companions as if he hoped they'd back him up.

"I know *you* are." Onyx tone lost its icy edge. "If you'd come by yourself, I'd have been delighted. You could have at least left Ash behind. He's never here to say a friendly hello."

Ash muttered something undecipherable.

Dante slipped an arm around Ollie's shoulders, eyes on Onyx. "You didn't answer your phone."

Onyx stalked to the reception desk. "If only you'd take the hint."

Scott, Gallery Four's curator, wasn't working today. If he were, Onyx might have forced everyone out. This visit smelled of magic business. Scott was human and provided a nice buffer, an excuse not to talk about whatever shit Ash and Dante were trying to saddle him with this time.

Onyx sat behind the desk and opened the laptop, waking the screen. "I have things to do. I'm showing a new artist soon, and there's a lot to coordinate before the opening. Unless you're buying one of the pieces on display, you need to leave. We aren't open to the public."

Gallery Four operated by appointment only.

Ollie extricated himself from his mate's hold and approached the desk. "Come on, we aren't the public. Harper is on his way. After we talk, why don't the three of us get lunch?"

Onyx's lips twitched, but he recovered his scowl. "Depends on where we're going."

"Your choice. I don't know any good restaurants in this neighborhood."

Onyx stole a glance at Ollie. Fuck, he had a face that was impossible to say no to. Soft, round cheeks cut with dimples and tumbling hair befitting a stylist. "We'll see. I'm not lying about being busy."

"I didn't think you were. But if you don't want us stopping by, bothering you, then you have to return the demons' calls."

Onyx focused on the computer screen, ignoring the twinge in his gut. He didn't care if his so-called brothers only came around if they had to. Only if they wanted something. It wasn't like Onyx wanted to spend time with them.

The front door opened, saving Onyx from responding to Ollie as Harper walked in, his gaze immediately landing on his mate.

Onyx couldn't imagine what Harper saw in Ash—the universe's most insufferable being—but Onyx was glad Ash made Harper happy. The young witch deserved it.

"Sorry we're late." Harper planted a kiss on Ash's cheek.

A second witch entered Gallery Four.

Onyx's spine stiffened. "What is *he* doing here?"

Nico Velázquez glanced around the gallery, running a hand through his short dark brown hair. "I thought we were having a meeting?"

Dante flipped the sign in the window to closed. "We are, and we're glad you could make it."

The nerve!

Onyx stood, his demon fire flaring within. "Excuse me. I didn't invite any of you here. You don't get to close my gallery whenever you feel like it."

"I thought you wanted me in on this." Nico turned his warm gaze on Onyx, whose inner fire burned to the point of pain.

"What would I want with you? You're no one but the witch who discovered my identity without my consent. Nothing going on here concerns you."

Nico's brow furrowed. The guy was annoyingly handsome with his brown skin and captivating dark eyes, his face soft and inviting like he was begging for your secrets. Onyx liked the look of his rough, stubble-lined jaw a little too much.

Onyx curled his lip at Nico's sheer size. Another tall menace. The group had too many of those—everyone but Onyx and Ollie—and Nico's thick build didn't help. Onyx was sick of men who acted like being big was impressive.

Nico stood like he had authority. Over what, Onyx couldn't imagine. Handsome or not, his presence made Onyx's nerves itch.

"Things concerned me the moment hordes of demons entered the Human Realm," Nico said as if the exodus from Hell was dire news. To him, it probably was, but that wasn't Onyx's problem.

Onyx marched from behind the desk, gaining on Nico until they were almost chest to chest. He pointed his nose in the air imperiously. Onyx wasn't looking up because he was short; he was posturing.

He fixed Nico with a flame-flecked stare, his magic rising to the surface. "I didn't give you permission to be here, so why don't you go be concerned about demons somewhere else?"

Nico swallowed, and Onyx tracked his bobbing Adam's apple. The witch was nervous. Good. An overpowering waft of citrus and earth filled the air, and electricity zipped along Onyx's spine.

That was odd.

Nico cleared his throat. "Sorry to bother you. I'll see myself out."

The waver in his voice was disproportionately satisfying. At least Nico wasn't stupid.

"No, wait." Dante moved to block the door. "*We* invited you. Onyx, we need to talk, including Nico. Can't you behave?"

Onyx's cheeks flamed, and fire threatened to erupt from his fingertips. "I'm not the one being rude."

Harper appeared at Onyx's side, reaching out and lightly brushing his arm. "Please, Onyx. It's not Nico's fault he found out your identity. It's mine."

Onyx deflated. He didn't want to hate Harper and needed to stop fucking up with him. "It's no one's fault. It's fine. Whatever. Just tell me why you're invading my gallery and then leave me alone."

Harper flashed him a small smile, and Onyx's gut twisted. He hadn't exactly succeeded in being nice. Harper was too sweet to him.

To Onyx's surprise, Nico spoke first, his nervousness banished or at least hidden. Onyx would need to work on that, keep the man off balance. Scaring Nico the night they met had been the most thrilling thing he'd done in quite a while.

As an immortal, you had to chase any high you could. It was the only way to keep eternal life interesting.

"I need to tell Rowan what happened in the Realm of the Damned," Nico said. "The magic world has to know that demons returned to Earth en masse. Shearwater Landing has to prepare if more demons are settling here. We can't wait much longer, or we risk people being caught off guard and lashing out."

"What good is telling a vampire who owns a strip club?" Onyx crossed his arms and glared at Nico. "Getting the word out is a lot more complicated than telling your buddy. Not that the public needs to know what happened between Lucifer and the three of us."

"I don't even know what happened between you and Lucifer," Nico said patiently. "All I know is demons escaped confinement. After a thousand years without demons, the world is going to change. The balance of power is going to shift, and I don't want it to blow up."

"We can take care of getting the word out." Onyx turned away, wishing there was clutter around, anything to busy himself with. "You and your stripping vampire friend don't need to get involved."

"Rowan doesn't dance at the club. At least not often. But he does need to be involved. His coven is well placed to spread the news and powerful enough to help us control how this goes."

"Then we'll talk to him." Onyx spun back around, making a shooing gesture. "You can go."

Ash lumbered forward. "What is your problem today?"

"You're my problem every day, Ash."

"We need an introduction to Rowan," Dante cut in, trying to keep the peace as usual. "He can help, but he doesn't need to know all our identities or personal troubles with Luc. Onyx, you can go with Nico to talk to him—"

"*Me?*" Onyx didn't know who to glare at. Dante, Ash, and Nico were all pissing him off. "Why don't *you* go? You love shmoozing."

Dante's jaw muscle ticked. "Ash and I are busy tracking Lucifer, and I'm trying to see what I can teach my flock about recognizing demons when they're hiding their power and we don't have specific descriptions to go on."

Of course they were conveniently occupied. "I'm busy too."

"Planning parties?" Ash sneered.

Onyx might actually kill him one of these days. Not permanently, but still. "I'm busy running a renowned gallery."

Nico stepped closer. Did the witch have a death wish? "It would be good to have your help. You can make sure Rowan doesn't find out anything you don't want him to know about you, and you'll be up to speed on exactly what's happening."

It would be nice not to be left out of the loop for once.

Onyx shook his head. "I'd be up to speed if people updated me." He shot a look at Dante.

But Nico wasn't done. "You're good with people, and your skills would be beneficial here."

Onyx whipped back around. "How the hell did you come to that conclusion? Good with people? I barely held back from setting you on fire when we met."

Nico swallowed again. Excellent, the nervousness was back. Nico gestured to a painting. "You run Gallery Four. You must be good with people. We need someone adept at moving between the magic and human worlds."

"Intermingling isn't exactly Ash's strong suit," Harper added, though kindly.

Ash had lived like a hermit for decades, so that was an understatement, and Dante spent too much time with his shearwaters.

"I am better with humans than either of you."

"See." Dante clapped him on the shoulder, and Onyx shook him off. "You're the best demon for the job."

Dammit. A tiny bit of praise, and he'd walked right into that. Now he was stuck.

2

———

NICO

Nico shouldn't have been satisfied to see the fight in Onyx fade, but it felt like a win.

"Fine. I'll come with you to talk to the vampire and be the demon face of this bullshit. But I don't want magical beings showing up here willy-nilly afterward. My life in the human world is separate, and the gallery is off limits." Onyx's stare bored into Nico, the chill palpable.

"Anyone with concerns can see me at The Herb Emporium," Nico assured him. "I'm more approachable anyway."

Onyx sniffed, and his lip curled. "Only because I aim for unapproachable."

It was funny that Onyx thought helping might bring him unwanted attention. Beings in the magic world finding out he was not only the aloof owner of a business catering to the elite, but a demon, would make him more intimidating, not less.

Onyx had nothing to worry about. Witches weren't going to come to him for help, especially when he acted like he was on the verge of biting everyone's heads off.

Nico shouldn't have found his viciousness hot. He wasn't usually into danger, but maybe a little fear would do him good.

Something had been missing in his life, and he didn't hate the idea of working with Onyx. Nico liked a challenge.

"Now that's settled, can we get lunch?" Ollie asked.

Onyx's hard edges softened as he turned his attention toward the human. "Great idea. Ash, Dante, you're dismissed."

Ash rolled his eyes and stormed out.

Nico wasn't sorry to see him go. He couldn't figure out if Ash liked him or not. Ash never passed up an opportunity to intimidate, seeming to love subtle and not-so-subtle threats alike. He acted as if Nico was about to betray Harper at every turn, even though Ash had to know that wasn't true by now.

Dante kissed Ollie and said goodbye, following Ash.

Onyx turned to Nico. "You can go too."

Nico crossed his arms, his brow raising. "You're dismissing me?" They didn't know each other well enough for that to be anything other than blatantly rude.

"Obviously." Onyx's hard edges snapped back into place. His fair cheeks flushed slightly, and his eyes darkened, not quite burning with blue fire, but cold enough to sting.

He was a head shorter than Nico, and if he hadn't been immortal—and in possession of the strength that came with that —Nico would have called him delicate.

Onyx's appearance was deceptive. His stature didn't make him any less intimidating than Ash or Dante. If anything, Onyx was the one Nico feared most. He had the air of a man out to prove himself, and the way he'd lashed out when Nico had first met him on the rooftop of Rowan's club told him that Onyx was unpredictable and had a serious temper.

All up, it was a dangerous combo.

But it wouldn't be good to show any hint of fear. Someone like Onyx would pounce on it.

"Why don't I go to lunch with you guys, and we can meet Rowan after?"

Onyx bristled. "Meet Rowan today? Did no one hear that I was busy, or are you purposely ignoring me?"

Nico didn't acknowledge the challenge in his tone, remaining calm. "I'm not ignoring or dismissing you. I'm sure you have a lot to do for your opening. I can't even imagine running a gallery. But we need to get on this. If we didn't have to give Rowan a heads up that we're coming by, I'd say we skip lunch and talk to him immediately."

Even as a friend, Nico didn't like dropping in on Rowan unannounced. Between running the Valero Coven and his various enterprises, Rowan had a lot on his plate. It made Nico glad he wasn't associated with a coven. The freedom to duck in and out of Rowan's business suited Nico and allowed him to look after his own priorities.

Besides, to join Rowan officially, Nico would have to become a vampire, and that was never a life he'd wanted.

Onyx swept back his blue hair, and Nico wondered what his natural color was. Dark like his eyebrows, or were they dyed too? "Fine. Lunch, then the vampire strip club, then everyone leaves me the fuck alone."

Nico grinned. "That wasn't so hard, was it?"

Onyx's mouth opened and shut, his cheeks darkening. He pushed past, looping an arm through one of Ollie's and one of Harper's, and guided the two young men toward the door.

Nico followed. Seemed he'd struck a nerve.

Did Onyx actually mind helping, or was there some other reason he fought so hard against every suggestion? Nico shook off the question and pulled out his phone, shooting off a text to Rowan.

After locking up, Onyx led them to a small bistro around the corner, where they were seated in the courtyard.

Nico lifted an edge of the crisp white tablecloth. "Fancy lunch."

"Hardly." Onyx unfurled his napkin with a flourish and set it on his lap. "My treat, little mates." He nudged the menus closer to Harper and Ollie, then frowned at Nico, his brow scrunching.

Nico swallowed a laugh. "You don't have to buy me lunch. I'm a big boy."

"Good because I wasn't going to." Onyx picked up his menu. "Not that I'm babying you," he said to the others.

"We know." Ollie looked like he was fighting a smile. "It's no secret that neither of us can afford to eat at half the places you like."

Nico glanced at the menu. Fuck. One meal wouldn't break the bank, but he wasn't coming back here in a hurry.

Onyx pointed out various dishes to Harper and Ollie, explaining what was good about each one. He seemed to know the boys' tastes well.

"Do you three go out together often?" Nico asked.

Harper put his menu down. "Not yet. Ollie hasn't been mated long, and with everything going on, some of our plans got delayed, but Onyx is going to take us on a food tour of the city."

"How nice of you."

Onyx squirmed in his seat. "Whatever. It's not an open invitation."

"Didn't think it was. Besides, Ash might not like me tagging along. He probably thinks I spend enough time with Harper at work."

Onyx's head tilted. "Ash doesn't like you?"

Nico shrugged.

"He likes you," Harper insisted, not for the first time.

"Well, it doesn't matter because Ash isn't invited either." Onyx disappeared behind his menu.

Interesting. Did Onyx not like the other demons any more

than he liked Nico? Either way, he definitely had a soft spot for their mates.

Relief loosened the tightness in Nico's chest. He worried about Harper and Ollie. They were young, at least ten years younger than Nico's thirty-five, and they'd been swept up in this whole fated mate thing so quickly.

Ash, Dante, and Onyx were legends in the magic world. The Hounds of Hell, formerly Lucifer's closest allies, and now apparent enemies. They were thousands of years old. Being bound to one of them came with a huge risk of being taken advantage of. It was so much worse than the risk of binding yourself to your sire to become a vampire.

Nico didn't like the power imbalance between the demons and their mates, especially human Ollie, and especially considering the telepathic element and irreversible nature of the bond. Everyone—including Harper and Ollie—claimed Ash and Dante treated the boys right, and Nico had never seen anything to the contrary, but the mating bond was hard to get his head around.

How could you trust someone enough to go through with it? How could you be meant for one person? Had Harper and Ollie accepted immortality easily? If they hadn't, Nico wasn't aware.

Harper knew he could turn to Nico with anything—Ollie, too. If the situation turned out to be problematic, Nico would get them out. Somehow.

It was a relief that Onyx's animosity didn't extend to the boys. If it came down to it, perhaps Onyx would take their side, even against the other demons.

When the waiter came, Nico ordered a side salad and water. He had plenty of food at home, and considering it was Sunday, Lucia, his older neighbor, was probably going to saddle him with half of whatever she was cooking.

Onyx's stare burned into the side of Nico's head as he ordered, but Nico refused to look at him. He didn't care if he couldn't afford this place and ordered accordingly. Onyx judging him for it knocked Nico's opinion of him back down.

As everyone else ordered, Nico checked his phone.

ROWAN:

It's not often you ask for my help. At least not on your own behalf.

Nico frowned. Rowan was busy enough, and Nico never had any serious problems of his own, so why bother Rowan with them?

NICO:

This isn't personal. I'll be bringing someone with me. Can't say more now, but it's big.

ROWAN:

Intriguing. I'll clear my afternoon.

NICO:

See you in an hour.

Nico let the others talk. Onyx was clearly content to ignore him, though Harper kept trying to rope him into the chatter. Normally, Nico would try harder, but unease ate at him.

Earth's demon population going from three to hundreds, maybe thousands—he wasn't sure how many demons had been in Hell—wouldn't go smoothly, no matter what they did. The most powerful covens, both witch and vampire, were going to be angry that they no longer sat at the top of the magic world's hierarchy.

The food arrived, and Nico's salad turned out to be more aesthetic than anything that would fill him up. Harper and Ollie had paninis, and Onyx seemed to have ordered the entire small plates menu.

"Everyone try these." Onyx passed a dish of small pastries around. "They're my favorite."

Harper and Ollie dutifully grabbed one each. "Oh, yum." Harper covered his mouth, eyes going wide.

Onyx thrust the plate at Nico. "Try one." He shook it like Nico was putting him out by not taking the food.

"You don't have to share with me."

"Of course I don't, but I'm not an asshole. Take a pastry. Unless you're allergic to gluten or something." Onyx narrowed his eyes as if he might spot a gluten intolerance lurking within Nico.

"No allergies." Nico took a pastry, buttery crumbs flaking onto his fingers. "Thanks."

Onyx popped the last pastry in his mouth, not bothering to reply.

They didn't linger over the food. Maybe Nico wasn't the only one anxious to get to their next task. Onyx shared everything he'd ordered, glaring at Nico if he didn't try a dish fast enough. If there wasn't so much on his mind, Nico would have laughed.

As their plates were cleared, Onyx slipped the waiter his credit card.

Nico hadn't even gotten his wallet out. "You paid for my lunch."

Onyx dabbed the corner of his mouth with a napkin. "Yeah, well, this isn't the sort of place where you split the bill. I come here too often to embarrass myself."

"You're ridiculous."

Onyx ignored him, smiling at Harper and Ollie and seeming to give his full attention to what they were saying. His blue eyes weren't as cold when they were lit by the summer sun, and he had the faintest freckles along his cheeks.

Nico's chest tightened, a sensation like something was tugging on his insides. He rubbed it absently. It'd be good it get this meeting over with. He wasn't used to feeling like this.

3
______

ONYX

Why had Onyx shared his food with Nico? It gave the wrong impression. He hadn't planned to, but the witch actually needed to eat to survive, and Onyx didn't. The hollow feeling currently burrowing its way inside him wasn't about food. He probably needed a drink of blood when he got home.

"Will Rowan be offering refreshments?" Onyx could go for a glass of blood sooner rather than later. This aching hunger wasn't usual for him.

"Probably." Nico sat tense in the seat next to him as they rode through the city in a rideshare. They'd left Ollie and Harper to make their own way home.

He could practically feel Nico's apprehension wafting off him.

Onyx rolled his shoulders. On second thought, it would be too friendly to accept blood from the vampire. He'd have to wait until later.

Eventually, they pulled up in front of an old-style building. Onyx doubted it was historic. Given the lack of genuine character, it was likely a modern dupe.

"Classy." Onyx opened the door and stepped out.

Nico climbed out the other side. "Not everyone can own a building as sleek as yours."

"More's the pity." Onyx gestured toward the entrance. "Lead the way. I don't want to explain to the plebs at the door who I am."

Nico shook his head, mumbling something that sounded a lot like *can't be serious*, but led the way without otherwise complaining.

They bypassed the closed strip club, entering a door to the side, leading to a stairwell where a couple of vampire plebs were indeed lurking. Seemed Rowan was more than a strip club owning—sometimes performing—vampire if he owned and utilized the whole building.

Onyx had a feeling his brothers and their mates had discussed the vampire's business before coming here last time, but Onyx hadn't paid close attention, and once they'd gotten here, he'd been too focused on scaring Nico to absorb much else.

He followed Nico up several flights of stairs and down a red carpeted hall. The building was quiet. Other than the muscle at street level, no one was around.

Nico knocked on a polished wood door, paused, then entered. Onyx stepped after him, head high but not quite putting his nose in the air. He suppressed his magic, making himself appear human to other magical beings.

Rowan stood from a large antique desk in the corner of the room. Dammit, he was tall too. It was natural for Eternals, and therefore demons, to be on the larger side, but other magical beings should vary as much as humans.

"Nico, it's good to see you." The vampire stepped out from behind the desk. He wore a gray suit made of expensive-looking fabric, the fit suggesting custom tailoring. Rowan's dark hair fell several inches past his shoulders, his brown cheeks flushed with life. He smiled politely but with no warmth.

"I appreciate you making time on short notice. Shall we sit?" Nico gestured to the leather couches next to a pair of bookshelves.

"Please." Rowan stepped toward the seating area.

Was Nico not going to introduce him? That was fucking rude after insisting Onyx come.

Nico nudged Onyx with his elbow, and Onyx snatched his arm out of reach.

Rowan perched on the closest couch, and Nico sat opposite him. Onyx sat, spine straight, next to Nico, leaving enough space for another person to fit between them.

"What can I do for the owner of Gallery Four?" Rowan asked smoothly, turning his attention to Onyx.

So he recognized him. Was that supposed to be endearing or a power play, displaying his knowledge of the who's-who in Shearwater Landing?

Nico glanced between them. "I wasn't aware you and Onyx had met."

"We haven't," Onyx corrected.

"No, but it's a pleasure." Rowan held out his hand.

His magic flared. If Onyx were human—as Rowan no doubt believed—he'd have felt inexplicably unsettled with the way the vampire was trying to intimidate him.

Onyx shook Rowan's hand. "I'm always a pleasure."

Rowan sat back, arms spread out on the back of the couch. "So, what can I do for you gentlemen?"

Nico scrubbed a hand over his face. "There's some serious shit going on."

What an astute assessment. Onyx blinked to keep from rolling his eyes.

"In the art world?" Rowan hedged, brow cocking.

What, did he think there was an art thief on the loose? If there was, it was more likely that Onyx was the culprit than the victim.

He'd robbed a few museums when he'd first escaped from the Realm of the Damned. Ash had a field day, refusing to acknowledge that Onyx had stolen items that had once belonged to him and other demons, therefore canceling out any claim of theft.

Onyx had no excuse for his stint as a jewel thief. That had been for fun.

"It's a problem for the Human Realm," Onyx said.

Rowan blinked a few too many times but otherwise didn't show any surprise. "You're aware of the magic world?"

"That should be obvious given I referenced the Human Realm." And the fact that he was here at all. Unless humans came to this guy for favors, not knowing what he was. Onyx turned to Nico. "Why don't you explain?"

He'd see how Nico wanted to approach this, and go from there. Maybe they should have discussed a game plan, but Onyx didn't think it mattered. He wasn't the one worried about the demons' return.

"Have you ever heard that demons live in Shearwater Land-ing?" Nico asked Rowan.

"There've been rumors that the sooty shearwater flock is under demon enchantment, but I've never heard more than whispers. Why?"

"The Hounds of Hell all live here." Nico glanced toward the windows like he'd rather be elsewhere. "I've met them."

Rowan lurched forward, his movement too fast to pass for human. "You've met the Hounds of Hell?"

Onyx narrowed his eyes. "He has, but *you* don't get to meet them. The Hounds aren't the problem. All demons were freed from the Realm of the Damned and are now on Earth. Some might be headed here. Nico wants to put together a PSA so people aren't caught off guard."

"A PSA," Nico muttered. "What a way to put it."

Rowan didn't acknowledge the comment, not taking his eyes off Onyx. "What does that have to do with you? How do you know anything about demons?"

Onyx leaned forward. "I am one." He smiled, letting his fangs drop and his eyes burn.

Rowan was silent for a good thirty seconds. He didn't move a muscle. "I can't detect your magic."

Onyx flicked his wrist dismissively, putting his fire and fangs away. "Demon trick. Our powers surpass anything you're familiar with, since we were the ones to give them to you. If you can call it giving, in your case."

The original vampires were a group of witches who'd slayed a demon and drank his blood in order to gain immortality. Killing a demon or Eternal was an unforgivable crime, even if the Eternal Realm had decided not to smite the perpetrators in this particular case.

Onyx liked to bring it up to make vampires uncomfortable, and hadn't had the pleasure in a long time.

Rowan frowned. "I'm not that old. The origin of my species is hardly my fault. How do you know Nico?"

Onyx cut a glance at the witch. Nico looked tired. Was he genuinely stressed about all this? Really, there was only so much he could do about any coming upheaval. He should relax.

"Nico is..." Onyx trailed off. It was to their advantage for as few people as possible to know who the Hounds actually were. Lucifer was still looking for them, and who knew if any other demons would come sniffing around. "We have a mutual friend."

Rowan studied Nico. "The boys from the other night?"

Well, it appeared Rowan wasn't stupid. They might have to trust him with who they all were, given they'd gotten him involved the night they went to hunt Luc in the Realm of the Damned. If he knew Harper and Ollie were involved, it wouldn't take much sleuthing to get a glimpse of their mates, even if they weren't detectable as demons.

"The night we had that strange disturbance behind the club?" Rowan continued.

"Yes. That was the night the demons were freed," Nico said.

"None of that matters," Onyx cut in before Rowan could ask anything else. "We're here to get the word out. There's going to be an adjustment now that the rest of my kind are back."

"An adjustment?" Rowan stiffened. "How can it not matter what happened the night the demons were freed? Did *you* free them? Why did demons fall to Earth in the first place? Does it have anything to do with their return? What about the witch souls in Hell?"

Fuck, he had an inquisitive mind. What a nuisance. They weren't going to get away with keeping this guy completely in the dark. Onyx should have refused to deal with this.

"Demons fell to Earth to—"

"It's no one's business why we fell from the Eternal Realm," Onyx snapped, glaring at Nico.

Nico glared back. "Why can't we tell him? What's the big secret?"

Onyx didn't want to talk about mates. It was irrelevant. "Why we came originally isn't the issue. It's literally ancient history. We lived among you before, and the world ticked along fine. Our return won't be an issue unless witches and vampires make it one."

"You don't know that," Nico argued. "Demons could start conflict as well as anyone. And I think people need to be aware of mates."

Fucking witch. Onyx briefly contemplated strangling him. "Why the hell am I here if you're going to say whatever you want? What happened to deciding what to share?"

"I agreed to let you decide whether to share your identity or not. I didn't say I'd keep anything else quiet." Nico shifted uncomfortably. "Why can't we explain mates? Isn't that why the demons were freed?"

Onyx clenched a fist at his side. "You don't know shit about mates."

"Well, it's clear the subject is a touchy one for you," Rowan interrupted.

Onyx's eyes flamed. "Watch it, vamp. I could end you without breaking a sweat."

Rowan didn't even flinch, damn him. Though Nico sucked in a sharp breath.

"We're surrounded by my coven," Rowan said levelly. "You can't take on a whole group on your own."

"Watch me." Onyx's body flashed hot. He needed to get his emotions under control, but everything was so sharp today. So overwhelming. "Andras was a pacifist. Caught off guard after trusting the wrong witch. Your coven couldn't overpower me. Don't let history make you bold. One slayed demon is hardly a precedent."

Rowan relaxed his posture, so calm you'd think he hadn't been threatened. What was his angle in backing down?

"My apologies. I clearly have no idea what's going on here. I don't even know what mates are. Of course, I'll help get the word out about demons returning, but it seems we need to agree on a message first. How about a drink?"

Nico nodded, and Rowan stood, heading for the small bar on the other side of the room.

"Bourbon, please." Nico sounded relieved.

Rowan began pouring two glasses. "How about you, Onyx?"

"Nothing for me." Onyx didn't drink anything but blood and the occasional intoxicating potion.

The hunger filling him intensified. Maybe Onyx should ask Nico to personally quench his thirst. That would really piss him off. But the possibility of sampling Nico's blood tugged at him, as if he really wanted it, and hadn't entertained the idea purely because it was inappropriate.

Onyx shifted his weight, leaning closer to Nico. His citrus cologne was overpowering. He must have doused himself. Onyx hated how pleasant the smell was. He didn't usually gravitate toward such bright scents.

Nico accepted his drink and raised his glass to Rowan. The vampire did the same, and they drank.

Rowan settled back in his seat. "Can you tell me how the demons were released? If they're worried about re-confinement, that could change things. Lucifer trapped them in the first place, correct?"

Onyx pulled his mind away from Nico's scent and the weird effect it was having on him. "Yes, Lucifer trapped us. He also released everyone. My brothers and I planned to free our fellow demons, but he beat us to it."

Nico cocked his head. "You planned to release the rest of the demons?"

Onyx shrugged. "It was the right thing to do. They didn't deserve to be imprisoned."

"Lucifer agreed with you?" Rowan asked.

"We didn't exactly discuss it. He's the one who deserves to be trapped, and he released everyone, at least in part, as a distraction to get away from me and my brothers."

"Brothers? You mean the Hounds?"

Onyx's eyes narrowed. "We don't like that term."

"Apologies." Rowan sounded frustratingly genuine. "So,

Lucifer changed his mind about holding the demons in Hell? Why?"

That was the question, wasn't it? "If you meet him, you can ask."

Nico set his empty glass on the coffee table. He drank that quick. "It has to be mates, right? Ash and Dante said they're the only ones to find theirs."

Onyx's fire flared. Fine, he'd talk about mates. "Freeing the demons could be in response to discovering Ash and Dante are mated. But the way Lucifer released them wasn't completely spur of the moment, not with how the gateway was constructed. He could have planned it before discovering Ash and Dante's mates."

And Lucifer hadn't believed either demon was mated. His conviction that they were lying had been so strong. Would he really change his tune that drastically? If not, why had he been planning to release everyone?

He must not have been. Onyx had to have it wrong.

Rowan shifted closer, perching on the edge of the couch, and Onyx could practically feel his questions coming.

"We fell to Earth to find our mates," he said to head Rowan off, bitterness eclipsing the hunger gnawing at him. "Eternal beings have fated mates. Destined matches. It's all very political in the Eternal Realm, so some of us came here to find and claim our partners freely. But we never found them. Everyone assumed the silly quest was hopeless. We were being punished for falling. Blah, blah, blah. Apparently, all it took was a few thousand years of waiting."

Rowan sipped his drink. "So the freed demons will be looking for mates. For love?"

Onyx ground his teeth. "I guess." Mates were still the driving force behind too much. Onyx was over it. Had been for a long fucking time.

Rowan took a second to digest this before turning his attention to Nico. "Why do you think the magic world should be aware of fated love?"

Nico ran a hand through his hair, glancing between them. "Mating means binding yourself to a demon irreversibly. It's not like any other magic I've heard of. People should at least be aware that this kind of bond exists. We can't do much about informing humans without revealing our whole world, but it would be better for fewer mates to be caught off guard."

Rowan nodded slowly. "You don't trust it. Do you not think the fated connection is as genuine and as purely love-based as Onyx says?"

"I don't doubt Onyx and the other demons are telling the truth, but I don't like the idea of powerful beings binding themselves to unsuspecting people." Nico seemed to brace himself for Onyx's reaction, hand tightly gripping the leather armrest.

Onyx smiled. Nico's suspicion was like a breath of fresh air. For millennia, all Onyx heard was how great the connection would be and how important finding their mates was. He didn't exactly disagree, but he didn't need a mate. Mating wasn't more important than any other aspect of his life.

He didn't care much one way or another. He saw no reason to be heartsick over not having a mate when there were so many other ways to enrich his life.

"Sounds like you have a healthy critical eye." Onyx turned away from Nico, but not before noting the man's surprise. "I'll tell my brothers you think mates should be common knowledge, and see what they say. Though it's not really up to us if it should be secret or not. We aren't demonkind's representatives."

He paused. "I will say, if you're spreading stories, make sure you present being a demon's mate as rare. There have only been two since we fell, and just because they were found recently doesn't mean we're all going to suddenly pair off."

Rowan nodded, setting his empty glass down. "Noted. I'll discuss this with my coven and see if we can decide where to start getting word out, emphasizing the exodus, not mates. Passing things along to my allies here and overseas will be easiest, and Nico, if you could talk to the Lockwood Coven, that would be helpful."

"They've been having a hard time lately, but I'll see who I can speak with."

Onyx hadn't heard of the Lockwood Coven. Until recently, he'd kept almost completely out of the magic world.

Which reminded him.

"I don't want people knowing who I am." Onyx straightened his posture, letting his eyes burn in Rowan's direction. "I suppose some of your coven saw me come in, so that cat's out of the bag if they're also aware I own Gallery Four. But no one else."

"Not a problem. My coven will keep your visit and identity confidential."

"Thanks, Rowan." Nico stood, and the vampire followed suit. Onyx hurried to follow. "Let me know how talking to your coven goes and when you plan to start passing things along."

"Of course." Rowan clapped Nico on the shoulder, winning a small smile in return. "I'm happy for the Valeros to be the point of contact here in the city, and won't spread around that you're in contact with Hounds—uh..." He looked apologetically at Onyx. "What do I call you and your brothers?"

"I'd prefer if you didn't refer to us."

Nico let out an irritated sigh.

"Right." Rowan only nodded. "Shall I contact you through Nico if I need you?"

Onyx gave him a look that told the vampire not to need him. "Sure."

"Excellent." Rowan led them toward the door. "Poker this week?" he asked Nico.

"I'll be there. If I'm not, Leo will hunt me down."

Rowan chuckled, and irritation flared in Onyx's chest, his hunger growing from a pit to a chasm.

He couldn't believe these two were actually friends. Why was Nico so cozy with a mobster-esque vampire? The two were nothing alike. Nico had stains on his jeans and obviously fretted about Ollie and Harper—given his opinion of mates—while Rowan was busy building his empire. He clearly had a lot more going on than a strip club and whatever else was in this building, talking about allies like he had enemies.

Nico should have better friends.

"As Leo should. We'd miss you otherwise. And, Nico"—Rowan paused at the door—"if you start getting a lot of requests after this comes out, let me know."

"Yeah, I'm sure it'll be fine. We aren't advertising my connection to the demons."

"Still. People come to you."

Onyx's pulse thumped. They were acting like he wasn't even there, and this was the second time people coming to see Nico had been mentioned. Was he so accommodating and helpful that he let people ask him favors all the time? Would they come to him if they heard about demons, not even knowing Nico was connected to this mess? How infuriating. Onyx wouldn't stand for anything like that if it were him.

"I have to get back to work," Onyx announced, refusing to be so easily forgotten. "It was interesting to meet you."

"Likewise." Rowan grinned, showing fang for some dumb reason.

"Talk soon." Nico turned and headed into the hall.

Onyx followed, the door shutting behind him.

Nico continued down the corridor without waiting. "Didn't you agree to help because you were good with people?"

Onyx made a face at his back. "No, you said I was good at moving between worlds. And I am. This wasn't a *human niceties* conversation. Rowan was posturing from the get-go. Acting meek isn't how I work."

Nico huffed. "It's not meek to be friendly."

"Agree to disagree, witch."

4

NICO

Nico left Onyx outside Rowan's and caught a rideshare home. Was Onyx booking his own car or flying back to the gallery?

Nico hadn't seen his wings the night the demons had dropped off Harper and Ollie before going to the Realm of the Damned. He hadn't even gotten a good look at Ash or Dante's, too distracted by Onyx's fury.

Would Nico see any of the demons in their full forms again? They were private enough that he doubted it. Especially Onyx.

A twinge of disappointment cut through him. Why should he care? He was relieved the meeting was over and to be away from Onyx's biting remarks. He'd had enough for one day.

Nico lived around the corner from The Herb Emporium, in the Banks by the river. The car dropped him in front of his apartment building, and he detoured to the coffee shop on the corner. Nico was wiped out, despite having achieved so little, and he wasn't looking forward to getting in touch with the Lockwood Coven.

After ordering a double espresso, he sat at a table outside. It would have been smarter to skip the bourbon, but he'd needed to take the edge off.

Now that Onyx was gone, Nico didn't feel so... He couldn't put his finger on it. He hadn't been on edge exactly, more like his reactions were heightened, making him hyperaware. Usually, no one got under his skin, but Nico was still thinking about Onyx's unwillingness to be polite.

Onyx's abrasiveness was impossible to ignore, practically begging for Nico to smooth it out.

He scrubbed a hand over his face. Fuck. It was probably best to stay away from the pretty demon. He was likely a challenge Nico didn't need, no matter how tempting it was to decipher what was behind his prickliness.

Draining the last of his coffee, Nico went home. He lived on the second story of a small apartment building, and sure enough, the smell of spices filled the hall between his and Lucia's doors.

Nico's smile died as he pulled his keys from his pocket and noticed his door wasn't closed. It was open the tiniest crack. There was no way he'd left it this way.

He pocketed the keys and called on his magic, reaching out for the protective spell he'd placed on the apartment.

The protection was gone.

It had been a basic spell, not linked to intruder alarms he could sense from afar, but it would have taken a decent effort to break.

The hairs on the back of Nico's neck stood as he slowly pushed the door open. Nothing was visible from the entryway but the coats hanging on the hook by the door.

Before he stepped in and rounded the corner, he sent a quick spell ahead. Any living being should register, as long as they weren't cloaked. It was better than scanning for magic, in case the intruder was suppressing theirs.

The spell detected nothing.

Nico crept forward, pulse thumping. He was careful not to step on the squeaky floorboards and left the door slightly ajar.

He turned into the open-plan living and kitchen area. It was empty, but fuck, the place was trashed.

The furniture was upended, papers and books strewn all over the floor. His PlayStation was tipped on its side, and games were thrown across the room. Nico's face flushed in anger. The rug was crumpled in a corner, a vase of dried flowers smashed, his food taken from the pantry and scattered on the countertops, spilling onto the ground.

He turned from the mess and inched toward his bedroom. The door was open, and no one was visible inside. Nico slipped into the equally trashed space. His clothes were everywhere, drawers pulled out of his dresser, mattress askew, and curtains ripped from the wall fastenings.

The bathroom was a mess, but also empty. Whoever had been here was gone.

Nico returned to the front door and closed and locked it. He had to recast his protections.

Fuck.

Who could have done this? His electronics were possibly broken but still here, so this wasn't about taking easy-to-sell valuables. The intruder seemed to have been looking for something, but what? Something small?

Nico would have to go through everything to see if anything less obvious than the TV had been taken, but he couldn't think of anything that would attract this kind of attention. He didn't have rare magical artifacts or anything worth a great value.

Robbing The Herb Emporium would've made more sense. The stock was easy to resell, some items were powerfully enchanted, and he had cash on hand. Dammit, he'd have to check the shop.

Nico slumped against the door. He didn't need this.

After a long moment, he straightened and went across the hall, knocking on his neighbor's door.

Lucia flung it open. She couldn't be more than five feet and was as old as Nico's parents would have been. "Nico. About time you wandered over. Can you guess what I'm making?"

Nico couldn't help grinning at the older woman. She had gray streaked hair and wrinkles around her mouth and eyes from a lifetime of smiling.

"Smells like your pozole. How can you stand over the stove on such a warm day?"

Lucia shook her head and pulled him inside. "It's like you've never cast a cooling charm. Besides, I'm never hot anymore. Summer is the season for my light sweaters."

The woman did have an impressive array of cardigans.

"I run warm, so I guess I can't talk." Nico followed Lucia to the kitchen. "Did you hear anything out in the hall earlier?"

Her manner turned shrewd. "No, why?"

"Nothing. I was wondering if someone came by my place." Nico wouldn't worry her if there was no reason to think whoever broke in was a danger to anyone else, and it didn't seem likely they'd rob Lucia if they hadn't taken Nico's TV or anything obvious.

Nico wasn't even sure if he'd been robbed. Trashing his place felt personal.

"I didn't notice anything, but the music was on and I had lunch out on the balcony."

Lucia had protections on her apartment. Probably more complex ones than Nico. Her children were always in and out, the grandkids too.

Of the two of them, Nico was the lonely neighbor, though he disagreed with that assessment. He had friends, just not ones he invited to his place. That didn't stop Lucia from looking after him like he was another one of her kids.

"Are you off to Emilio's tonight?" Nico asked. He was Lucia's son, who also lived in the neighborhood.

"He's picking me up at four. You should come."

Nico shoved his hands in his pockets. "Maybe next time. I have to stop in at work."

"But it's Sunday. Isn't the shop closed?"

"It is. I need to check a few things, that's all." If The Herb Emporium had been broken into, he'd have to tell Harper. Nico hoped he wouldn't have to. Harper didn't need more stress after escaping his abusive coven.

"We love having you," Lucia said as if she worried Nico thought it was a pity invite. "If you'd grown up across the hall, you and Emilio would have been great friends."

Emilio was Lucia's oldest child, and around Nico's age. He had a feeling she was right, but Nico hadn't grown up here. His parents had lived on the other side of the river.

"I'll see if I can do next week."

"All right." Lucia turned toward the kitchen. "Don't leave without your food." She collected four containers of pozole, each a dinner-sized portion.

Nico took them. "Did you leave any for yourself?"

"Yes." She rolled her eyes. "You can put a couple in the freezer."

"I will. If there's space. Sorry, I forgot to grab the clean containers to give back." He hoped they hadn't been broken.

Lucia opened the door. "Don't worry. I know where you live. I'll be 'round the shop to pick up my potions on Tuesday. That handsome young man still working there?" She raised her eyebrows, face the picture of innocence.

"Yes. Like I said, Harper isn't going anywhere. And he has a boyfriend."

Lucia pouted. "I suppose getting involved at work wouldn't be like you. It's been a while since you dated. Unless you're keeping secrets?"

"No secrets." Onyx's scowl crossed Nico's mind, and he blinked him away. "I'll see you soon. Thanks for dinner."

She watched him cross the hall. "You're welcome."

Nico went inside and put the pozole in the fridge. Luckily, the intruder hadn't thrown the contents on the floor like they had with everything from his pantry.

He gathered his magic and recast the protection spells on his apartment. It would be smart to get someone stronger to come around and beef up his security. Maybe he could hire a witch rather than ask a favor.

Once the protections were in place, Nico left his trashed apartment and walked to The Herb Emporium. Moving calmed him, even though he was only putting off cleaning his place and figuring out if anything had been taken.

The walk was too short to relax him completely. Nico couldn't stop his muscles tensing as he raised the metal grate covering the shop's entrance.

At a glance, everything seemed fine, and a quick inspection showed his protective spells were still in place. Nico unlocked the door and strode through the shop.

Everything was as he'd left it. His displays of dried plants and candles were as crowded as usual, but nothing appeared out of place. He checked the back room and the potions stocked behind the counter. All fine. He counted the cash and double-checked that all his log books were present.

Satisfied no one had been there, Nico locked up. He thought he'd feel relieved, but was instead left with a sinking feeling as he went home to face the mess.

5

___

ONYX

On Wednesday morning, Onyx flew from his loft to the gallery at top speed, beating his wings until they burned. It didn't help.

He landed on the gallery roof, shoes hitting the building hard. Burning off that smidge of energy left him even more restless. He ruffled his feathers, stretching his wing muscles, and concentrated on the breeze swirling around him, trying to find any hint of calm.

There'd been no word from anyone since Sunday. He cracked his knuckles. Why the fuck did he think he'd hear from his brothers? They obviously didn't need anything more from him after pawning off their task.

Nico had been silent as well. Onyx's fire flared every time he thought of the man. He hadn't exactly given out his phone number, but still. Shouldn't Nico have updated him by now? Had he talked to that coven? Had Rowan been in touch?

It didn't matter. Onyx didn't even want to be involved, which only made his obsession more infuriating.

Onyx retracted his wings, skin itching as they transformed into large tattoos spanning his back—his other demon features were always hidden—and slipped on his shirt. His fingers flew over the buttons, pale lavender fabric crisp against his overheated skin. After tucking the shirt in and rolling the sleeves to his elbows, Onyx ran a hand through his hair.

There was no need for a mirror. He always looked amazing.

He didn't have to think about his brothers or Nico. He was important in the human world, and there was more than enough to focus on with the gallery.

Onyx descended the ladder from the roof and climbed through the window to his office. It was barely after sunrise, so there was no risk that Scott would be around. Onyx crossed the room and opened the small fridge hidden in the wood-paneled shelving. He pulled out a bag of blood and reached for a crystal glass.

On second thought, he abandoned the glass. He'd been famished lately. Nothing seemed to fill the pit inside him.

Onyx flopped into his desk chair and grabbed a metal straw out of his top drawer. He pierced it through the bag and cast a spell to heat the contents.

Maybe he needed to feed from a donor rather than a bag. It had never mattered before, but there had to be a reason everything was so *off*.

Onyx bought his blood from a vampire-run organization that sourced its product from magical community members. It was the easiest, most ethical way to feed. Onyx hadn't fed from a person in decades. Perhaps the sheer length of time since feeling a pulse beneath his fangs was the problem.

As he sipped, he pulled out his phone. No messages.

He sucked on the straw until the blood was gone, drinking so fast his stomach cramped, leaving him no more settled now that he was full.

Onyx put the empty bag in the fridge to throw away later and pulled up his chat with Ollie and Harper. He'd named it

Your Favorite Group Chat upon starting it, but figured it was time to change it up. He typed *Not My Mates* into the name field, then sent the group a text.

ONYX:

> Let's start our food tour with sushi. Dinner tonight?

Neither man would reply at this hour, so Onyx didn't hold his breath. He set the phone down.

Ollie and Harper were growing on him. He'd been suspicious of Harper at the start, but who could blame him? It hadn't helped that *Ash,* of all demons, had been the one claiming he'd found his mate.

He'd never admit it, but being around the little mates gave Onyx a soft, warm feeling. He loved knowing his brothers would care for the two young men better than anyone else ever could. He even liked knowing Ollie and Harper would care for his useless brothers.

Onyx didn't need a mate like they did. He hated so many things about what the quest for mates had done to everyone, and to the world, but part of him still went mushy over the reality of the mating bond.

His brothers were assholes—well, Ash was, Dante was all right—but they still deserved happiness.

Onyx couldn't suppress his joy that their little group had expanded. Ollie and Harper had the potential to be true friends, loving brothers like he'd always wanted. People who wouldn't cast him aside or treat him as an afterthought.

Maybe that kind of family didn't exist. Maybe real family was Lucifer, a brother who'd betrayed Onyx even after he gave up everything for him. Maybe real family was Ash and Dante, who made him want to scream more than anything else.

Maybe Ollie and Harper would get tired of him, too.

But until then, Onyx would enjoy the little mates. What else could he do? Wallowing was a stupid waste of time. He'd made his choice to fall from the Eternal Realm, so he'd make the most of his life on Earth.

Later that morning, Ollie texted to say he had plans tonight with a friend from work, but was free tomorrow. Harper eventually replied, apologizing profusely for being asleep and rushing off to work before responding—he really was a sweet, earnest young thing—and said tomorrow worked for him too.

Onyx agreed on tomorrow and tucked his phone away.

"You seem pleased," Scott commented from his desk in the main gallery space.

"I am. Nothing business-related. I'm organizing my social calendar."

Scott hummed. He looked impeccable as always, his silver hair styled and clothes flattering his trim form. If Onyx were to ever age, he'd have hoped to do it as Scott had.

"You're always busy. How do you have the energy? Most nights I'm curled up with my cat."

"So? That's where you want to be. Maybe I need a cat." Onyx imagined having a pet. It wasn't something he'd ever done in his long life.

"If you're serious, I can put you in touch with my friend who runs a shelter."

"Let me mull it over." Onyx wouldn't get a pet on a whim, but maybe a cat would help fill the void that had opened inside him this week. He was beginning to suspect it wasn't hunger after all.

But he needed something.

Maybe he needed to get laid. He hadn't bothered since Ash had come into town and started pestering him with all the Lucifer nonsense, other than the one night he'd dragged his brothers to a club and found a delectable human couple to play with.

It had been too long since he'd relaxed like that.

Onyx had finalized the guest list for the new opening yesterday and emailed catering suggestions through to Scott, who'd handle the logistics of moving their current pieces into storage and staging the show with the artist. With no appointments that afternoon, there wasn't much else Onyx needed to do, and Scott hated when he hovered aimlessly.

"I might head out early. If you have everything under control?"

Scott lifted a brow. "I always have this place under control."

"I know, otherwise I wouldn't have hired you." They shared a smile. "Call if you get lonely."

"You're on my speed dial," Scott assured him, and Onyx strolled out the front door.

There was an exclusive kink club he frequented, where he knew more than a few Doms who could get the job done, but it was too early in the day for that, and apps always soured his mood. Perhaps this was why he hadn't gotten off in so long. He couldn't seem to muster any enthusiasm.

Onyx checked his phone again. Still no word from anyone about telling the magic world that demons had returned.

Renewed anger jolted through him. Hadn't Nico said they'd needed his help? Had Onyx fucked up the meeting with Rowan or something? Maybe Nico had gotten annoyed and decided he didn't need Onyx after all.

Bitterness twisted Onyx's insides. Why did he care if the witch was avoiding him? Onyx was good at not being left behind. If people didn't like him, too fucking bad. He'd get that much more pleasure out of showing up unannounced.

Onyx searched The Herb Emporium online and booked a ride. He preferred navigating the city on the ground, rather than flying—except for his morning commute to work. Feeling like an actual part of human society kept Onyx in the moment. He liked experiencing the city as humans did, even when that included the subway or midday traffic.

When he got there, The Herb Emporium turned out to be a small, rundown shop on a busy street. Nothing fresh paint wouldn't fix. The building itself wasn't badly designed.

How long had the shop been there? Had Nico bought the business from someone? He couldn't have been running it since the sign was last painted. Nico wasn't that old.

Onyx entered the shop. He preferred minimalism but acknowledged the homey charm of the packed shelves and handwritten signs.

Nico appeared from behind a curtain. "What are you doing here?"

Onyx's spine stiffened. "I'm here to see Harper. Is that all right with you?"

"You don't need my permission." Nico leaned forward, arms braced on the counter. "Harper's on his break."

"Oh." Onyx glanced around, heat rising in his cheeks. Why was he embarrassed? Fuck, he hoped it didn't show. "When will he be back?"

"Half an hour."

It was too long to wait. Onyx stalked toward the counter anyway. Nico had a stain on his apron. Probably good that he was wearing it, or he'd ruin his T-shirt.

Nico smiled at his approach, and Onyx wanted to wipe the look from his face. What was he so pleased about? Maybe he always smiled like that, which was even worse.

Onyx crossed his arms. "Did you talk to that coven?"

Nico pushed off the counter, his smile disappearing. "Yeah."

Yeah. That was it? Onyx waved his hand. "And?"

Nico's brows pinched. "And their leader died recently, so

they have a lot on their plate. I didn't want to saddle them with more bad news."

"Demons returning isn't bad news."

Nico shrugged. "Maybe not."

There was a beat of silence.

"That's all you have to say?"

Nico frowned. "Did you want meeting notes?"

Onyx's fire sparked in his gut. "No, I'm supposed to be helping. You were all worried about telling people, and what, now it's fine? You told your friends, and that's the end of it?"

Nico's lips twitched like he was holding back a smile. Like he was laughing at Onyx. The nerve. "It's not the end of it, but I feel better now that I'm not the only one aware of what's happening."

Onyx was momentarily glad Nico felt better before he remembered he didn't care.

"Is that why you're here? To see how spreading the word is going?"

Onyx pursed his lips. "I'm here to see Harper."

"Okay. Feel free to browse the shelves while you wait." Nico turned his attention to a notebook lying open on the counter.

Onyx wouldn't be dismissed like that. "So, do you not need my help anymore, or what? Because it seems like you could have done without harassing me. Have you even talked to Ash and Dante?"

Nico looked up. "I talked to them yesterday."

Had they all met without him? "Sounds like it's all taken care of then." He couldn't keep fury from tightening his words. He turned to go.

"Hey," Nico called.

Onyx stopped but refused to turn around. Why couldn't he

control his temper? He wasn't usually this short unless Ash was in the room.

"What?" he snapped.

"I'm seeing Rowan tonight. Come with me?"

"Why?" Onyx spun slowly. His stupid heart fluttered at the invitation as if he had no friends, but Scott was right. His social calendar was always full.

"You can ask him how things are going. Meet some more of the Valero Coven, too, if you want."

Onyx wrinkled his nose. "More vampires?"

"You don't have to." Nico shrugged like he didn't care much either way.

"I probably should, since everyone decided I need to be involved. I want to keep an eye on Rowan. Don't need him trying to twist things to his advantage."

Nico tapped his notebook thoughtfully. "He wouldn't twist the situation, or make trouble where there is none. He's not like that, but he does look for advantages in everything."

"That doesn't bother you? I thought you were out to help people."

Nico chuckled. "Rowan helps people, too. Just in a different way. I don't need my friends to all be exactly like me."

"Good because if they were, I wouldn't come tonight." Onyx shuddered. Nico's sincere kindness was off-putting.

Nico laughed more loudly. "Why do you hate me?"

"Why do you care?"

Nico grinned, and Onyx's lips curved upward to match. He couldn't help it. Damn witch.

Nico pulled out his phone. "Give me your number."

Onyx did as he was told, rattling off the digits before he thought better of it.

"There." Nico sent him a text, and Onyx's phone vibrated.

"I'm sorry I didn't keep you updated. There's been a lot happening this week."

The apology soothed some of Onyx's agitation, quieting the flames inside him. "A lot happening? It's only Wednesday. Was there a dried herb emergency?"

Nico snorted. "Nothing that dire." He paused. "I'll make sure to keep you in the loop, even if it's to confirm that I followed through on what we discussed."

Again, the reassurance soothed Onyx, loosening the tightness in his chest. He took an involuntary step closer to the counter. "I'll hold you to that."

"I'd expect you to." Nico leaned forward once more, forearms on the counter. "While you're here, can I ask what happened when you went to the Realm of the Damned? Ash and Dante won't tell me what's going on with Lucifer."

On the one hand, keeping the details within their inner circle was probably best, but if Ash and Dante didn't want Nico to know, it gave Onyx the opportunity to rock the boat. They deserved it after messing him around.

He shrugged. "Why does it matter? Lucifer isn't going to come knocking on your door."

"Glad to hear it, but he might come after Harper and Ollie, right?" Nico's voice dropped, like he was afraid of the answer.

Onyx inched closer. "You're very concerned about them, but you don't have to be. Luc would be a fool to go after the mates again. I had to stop Dante from killing Luc just for hurting Ollie. He was out for blood. Ollie and Harper are safer than they were before they mated. My brother's issue is with us, not them."

"Brother?"

Onyx cursed himself for letting that slip. "Yes, brother. Luc and I share the same unfortunate parentage."

Nico looked fascinated by this news, and Onyx's tension returned.

"What's Lucifer's issue with you?"

"There isn't enough time in your mortal life to unpack that." Onyx shook himself. He shouldn't get personal. Nico's kind face must have lulled him into a sense of false security. Still he said, "Luc wanted to drag us back to the Realm of the Damned."

"But he won't drag you back now that everyone is free. Right?"

Unease swelled inside Onyx. He hated speculating on Luc's plans. "It seems unlikely."

Nico almost looked relieved, but why would he be? "Is the conflict between you over?"

Onyx was suddenly exhausted. It took effort not to let it show. "Our conflict will never be over unless we trap him."

Nico's eyes widened. "Trap Lucifer?"

"Yes." Onyx probably shouldn't have revealed that, but whatever. Everyone else gave away their secrets. It wasn't like Nico would do anything bad with the information, and Luc already knew imprisonment was their aim after their failed attempts.

Nico made an understanding sound. "You want to trap him as payback for him imprisoning you?"

"In part. It's also because he betrayed us. It's because...of a million reasons that I don't need to explain."

Onyx's fire flared once more. He didn't need Nico's approval or understanding. How had he gotten sucked into saying any of this? He hadn't come here to talk to Nico at all. "Tell Harper I stopped by, and text me the details for tonight. I have to go."

Nico seemed startled by his abruptness but recovered quickly. "Sure thing. See you later."

Onyx stormed out of the shop.

Finding a deserted alley, Onyx cast an invisibility illusion over himself. He stripped off his shirt, freed his wings, launched into the air, and flew toward Dante's otherwise inaccessible clifftop home.

He shouldn't have said anything about Luc. Nico didn't really care what Luc had done to Onyx. He wanted to hear the sensational tale of the Devil's origins, and Onyx was sick of that side of the story. He was tired of hearing how Luc had led them on a noble quest for their mates and freedom before it all went wrong.

That wasn't how Onyx saw it.

Luc had never liked being told no. He didn't like their parents' authority—neither did Onyx, to be fair—and especially disliked that their seats on the council gave them power over granting him his mate. Luc's rebellion had been personal. It wasn't about freeing Eternals from a controlling society. Luc longed for his fated mate, but he also wanted to spite their parents and get his own way no matter what anyone said.

Ash and Dante had been heartsick, clinging to the idea of a perfect love. No one had been happy with what they had, and were quick to leave it all behind. To leave Onyx behind.

Onyx had never sought approval from the council to mate— a secret he'd kept to himself. He was younger than Luc and the others and hadn't been restless like they had been. He'd only wanted their love, their companionship. He'd wanted Ash and Dante to treat him like a friend in his own right, not an extension of his brother.

He hadn't wanted them to leave.

Nothing Onyx had said convinced them to stay. They saw Earth as a place of limitless possibilities. They proclaimed the bond between the four of them to be strong, but not enough without their mates. They didn't think they were giving anything up by leaving.

But Onyx had wanted to stay, and they would have left him behind. How was that not giving something up? Was he nothing to them?

Luc would have happily left Onyx to deal with their parents' fury once they discovered Luc had fallen. Luc knew as well as Onyx that Onyx would have been punished in his brother's stead.

Onyx would have had no one. Even if he'd stayed and been granted his mate—which seemed unlikely after his parents learned he'd failed to prevent his brother's fall—he hadn't wanted to lose his brothers. A mate wasn't everything.

So Onyx fell with them, and it was the stupidest thing he'd ever done.

Luc had hurt Onyx well before his betrayal, stealing their power and turning them into prisoners. Onyx should have seen that coming. He shouldn't have gone. They hadn't wanted him, and that never changed.

These days, Onyx wasn't so young or naïve. He hated chasing people, but he still did it. Not because he hoped Dante and Ash might love him one day, or respect him as they did each other, but because he would not allow anyone to ignore him.

He was in control of who came and went from his life.

Onyx landed on Dante's deck. The sliding glass door stood open, but neither demon was in sight. Onyx retracted his wings and put his shirt back on, striding into the house as if he owned it.

A tray of mushroom tarts sat cooling on the kitchen island. Ash must be around. Onyx popped a tart in his mouth. They were still hot from the oven and not bad considering they were baked by such an oaf.

He selected another tart.

"Those aren't for you," Ash growled from behind him.

Onyx stuffed the second tart in his mouth and turned, staring Ash down as he chewed.

Ash pushed past him and moved the tray to the other counter. "You can't come in and steal things."

"Steal? Please. Harper would have shared them with me. He can't eat a dozen tarts by himself."

"It's still rude."

"Oh no. I feel so bad about it," Onyx sneered.

Ash crossed his bulging arms. "Why are you here?"

"To steal all the treats."

Predictably, Ash's eyes burned orange.

"What is wrong with you two?" Dante strode in from the deck, shirt off and wings out. Ash was similarly undressed. "I eat your baking all the time, Ash."

Onyx used to take Dante coming to his defense personally, but Dante did it for everyone.

"I wanted to see how things were going," Onyx said before Ash could respond. "You barged in on me first, so you aren't in a position to complain."

"You aren't barging in." Dante's brow creased, probably fretting over Onyx's irritated tone. "You're always welcome here. If you want to stay now that Luc is back, there's plenty of room."

"No, thank you." Onyx made a show of shuddering. "My place is nicer and there's no risk of running into Ash with his clothes off."

"I'm dressed," Ash muttered.

Onyx ignored him. "So, what's happening? You wanted me involved, and here I am. Or did you forget?"

"Of course we didn't forget. I was going to call you today," Dante insisted.

Sure he was. "Don't hold back now. Where's Luc? You've been tracking him for ages."

Dante grabbed a soda from the fridge and plopped onto a barstool. "We can't track Luc. He figured out another way to hide."

Damn his brother. It was too bad he was clever. "But he can't hide behind our magic anymore. That illusion was broken."

"No, he can't hide behind the magic he stole from us. He's using everyone else."

Onyx took a staggering step back. "He stole magic from all the demons he released?"

"No." Dante gave him a horrified look. "We're lucky it wasn't that. Fuck. No, he did the reverse. The spell must have been built into the gateway. When we've tried to track Luc, we get hundreds of locations."

"It seems like Luc branded every demon that flew through the gateway with his magic," Ash added. Or overexplained, Onyx would argue. But he kept quiet as Ash continued. "Several groups of demons are headed this way, but there's no way to tell if one is Luc. We'd have to hunt them down in person and see who we find at the end of the trail."

"Well, that's useless."

"Thank you, Onyx, but I'd already worked that out."

"Good for you. Not as dumb as you look." Onyx turned his attention back to Dante. "So are you going to scope out every demon that comes to the city? How long have you known this was an issue?"

Dante ignored the second question, and Onyx feared the evasion was deliberate. "My flock will recognize Luc by sight, as long as he's not invisible, so I'll have my birds discreetly check any new arrivals. I don't want to seem aggressive, turning up in person and demanding to know what every demon is doing. We don't need to create enemies."

"We'll have enemies whether or not we create them. What if more demons are here to hunt us down like those last three?" Onyx asked.

"Then we'll deal with them." Dante paused, his tone taking on an edge of concern. "You can stay here if you want. It might be safer."

Onyx wrinkled his nose. "Again, no thanks. My place is guarded."

No one argued with him even though they knew his home wasn't as well protected as Dante's. Maybe Dante's offer was insincere despite how it sounded.

"I guess I'll keep an eye on the witch situation," Onyx continued. "Make sure our fellow magical beings don't freak out about demonkind's repopulation of the planet."

"Great." Dante smiled, all supposed concern vanishing. "Nico said he'd keep us updated, too."

Was he trying to say they didn't need Onyx? But they'd made such a big deal out of it. "Yeah, well, my assessment should be less biased than Nico's." He turned to go. "If you spot Luc, don't forget to tell me."

They'd need him to help open the prison for Luc, so it wasn't likely they'd forget, but honestly, if it weren't for that, they probably would.

Onyx left before they could dismiss him.

6

NICO

Was inviting Onyx to poker night a mistake? Probably. It was too late to do anything about it now.

Nico wished he could say he didn't know why he'd done it, but that wasn't true. Onyx had pushed him away and then gotten mad when he'd left him alone. Onyx clearly wanted to be involved despite all his proclamations to the contrary.

Was it a test or something deeper? Nico needed to figure it out. Onyx had been on his mind all week. If Nico didn't know better, he'd almost believe his incessant thoughts had summoned Onyx to his apothecary shop.

Nico arrived at Rowan's club and found Onyx sitting at the foot of the center stage, sliding money into a dancer's thong. The demon looked downright gleeful, smiling smugly, eyes bright. Another dancer, wearing a tiny blue outfit that matched Onyx's dyed locks almost perfectly, sat on the arm of his chair, playing with his hair.

Onyx seemed to bask in the attention.

Nico strode over, hands in his pockets. "Enjoying yourself?"

Onyx spared him a darting glance before refocusing on the woman on the stage. "Is it a crime?"

"Certainly not." Nico grinned.

It was early in the evening, and the club wasn't busy. The dancer performing ignored the few other men hanging around in favor of Onyx. He threw money at the stage, and Nico caught sight of more than one twenty-dollar bill.

A woman with bright pink hair approached. "Are you two together? Pull up a chair, handsome." She batted thick lashes at Nico.

"We aren't together." Onyx slipped more money into the performer's thong. "At least not like that. I don't even know if he's gay."

She probably hadn't meant it like that, but okay.

"Either way, want a dance?" the pink-haired woman asked Nico.

"I'm actually here to drag my friend away."

She pouted, and Onyx beckoned her closer. She leaned forward, and he slipped money into her top. Beaming, she blew him a kiss.

"You're here to see Rowan, aren't you?" asked the woman in blue, eyes sweeping over Nico. "Thought you looked familiar."

"Yeah. You've probably seen me around."

Not everyone who worked in the strip club knew about the magic world, and a quick, silent spell looking for any signs of magic showed both women were human.

"I'll be back another time," Onyx promised them. "Especially since no one I'm here to see holds a candle to any of you gorgeous girls."

The women giggled.

Onyx stood and brushed back his hair. "Lead the way."

Nico showed Onyx to the stairs. "Was that you asking if I'm gay?" He hadn't known how Onyx identified, and couldn't help the spark that had ignited at the confirmation that Onyx wasn't straight.

Onyx's eyes went wide. "No, I wasn't asking or making any assumptions. I only mentioned it when I arrived so the girls knew they could give me as much attention as they liked without worrying I'd get inappropriate."

"I think tipping with twenties was getting you more attention than anything else."

"That too." Onyx didn't sound bothered.

As they reached the first landing, Nico found himself saying, "I'm bisexual."

"Noted." Onyx proceeded upward. When Nico didn't immediately follow, he paused. "We aren't playing poker in the strip club, are we?"

Nico had stopped outside the club's second story, which housed the men's stage. "No, we're playing in the casino."

A funny sensation spread within him, almost as if he'd anticipated something changing now that everyone's sexual orientation was out in the open. Nico shook it off and continued up the stairs, but that little spark inside him remained.

Onyx matched his pace. "Good. I'd be distracted otherwise. Seems rude not to give the dancers the attention they deserve."

Clearly, confirmation that Nico liked men wasn't of any particular interest to Onyx. Nico bit back a misplaced swell of frustration. It didn't matter.

Except apparently, it did. Possibilities opened in Nico's mind, and he tried to ignore them.

At the next landing, Nico nodded to the vampires guarding the casino door. Their gazes lingered on Onyx, but he either didn't notice or did a good job of pretending he didn't.

"Good luck," the man on the right said as he opened the door.

"Thanks, Jack." Nico led the way inside, the demon at his heel. "Would you like a drink?"

"No." Onyx wrinkled his nose. He was cute all scrunched up like that.

It wasn't as if Nico hadn't noticed Onyx's attractiveness before—far from it—but now he wanted to do something about that attraction. Nico's insides fluttered. Damnation, it was like he couldn't stop his train of thought now that it had started.

"You sure you don't want anything?" He had to say something other than what was going through his mind. "There are non-alcoholic beverages too."

Onyx took in the casino with an assessing eye. "I figured as much."

"Do you not drink?" He'd bypassed refreshments at lunch and the meeting with Rowan.

Onyx's sharp gaze finally landed on Nico. "Only blood."

A shiver wound down Nico's spine, his heart rate picking up. He tilted his head, cracking his neck to ward off the pleasurable sensation. *Fuck.*

Onyx laughed. "Don't worry, I'm not after your life force. I'm perfectly capable of feeding myself."

"Of course you are." Nico was suddenly hot in the cool casino. "I'm going to grab something. Have a look around and I'll show you to the private room after."

Onyx didn't hesitate to wander off, and Nico stalked to the bar and ordered a bourbon.

He wasn't usually into blood or biting, and couldn't even blame his reaction on curiosity. Being friends with vampires his whole adult life, it had been inevitable that he'd let a partner or two bite him during sex. He'd enjoyed it well enough. But he'd never craved anyone's bite.

Onyx's fangs piercing his flesh was another story. A second shiver raced through him. Onyx was beautiful and very much Nico's type. Even remembering Onyx's terrifying glowing face from the night they met didn't make his bite less appealing. Onyx's fury was as intriguing as the rest of him.

Did his and Onyx's tastes align?

Just because Onyx acted like a brat didn't mean he wanted to be disciplined. He probably had no interest in Nico hauling him over his knee and spanking his ass until it turned red. Right? But if he did...and if Onyx was good for Nico, he could reward Onyx with a taste of his blood, among other things.

Nico cleared his throat and braced against the bar.

He had to stop. It wasn't a good idea to find out what Onyx was into. Nico didn't want any drama, and Onyx seemed ripe for it.

Nico planned to be present in Harper and Ollie's lives as long as they allowed—even after everything settled down—therefore, he'd be in the demons' lives. Hooking up with Onyx even once would complicate his long-term relationship with the group, and it wasn't smart to get involved with someone who was waiting for a fated mate.

Sounded like a recipe for heartbreak.

Nico wasn't Onyx's mate and didn't want to be. He'd never been interested in immortality and had no desire to be bound to anyone.

Nico hoped to find a partner to share his life with long term, whether exclusively or more openly, in a relationship that included others. There was no reason to get attached to a demon who was destined to be part of a perfect pair when Nico wasn't the other half of the equation.

Scooping up his drink, Nico left the bar and found Onyx at a slot machine.

"The strip club was more fun," the demon complained.

Nico suppressed a smile. No doubt, Onyx could whine about anything. It shouldn't be charming, but it was.

"Come on."

A hallway lined with private rooms was situated at the back of the casino. High-stakes games, and ones where players wagered magical items and favors rather than money, were tucked away from prying eyes, though tonight wasn't anything like that.

In the last room on the left, Leo—one of the casino bartenders and a good friend of Nico's—waited with an air of excitement. Nico had texted to say he was bringing Onyx, and Leo must have come early to get a look at him before everyone else arrived.

"Glad you made it." Leo pulled Nico into a one-armed hug. "Who's this?"

Onyx braced a hand on his hip. "You mean my reputation doesn't precede me?"

"Okay, you got me." Leo raised his hands, palms out. He had pale skin and short brown hair, and was about Onyx's height. "You must be the demon, Onyx. I'm Leonardo Valero, but you can call me Leo."

"Pleasure." Onyx extended a hand, and Leo shook it.

Leo's eyes swept over Onyx. "I can't detect your magic at all. It's amazing."

"Most things about me are."

Nico hid a snort of laughter with a sip of his drink. Not well enough, going by the glare Onyx shot him. Nico smiled wider.

Leo ignored Nico's amusement. "Can all demons hide their magic?"

Onyx raised a brow. "Are you fishing for information?"

Leo's smile fell. It was more likely he was trying to show friendly interest.

But Onyx didn't wait for a response. "I already told your boss that suppression is a demon trick. So no reason to pretend we can't all do it."

Leo brightened. "It makes it nearly impossible for anyone to spot you."

Onyx hummed in agreement. "Unless we want you to."

Leo laughed. "Right." He turned his attention to Nico. "You weren't online on Sunday."

"Sorry." Nico rubbed the back of his neck. He'd been too busy cleaning his apartment to log in and play *World's End*.

He still had no idea who'd broken in. Nothing had been taken, or at least nothing noticeable, and they'd left no trace of magic behind. It seemed unlikely that any of the favors he'd done recently could have led to bad blood. All the requests had been low-key.

There was no point worrying Leo about it. "I got caught up with the neighbor. Hope you didn't miss me."

"We always miss you, but we did all right, so maybe we don't actually need you."

Nico shoved Leo's shoulder and rolled his eyes. Leo grinned.

Onyx's assessing gaze jumped between them.

"Do you play *World's End*?" Leo asked.

"No." Onyx frowned. "Not really my thing."

Nico wasn't surprised. "Ollie plays, right?" Harper had mentioned Ollie and Dante being into the game when Nico had brought it up the other day.

"Yeah," Onyx agreed, like he wasn't sure he wanted to give out the information.

"He should join us," Leo said without pause. "What side does Ollie play?"

Nico would love to include Ollie and get to know him better. "I'll have to ask."

Dante might not want to join if he were trying to keep his identity under wraps, but no one in the Valero Coven would take advantage of his trust. Besides, they'd only see his *World's End* character.

Onyx regarded Leo with newfound distaste, as if he didn't like the turn in the conversation. Was he being protective of Ollie? He didn't say anything or threaten Leo, and it wasn't as if politeness would hold him back.

Maybe it was something else.

A theory formed in Nico's mind. "Are you sure gaming's not your thing?"

Onyx narrowed his eyes. "I've never actually tried it."

"If you want, you're welcome at my place any time. Who knows, give it a go and you might enjoy it."

Leo's brows lifted. Yeah, Nico never invited anyone over, so what?

"I don't know. It sounds dumb." Onyx shifted his stance, almost nervously. "Why pretend to have powers when I can shoot fire from my fingertips?"

The warmth seeping into his tone didn't match his dismissive words. It seemed like he'd been jealous of Leo inviting Ollie to play, and was mollified by Nico's counter-offer. Not that the brat would admit it.

"Gaming's no dumber than any other hobby," Leo grumbled.

Onyx shrugged carelessly. "Not that you can control immortal fire. So what would you know?"

Leo shook his head and went to grab a drink from the bar in the corner of the room just as Rowan appeared in the doorway with Cecile, a tiny, lethal woman in charge of the coven's information gathering. Emile, Rowan's main enforcer, followed close behind.

"Onyx, welcome back." Rowan clasped Onyx's hand with a smile. "Let me introduce you to Cecile and Emile Valero."

Onyx greeted the other vampires with a frosty politeness.

Rowan's coven, like most vampire covens, wasn't based around mortal family ties the way witches' covens were. Members took the Valero surname upon joining, but only Rowan's children, to whom he'd gifted immortal life, were blood-bound to him.

Like the witches Harper grew up with, some vampire covens required members to swear blood loyalty upon joining, but Rowan didn't believe in forced connection.

Felix, Rowan's other enforcer, drifted into the room and was introduced. Everyone found seats at the table, with Nico situating himself next to Onyx.

Onyx wasn't aware, but Rowan had brought his three most powerful and trusted coven members. This wasn't their usual poker crowd.

"Can I get anyone else a drink?" Leo sounded nervous, likely having made the same observations as Nico.

"You're off duty, Leo. Relax. You aren't tending the bar tonight." Rowan pulled two cigars from his inner suit pocket and passed one to Cecile. "You don't mind, do you?" he asked Onyx.

"I'm not exactly worried about second-hand smoke."

Rowan smiled. "I suppose not. Would you like one?"

"Go on." Onyx held out a delicate hand, palm up, faint blue veins standing out against the pale skin of his wrist.

Rowan passed him a cigar. Putting it to his lips, Onyx lit it with a flash of blue fire.

Everyone stared. Fire was no vampire's friend, and no other magical being could conjure it from nothing.

The demon cut a smug look at Nico.

Nico shook his head, heat blooming in his chest. Fuck, Onyx looked hot when he was pleased with himself, those blue eyes shining, promising wickedness, and the slightest hint of a blush on his sharp cheeks.

Being around Onyx gave Nico a thrill. He was more aware of his body than usual, all his reactions bordering on primal, as if his subconscious recognized the predator in Onyx, yet wanted to move closer rather than flee.

What would it be like to master Onyx and coax sweet sounds from those snarky lips?

Rowan dealt. Usually, one of his employees oversaw the table and Rowan played, but this wasn't a regular game, and even though all the casino employees were aware of the magic world, many weren't in Rowan's coven, and couldn't learn Onyx's true nature.

Nico should have considered that before inviting Onyx last minute. A pang of guilt settled in his gut. What if Rowan had wanted to relax tonight?

They played the first few hands quietly, not talking more than was necessary to keep the game moving. The atmosphere remained tense. This wasn't exactly what Nico meant to invite Onyx to. He'd hoped for more fun, but of course, Rowan wouldn't relax around Onyx until they were better acquainted, if Rowan ever relaxed around him at all.

Maybe Nico shouldn't be so comfortable around the demon, but nothing he'd learned had led him to believe that the furious being he'd first met was the real Onyx. That wasn't the whole picture. Nico wanted to connect the dots between *that* Onyx and the one who got jealous of Ollie being invited to play video games.

"So, has our return caused a big stir?" Onyx asked as he folded his cards, his tone dripping with sarcasm. "Are you gathering your allies to strategize, preparing to counter our play for dominance?"

Damnation, did he have to be so abrasive? Maybe the furious Onyx was closer to the real him. He didn't exactly try to get along with anyone. At least not from what Nico had seen.

Rowan's turn was next, and he folded, tossing his cards into the middle of the table. "I've informed the covens I'm on the best terms with. Word hasn't gone wide enough to cause a stir, and since you gave no indication that demons wanted to dominate the magic community, I have no reason to move against you."

"Maybe not. But that doesn't mean you aren't. Are you really going to take my word for it and do nothing? You believe me when I say you won't notice most demons?"

Rowan raised a shoulder in a half-shrug. "Being prepared for all potential scenarios is always best."

"In other words, I suspected correctly." Onyx puffed on his cigar. "It's like you've forgotten demons have been in this city longer than your coven, and you didn't notice or have any trouble."

"Not every one of your kind is going to spend their energy making a name for themselves trading paintings."

"Of course not," Onyx snapped as if he thought Rowan was taking a dig at him. "But there will be more demons interested in the arts than in magic world politics."

"And finding their mates, right?" Leo cut it. He'd never liked tension. "It doesn't seem so bad if demons are going to be focused on finding partners. Onyx is right, most of the magic world probably won't even notice the demons' return if that's all they're doing."

"You make it seem like demons keep to themselves, Onyx." Nico had to agree, even if he worried that the transition was bound to be rocky.

Onyx waved his cigar. "Why wouldn't we? You all aren't as interesting as you think."

Cecile snorted, a hand covering her mouth.

"So, how does finding your mate work?" Leo asked.

Onyx blew out a plume of smoke. "Who knows? Magic, fate? I don't care."

"You don't?" Leo smiled like it was a joke, then his face fell. "How can you not care? Mates are why you came here in the first place."

Onyx's eyes glowed behind the wafting cigar smoke. "What do you know about why I do anything?"

"Sorry. I suppose I don't." Leo looked away.

Onyx set his cigar in an ashtray at the center of the table and stood. "It seems I'm killing the party. Why don't I leave so you all can relax? Unless your poker nights are always this *fun*. In which case, I'd rather spend my time with humans."

"Wait." Nico stood, but Onyx was already through the door. Nico followed him into the hall. "Do you always have to get under everyone's skin?"

Onyx stopped. "Yeah, pretty much."

"Why?"

He turned, eyes glowing with blue flame. "Because I can, and there's nothing anyone can do about it."

That was true. As a powerful immortal, Onyx could get away with anything, but Nico swore he'd said it as if he was begging someone to try and stop him. Was that what he wanted? To be included even when he pushed people away? Did he want someone to challenge him?

Nico stepped forward until they were chest to chest. He peered into Onyx's stony face. "Sounds like someone needs to teach you some manners."

Onyx took a step back, mouth open in offence, eyes flaming brighter, casting that eerie glow on his cheeks. "Like who? You? Try me, witch."

My fucking pleasure.

Onyx's power flared, electrifying the air, but it didn't scare Nico like it had on the rooftop. Onyx was so full of emotion, it was beautiful, enticing, practically pulling Nico into his orbit. Onyx's dark lashes framed his glowing gaze, and Nico wondered how they'd look fanned out on his cheeks.

What would Onyx look like when he let his emotions fly without the barrier of his indignation?

"Why does talking about mates bother you so much?"

Onyx clenched his fists, fire sparking, voice barely audible as he spat, "Because I don't need one."

Was that true? Was a mate not what Onyx wanted? The way he said it was different than his other protests, suggesting he didn't always want to be challenged.

Nico raised his hands in surrender. "Okay."

"Okay?" Onyx's cheeks flushed, fire dimming, the blue that remained transforming his blush from pink to lavender.

Had Nico guessed right? He wanted to prove he could recognize when Onyx was goading versus setting an actual boundary. "Yeah, I hear you. You aren't interested in mates the way other demons are. If talking about it bothers you, I won't bring it up."

Onyx's fire went out, but he covered his apparent surprise with a sneer. "Damnation, you always have to be so *reasonable*."

Nico scratched the stubble lining his chin. "You say that like it's a bad thing."

Onyx made a frustrated gesture with his hand. "It's annoying."

Yeah, he'd read Onyx correctly. "So it's annoying when I don't understand and say things that bother you, but also annoying when I try not to?"

"Yes, keep up. You're insufferable no matter what you do."

Nico bit back a smile and dammit if Onyx didn't too. "You like that I'm annoying."

Onyx looked comically horrified. "Eww, no, I don't. I like when you leave me alone."

"Liar," Nico teased, and Onyx actually grinned, anger seemingly forgotten.

Then his face closed off, fury snapping back into place. "Whatever. I'm going back downstairs." Where he could get the uncomplicated attention from humans he apparently preferred.

Nico hoped Onyx enjoyed showering the dancers with money as much as he seemed to. "All right, I need to speak to Rowan."

Onyx turned up his nose. "I don't care. I wasn't asking you to join me." And with that, he left.

Nico scrubbed a hand over his face. He was sure Onyx wanted him to follow. In fact, saying he wasn't inviting Nico was practically a formal invitation, at least based on everything Nico had seen of the demon.

But why did Nico *want* to follow? He wasn't trying to win Onyx over. He didn't need to be on good terms with him in order to look out for Harper and Ollie, and Onyx wasn't exactly helping spread the word about demons or manage the fallout.

That didn't stop Nico from wanting to get through to Onyx and break down his walls. Nico wanted to show Onyx he didn't have to push him away. He wanted... Nico wasn't sure. To make Onyx smile. To feel that crackle between them. That excitement.

Onyx's retreating form pulled on Nico like a magnet. Being around him was oddly enticing. Nico wanted Onyx despite it being a bad idea.

He craved the challenge Onyx presented. Nico was sure he could teach the imp a lesson, get to the bottom of what the demon really needed, and that both he and Onyx would more than enjoy the process.

But that wasn't his priority right now. Nico hurried back to the private room.

7

———

ONYX

Onyx found a new seat at the foot of the stage. A different woman was performing, and more people had crowded into the club. The energy coursing through the room was high, music thumping, but Onyx wasn't feeling it like he had been earlier.

A server appeared at his side almost instantly. "Can I get you a drink, darling?"

"No, thank you." Onyx handed her a tip anyway. He didn't bother checking if he'd grabbed a twenty or something larger.

The money disappeared into her top. "You must be the guy Star was talking about. How about a lap dance instead?"

"That's an excellent idea. Why don't you grab a few of your friends and take me to a private room?"

She beamed. "You got it, darling."

Onyx stood and followed the woman across the club. She grabbed Star, who'd changed out of her blue outfit into something cherry red, and beckoned another woman to follow them.

"I'm Angel, but the way," she said over her shoulder. "You've met Star, and this is Jade."

"Lovely to meet you all. I'm Onyx." He followed them into a

private room and sat on the cushioned bench seat, the bouncer catching his eye from beyond the partially open curtain.

Onyx extracted a wad of cash from his pocket and set it on a small side table. "How do you ladies like working here?"

"Oh, it's not bad." Star seated herself beside Onyx and ran her hands through his hair as she had earlier.

Jade glanced from the money to Onyx, fine black hair falling into her face. "Do you actually want a dance?"

"Not really." He dragged the table into the middle of the room and kicked his feet up. "So working for Rowan is all right?"

The women exchanged a glance. Jade sat beside Star and Angel perched on his other side, kicking her stiletto-clad feet up next to his, saying, "Working here is way better than anywhere else I've been."

Onyx had no desire to like Rowan, but was glad all the same. "Why's that?"

"The security here is next level." Star tugged on his hair, and Onyx closed his eyes briefly. It was like the woman had read his need to be touched the second he'd walked into the club. Fuck, he liked a head massage.

"Yeah, I've never worked in a club where half the bouncers weren't as bad as the patrons," Jade added. "Here, they aren't afraid to kick problems to the curb."

"And I consistently make more here than I have elsewhere." Angel took Onyx's cash and began counting it. "I got this job thinking I could move to bartending in the casino if I needed something more consistent, but why take the pay cut?"

"Not that they aren't paid well upstairs," Jade said quickly.

So Rowan wasn't scum. Onyx would have to work at hating him, not that it'd be a problem. He was a vampire and, therefore, annoying by default.

"How do you know Rowan?" Star asked.

"Friend of a friend. We've only met a few times."

Angel slid her feet off the table and divided the money into three piles. "What do you do, Onyx? That's such a cool name, by the way."

"Thanks." He grinned. "I run a gallery."

Angel laughed. "Fuck, it must pay well."

"It does. My artists make a killing."

Onyx didn't take much of a commission, less than other comparable galleries. It was easy to pass up the money when he'd had two hundred years since his escape from Hell to amass wealth, and magic to help him do it. He only bothered taking a commission to pay Scott and keep his business from drawing the wrong kind of attention in their circles.

Jade leaned forward. "Which gallery do you run?"

"Jade studied art in school," Star added.

Jade glared at her.

Onyx sat a little straighter. "I run Gallery Four. What medium did you study?"

Jade's eyes went wide at the gallery name. "Um, acrylics and a little bit of digital art."

Star paused her tugging on Onyx's hair. "Jade has such a cool style, and she does commissions."

"Really?"

Jade's cheeks turned pink. "Yeah, it's nothing much. I sell stuff online, like avatars and illustrations of people's OC's. I don't do many. I've only been doing commission for a few months."

Angel held her hand out in front of Onyx. "Give me your phone and I'll show you."

"No." Jade batted Angel's hand away. "Don't. They aren't that good."

"Yes, they are," Angel said firmly. "Especially your original work."

"I'd love to see." Onyx genuinely would. His favorite thing about his job was meeting artists, and he didn't hold onto pretentious ideas about some people being more worth his time than others. There were so many talented people out there, and Onyx preferred showcasing the ones who didn't already benefit from connections in the industry.

"Okay, if you want to see, I'll show you. Give me your phone." Jade took Onyx's phone and brought up a website. "I get commissions through social media and have an account showcasing my digital style that's linked under my contact page, but this shows more of my other work." She passed the phone back.

Onyx scrolled through the gallery showing a mix of line drawings and acrylic paintings, all of the human form, mostly women. There was so much emotion in each piece, especially the ones with two or more people. It was like getting a glimpse of various lovers at different stages of their relationships.

"These are stunning."

"Thank you," Jade breathed.

Onyx extracted his wallet and fished out a business card. "Why don't you send me a message, and we can meet at the gallery. I'd love to see some of these in person if that's all right with you?"

Jade took the card. "Fuck, really? I mean, sorry, thank you. I'd love that."

Onyx grinned, feeling a lot better than he had upstairs. Humans were his happy place. This right here was what mattered in life. Magical beings' priorities were too often lofty and stomach-churningly self-important.

After chatting idly for a while longer, they had to vacate the private room.

"Thanks for a great time," Onyx said as they reentered the main club.

"Come back and we can do it again sometime." Star blew him a kiss and sauntered over to a group of men standing near the bar.

"Yeah, see you around." Angel looped her arm through Jade's and pulled her away.

"Making friends?"

Onyx spun to find Nico smirking at him. Onyx's tense muscles loosened, and the hollow feeling that had been following him around seemed to fade. "I always make friends. Everyone loves me."

The witch raised his brows. "Is that what you were doing upstairs, getting everyone to love you?"

Onyx didn't need the magic world's affection. "I don't spend a lot of time with vampires. They don't count. I was talking about people who matter. *They* all like me."

"I see." Nico's expression turned shrewd, like he really did see. "And what about witches?"

Onyx's pulse sped up. "Depends. I won't hold being a witch against Harper."

Nico laughed, and Onyx's fire sparked inside him, the sound annoyingly beautiful. "Just Harper? I see how it is."

Onyx scowled, hiding the smile threatening to break free. "Aren't you busy with Rowan?"

"No." Nico shoved his hands in his pockets. "I figured I'd see if you wanted to go play *World's End?*"

Onyx's heart leapt. What was wrong with him? He hadn't expected Nico to come find him and hated being so glad to see him. All his reactions to Nico were baffling. He'd gotten under Onyx's skin in a way that shouldn't have been possible.

"I never said I wanted to play your little game."

"Oh, I know. But that doesn't mean you don't want to. Come on, I'm sure Ollie would love it if you played with him sometime."

How had Nico found the one argument Onyx couldn't say no to? Was Onyx that transparent in his desire to win over Ollie and Harper? Could Nico tell he wanted to be dragged kicking and screaming into being included? No, probably not. Nico was set on being kind and helpful. To everyone. It wasn't about Onyx specifically.

Hell, Nico was the worst.

"Fine, but don't try to invite me to play with that vampire, Leo."

Nico rolled his eyes. "Wouldn't dream of it."

Onyx followed him out of the club.

It wasn't as if more time with Nico was the worst thing to happen to him. The man was a treat to look at, and Onyx was curious about where he lived. Besides, the longer they hung out, the longer Onyx could pester him. Nico responded so well to everything Onyx threw at him.

Someone needs to teach you some manners.

Onyx's fire burned at the sheer audacity, his insides tightening with anticipation. Did Nico mean it? Did he care enough to make Onyx be good?

Probably not, but it was fun to mess with the witch either way. It was almost like Onyx was developing an addiction to him. That or some sort of magnetic pull had to be what drove him to follow Nico outside and into a rideshare.

The ride through the city was almost relaxing, and by the time the car pulled over in front of a small apartment building, Onyx's agitation was a distant memory.

They climbed out of the car, and Nico unlocked the gate barring the building's entry from the street. "No comments about my place?"

"Huh?" Onyx followed him into the small space separating the front door from the street, and the gate shut behind him.

Nico looked down at him. They were too close, trapped in

the narrow enclosure. "You had a lot to say about the look of Rowan's club."

"No I didn't. I made one comment." Onyx's skin prickled. He'd never insult the place where Nico lived. He took a shot at Rowan because he was an immortal and had chosen to spend his money on an architectural eyesore when he could, by all accounts, have afforded to set up somewhere nicer.

"Fine. Don't expect much and you won't be disappointed." Nico turned and unlocked the door.

Onyx seethed. Did Nico think he was shallow? He didn't go around the city judging people who had to actually work for a living. Of course they wouldn't have the same luxuries he had.

Nico led him inside, up the stairs, and down a hallway with worn carpet. He unlocked a door and stepped through, slipping off his shoes. Onyx followed and did the same.

The scent of citrus filled the air.

"I won't bother offering you a drink, but I'm going to grab something." Nico rounded the entry's tight corner and disappeared.

Onyx stepped after him. He took a deep breath, and the citrus scent deepened into something more earthy, soothing Onyx's foul mood as if it were a personally tailored balm made to inspire a creeping sense of comfort.

Déjà vu hit Onyx in the chest. A feeling he'd forgotten tugged at the edge of his senses. The Eternal Realm popped into his mind, bright blue skies, wispy clouds, and towering mountains.

For a second, it was as if Onyx had been transported home. Not to his loft or any other place he'd lived on Earth, but *home*. To the realm he'd never wanted to leave.

"I know it's small." Nico filled a glass with water in the kitchen area to the right of the open living space.

Onyx shook himself, and the feeling faded. "There's

nothing wrong with small. I don't live in a mansion, you know." He walked further into the room and sat on a leather couch that looked well-loved.

Nico joined him, pausing to turn on the TV and gaming console before sitting. "Where do you live?"

"A loft on the other side of the river." Why had he answered? He never told anyone where he lived, except Scott.

Nico's brows raised. "Across the river?"

"Yeah." Onyx's tone turned defensive. "Is that surprising?"

"It's not what I pictured." Nico set his glass aside and glanced toward the window. "I used to live right on the border of the South Banks and Port View."

It was Onyx's turn to be caught off guard. Those were the two Shearwater Landing neighborhoods that sat separated from the rest of the city by the river. They'd nearly been neighbors.

"I'm in the South Banks. Near Marlo's Bakery."

Nico ran a hand through his hair. "Shit, Marlo's. I haven't been there in ages."

"Marlo was the reason I moved there in the first place." Onyx was half kidding, but he did like the man's baking.

"You knew him?"

Oh, right. By the time Nico would have been born, Marlo hadn't been running the bakery anymore. "Not well. But I went by often enough that he recognized me."

Nico shifted, turning sideways to look at Onyx. "How long have you lived in Shearwater Landing?"

"This time? Maybe forty years? I've lived here off and on since the turn of the century. Last century, I mean."

Nico nodded. "What about Ash and Dante?"

Onyx's peaceful mood soured. "Dante hasn't left since they started building the place. We were all here then. Ash moved around. I didn't keep track of where. Though most recently, he was hiding in the woods."

Nico stifled a snort. "Hiding from what?"

"Who knows?" It was annoying that Nico cared.

He seemed to stare Onyx down. "What's that frown for?"

"It's just my face," Onyx snapped automatically, but for some reason, he added, "Ash said something about Harper growing up in the mountains where he'd been living. So maybe he wasn't really hiding."

Nico leaned closer. "Like Harper drew him to the woods?"

"Yeah." Onyx's world tilted, unease knocking him sideways. "Ash and Dante think it has to do with the mate connection."

"Is that why Dante was here in Shearwater Landing? The mate connection kept him in the city?"

"That's what he says. He always claimed he'd find his mate here. It took more than a hundred years for Ollie to show up, but Dante wasn't exactly wrong."

"Wow." Nico's brow creased. "I had no idea magic like that existed. Or that the bond was so all-encompassing. It goes beyond even meeting the person."

"Seems like it," Onyx muttered.

Before Ash and Dante mated, Onyx hadn't realized the bond could influence a demon's subconscious before crossing paths with their mate.

With Dante, being drawn to the place he'd find Ollie was somewhat logical. He'd always believed his mate was out there, so on some level, he'd been seeking Ollie this whole time. But the fact that Ash had hunkered down so close to Harper, even when he had given up on ever finding his mate, spoke to the cosmic nature of the connection.

Unease slithered around Onyx's heart.

He'd kept returning to Shearwater Landing because of his brothers, refusing to let them forget him. What if his determination to stay within reach meant he'd missed his mate?

No. He didn't need a mate, so it didn't matter. He'd had no

strong desire to be anywhere else, and surely ignoring an instinct like that was impossible. His mate probably wasn't out there.

Onyx liked his life in Shearwater Landing. He'd built something *good* this time around, something that brought him undeniable joy. Even if nothing had changed with his brothers.

Onyx pushed his discomfort to the back of his mind. "So, are we playing this game, or what?"

Nico jolted like he'd been in a daze. "Yeah. Unless you want to start with something more beginner level, since you've never played anything like this before."

"That might be a good idea." Onyx slumped into the couch cushions, the motion bringing him closer to Nico than he'd intended. "I don't want to suck at your stupid game."

Onyx felt Nico's laugh vibrate through the couch more than he heard it. "I'm surprised you don't want to get playing over with so you can tell me you were right, and gaming isn't for you after all."

But then they'd have one less reason to spend time together.

Fuck, Onyx wanted to spend time with Nico. How annoying. He couldn't even deny it to himself.

"You won't get rid of me that easily," he grumbled.

8

NICO

Nico handed Onyx a controller. "I'm not trying to get rid of you."

Onyx glared, like the reassurance was offensive. "Even if you were, it's not like I need you to entertain me."

"Of course not." Nico sagged into the couch. A moment ago, Onyx had been opening up, and Nico wanted that back. "Maybe I need *you* to entertain *me*."

Onyx didn't seem to know what to say to that.

Nico's face heated, and he turned his attention to the TV. Hopefully, Onyx wouldn't read into it.

He didn't *really* need anyone to keep him company. He wasn't lonely. But he wanted this. Onyx next to him on his couch was...not soothing—because it was *Onyx*—but welcome. The prickly demon fit, strangely like he belonged, even if Nico kept most of his friends out of his private space.

"Let's start with *Power*. It's by the same people who created *World's End*, but it's not as involved." Nico selected the game and started from the beginning. The intro music played, and Onyx watched the screen with apparent interest.

After a minute, he said, "Why are we watching a movie?"

Nico laughed. "Just be patient."

Onyx crossed his arms and slouched further into the couch. Once the intro was over, Nico attempted to guide Onyx through creating his character, but he didn't seem interested in any of the options. Nico quickly chose what he needed and passed him the controller.

"Play through the tutorial."

Onyx looked from the screen to his hands. "I don't get what it's telling me to do."

Nico scooched closer until he was almost pressed against Onyx. "The buttons are labeled." He pointed.

"Oh." Onyx pressed a mash of buttons, and the character on screen did a random mix of moves. "It's going to take forever to get good at this. How much damn time has Dante wasted learning so many games?"

"It's not like either of you are short on time."

"No. I guess not. And I do like to try everything once." Onyx made more of an effort to follow the on-screen instructions.

"Everything?" Nico couldn't help asking.

Onyx cocked his head, blue hair falling artfully to the side. "Pretty much. Though if it's sexual, I like to give it more than a one-and-done. To be sure. Things like ironing or building a ship in a bottle don't need further investigation."

"You've built a ship in a bottle?" Nico wasn't sure if mentioning it in the same breath as ironing or sex was weirder.

"Miniatures are fascinating, even if I don't particularly enjoy making them myself." Onyx turned back to the TV and tried again. "Don't look so shocked that I have hobbies."

"Sorry. I've never met anyone who's built a ship in a bottle."

"I guess I'll forgive you then. I'm sure it's not the last time I'll shock you."

Nico bristled. "I'm not exactly innocent."

Onyx's attention snapped back to Nico, glee brightening his face. "Oh? Are you a naughty little witch?"

"Fuck." Nico's body flashed hot. Not expecting that, he scrambled, "I-I'm not little."

Onyx's gaze raked over him, searing even without fire in his eyes. "Would you prefer young?"

Nico cleared his throat. "I don't feel young." His back certainly hadn't that morning, but the way his insides squirmed at Onyx's teasing left him out of his depth. Comparably, he was young and innocent.

Onyx's gaze dragged over Nico once more, and his skin tingled. "I guess that makes sense. You're an old soul. Too responsible and concerned to be youthful."

True, but ouch. "Make it sound less like a compliment, why don't you?"

Onyx pursed his lips. "I could, but I don't want to hurt your feelings."

Nico shook his head. "Your kindness really knows no bounds."

"Right?" Onyx gave him a feral grin. "I'm a gift unto this mortal plane."

Nico barked a laugh. He liked everything about this, even the shock of discomfort. He was a fool for thinking he could get a handle on an immortal like Onyx.

Didn't mean he wouldn't try.

A sound like clanging metal had Nico's head whipping around. He stared out the darkened window. The curtain wasn't shut, but he couldn't see anything with the lights on inside. Had that been something out on the fire escape?

"You okay?" Onyx asked.

Nico forced himself to look away. "Fine. I heard something, but it was probably a cat."

Onyx narrowed his eyes. "Are you scared of cats?"

"No. Don't be ridiculous."

"I'm not. You're the one who jumped like someone was about to appear in the window and say *boo*."

Nico rubbed his palms along his thighs. "What? I can't be startled?"

He stood and crossed the room. Opening the window, he stuck his head out and looked up, then down. There was nothing on the fire escape. He closed the window and drew the curtain.

"You should have your house better protected," Onyx said as Nico sat back down.

"Are you inspecting my spells?"

Onyx shrugged. "Yeah. They could use some help."

"Fuck off." Onyx was right, but the protection was the best Nico could do without hiring someone more powerful.

He had a solid magical ability, nothing extraordinary. Nico had studied hard and knew a wide range of spells. He was good at picking things apart and figuring out the best way to counter most magic. His skill was versatile. Strength wasn't everything.

"I'm not being rude." Onyx put the controller down. "All I'm saying is, stronger spells would keep the big scary cats out, if they've got you jumpy."

Nico ignored the cat comment. "I'm going to get someone to sort it out, but haven't gotten around to it."

He'd asked Rowan if the coven had any trouble recently, but it was no surprise that all was quiet. It was unlikely that whoever had broken in had been mad about something Nico had done for Rowan. If they were, why not go directly to the vampire they had a problem with?

The break-in seemed personal, but it had been years since Nico had fallen out with a friend, and his family wasn't among the living.

"I can protect your place for you," Onyx said with a flippant wave of his hand.

Nico's spine stiffened. "You don't have to."

The demon arched a brow. "Damn right. Seeing as I don't have to do anything, ever. I'm offering because I want to."

"Why?" Nico stared at him. Onyx didn't hate him, but whatever was building between them wasn't strong enough to garner a favor like this. "Aren't I annoying?"

"You can be annoying and well-protected at the same time. I don't see the issue."

Nico should accept. It would save him spending money on a security witch, and Onyx's spell would be stronger than anyone's, except possibly other demons.

"What do you want in exchange?"

Onyx blinked, like the question confused him. "Do you ask for anything in return when you do favors for people?"

"No." Nico helped people who needed it, not so he could gain anything for himself.

Onyx stood. "Didn't think so."

"But—"

"Sit back and relax, and I'll make you an impenetrable fortress. Well, not quite, but demons aren't after you. Just big scary cats. Besides, you've wormed your way into our little group, so you should be protected like Ollie and Harper."

Nico gaped at Onyx, his chest tightening. When was the last time he'd let someone look out for him? With Rowan, everything was mutual. Nico didn't ask for favors. He gave his time and talent to others but relied on himself.

He almost told Onyx that someone had broken in, then stopped himself. They wouldn't be able to violate his space after the demon cast his spell. Nico didn't want to worry Onyx, or even worse, find out that Onyx wasn't actually concerned, and this was some weird...Nico didn't know what, but he didn't want to ruin it.

9

ONYX

ONYX ARRIVED at the restaurant early and was shown to the table he'd reserved. Ollie and Harper couldn't be too far away. Once they were here, their Shearwater Landing food tour could officially begin.

Onyx ordered sparkling water for the table and opened the menu.

As kept happening that day, Nico intruded on his thoughts. He'd been so awkward about Onyx protecting his apartment. It should have been annoying, but was kind of adorable. Too bad Nico hadn't said what caused him to be so jumpy.

Maybe it was nothing, and Onyx shouldn't care. The witch could take care of himself. But Onyx hated not knowing. Hopefully, if he teased Nico about being afraid of cats enough, he'd give in and tell Onyx the real problem to shut him up.

"This place looks nice."

Onyx glanced up, finding a beaming Harper approaching the table, closely followed by Ollie.

Ollie pulled out a chair. "I love sushi. It's the perfect way to start our tour."

"Couldn't agree more." Onyx put down his menu and smiled at the little mates, feeling even mushier than usual.

"I've only had sushi a couple of times," Harper confessed. He wore eyeliner and what looked like mascara, making his eyes pop behind his glasses. Onyx hadn't ever seen Harper wear makeup before.

"You'll love this place. We can get a little of everything." Onyx reached across the table and tapped Harper's shoulder gently. "You're looking good, by the way. The liner suits you."

Harper's cheeks bloomed red. "Thanks. I'm—uh—playing around with it."

"As you should. Trying out different styles never gets old, especially as the decades go by." Onyx was still in his work clothes, a designer T-shirt and distressed jeans. He went back and forth between business casual and not, depending on his mood. At least at work.

Harper leaned forward. "What's your favorite style?"

"At the moment?" Onyx considered. "Nothing dinner appropriate."

Harper's eyes went wide, and Ollie snorted.

"I'm kidding. Kind of." Onyx was at his most free when he was wearing as little as possible. Contrary to what his brothers might think. "I like using clothes to fit in with human society. They help shape how they see me."

Harper seemed fascinated. It was the longest the two of them had ever talked without Onyx ruining it. "You like dressing human?"

Onyx willed his cheeks not to heat. "Yeah, maybe that sounds dumb, but I want to feel like I'm a part of their world, not just passing through."

Harper nodded as if this made sense. "You're so much better adjusted to the real world than Ash or Dante. I swear I have to remind Ash to put on a shirt every time we go out."

It was true. Onyx's brothers seemed happy to sit apart from humanity.

"They've been more involved with humans in the past than they are these days," Onyx admitted. It was hard when human friends died, or had to be left behind so they didn't notice the demons not aging, but Onyx never let that keep him away.

"Speaking of humans, how's your artist friend?" Onyx asked Ollie.

Ollie's dimples popped as he smiled. "Dex is good. I'd love to bring him to your next opening, if that's cool?"

"Consider it done. I'll send you both formal invitations." Onyx basked in Ollie's string of thank yous.

They turned to the menus, and dinner flew by in a whirl of delicious food. If Nico had been there—wait—why was Onyx thinking about Nico? He'd seen him yesterday. His addiction to the man seemed less like a joke all of a sudden.

As they left the restaurant, Onyx booked a ride home for the mates.

Harper seemed disappointed that dinner was over. "Next time we have to go out when we aren't working in the morning."

"Deal." Onyx gave him and Ollie an evil grin. "We can add a nightlife tour to our schedule."

"Yes, oh my gosh, we have to." Harper bounced on the balls of his feet. He had so much joyous energy, it was amazing. "Oh! How did you like Rowan's club last night?"

Onyx's stomach swooped. "What?"

"Nico said he was taking you to poker night." Harper waggled his eyebrows.

Ollie made a pleasantly surprised sound. "He did?"

Onyx crossed his arms. It wasn't like he had anything to be embarrassed about, so he pushed the feeling away. "Poker was dreadful, though I'll admit, Rowan runs a good show. No one at the club had any complaints about him."

Ollie's brow furrowed. "You were asking around?"

Onyx shrugged. "We don't really know the guy."

"True." Harper rubbed the back of his neck. "I'm glad the dancers don't hate him."

Ollie elbowed Harper in the side. "You and Ash going back again?"

Harper's cheeks flushed. "Yeah, but after watching everyone perform, I think I want to take pole dancing lessons."

"You should." Onyx loved how outgoing Harper was, even when he was bashful about it.

Ollie nodded his encouragement.

These little mates were going to be fun. They'd do Onyx's miserable brothers good.

"I'll keep you guys posted," Harper promised as the car pulled up.

The boys climbed in, and Onyx headed toward the nearest subway station. The train didn't cross the river, but he felt like a walk. He'd ride it as far as it went and take the footbridge.

Onyx zoned out, on autopilot as he moved through the night. He didn't mind the harsh lights of the subway or the drunk people singing in his car. Cities were the only place for him, where masses of people meant something was always happening.

The night air turned cool as he exited the underground station. Onyx walked lazily, not in any rush to get back to his empty loft.

He crossed the bridge, pausing to look out at the water. The idea of a pet nagged at him. He needed something. Ignoring the hollow longing that had taken up residence inside him never worked for more than a few hours. And if he got a cat, he could use it to tease Nico about his fictional fear.

Onyx smiled to himself, a garden of tangled feelings blooming in his chest, delicate and open, but with a razor edge, like he was afraid of where this change in him had come from.

Someone stepped up to the railing beside him. "Brother."

Onyx froze. Lucifer loomed next to him, taller even than Ash.

"What the hell are you doing here?" Onyx hissed.

Luc had never sought him out on his previous trips to this realm. Only Ash and Dante.

Onyx pretended that didn't hurt. It shouldn't, when he never wanted to see his brother's obnoxious face again.

"I wanted to talk to you," Luc said, voice low and concerned.

Onyx's rage bubbled like a cauldron about to explode. "Like fuck you do. Did you forget that the first time you saw me in two hundred years, you cursed me, knocked me unconscious, and left me on the fucking floor?"

"Onyx." Luc laid a hand on his shoulder.

"No." Onyx jerked away, glaring at his brother's familiar chiseled face and tumbling night-black hair. "Don't use that placating tone with me. Don't fucking act like I'm making shit up."

"I'm not. I'm sorry I cursed you, but I had to get away." Pain lined Luc's eyes, which were brown rather than flaming red. He looked like a damned runway model—beautifully human—in a sleek black coat that was completely inappropriate for summer.

"You're sorry, *but*. Story of my life, Luc."

"Onyx, I get that you're mad. We still need to talk. That's why I came to you."

"No, you came because I'm the only one you could be sure wouldn't try to kill you on sight."

Lucifer grimaced, his fine features twisting in a way that almost looked regretful. He was a master of emotion. A master of faking it. Lying.

"Leave us alone, Luc." Onyx took a step backward. "If you aren't trying to drag us back into your shit—"

"Then what? You won't imprison me?"

Onyx held his tongue. He should call Dante, but he hesitated.

"I need your help, Onyx. Please." Luc took two steps forward, bringing them too close together, and grabbed Onyx's upper arms, his touch deceptively gentle.

"H-help?" Onyx spluttered. He couldn't believe the nerve. "You want my help? Maybe you should have considered that before—oh, I don't know—every single thing you've done in your life."

"You can't blame everything on me. You chose to fall."

Onyx's fire burned, and Luc's wince told him he felt the sting.

"I've wronged you," Luc continued in a rush. "I'm sorry. Can't you believe I want to make things right?"

"No." Onyx pulled from Luc's grasp. "Stop trying to manipulate me. Just stop. Leave me alone!"

Luc ran a hand roughly through his hair, leaving it disheveled. He glanced around the empty bridge. He seemed jittery. Worried. Anxious even. Onyx caught himself, remembering not to believe any of it.

Then Luc disappeared. In a blink, he was gone.

Onyx's eyes burned, his vision blurring. "Fuck you, you miserable shit!" he screamed at the deserted spot where his brother had stood. His fire burned even hotter, and he sucked in a ragged breath.

Stupidly, he felt abandoned all over again, irrationally mad that Luc was gone even when Onyx had never wanted to see him in the first place.

Casting an invisibility illusion over himself, he ripped off his shirt, freed his wings, and shot into the sky.

10

———

NICO

The Herb Emporium was quiet first thing in the morning, so
Nico took the time to organize the new stock that had been
delivered the afternoon before, then brewed a pot of coffee in
the back room.

He had a steaming mug in hand when Harper bustled in.

"Morning." Harper slipped past Nico to put his bag away,
returning with his own mug of coffee, drowned in hazelnut
creamer by the looks of it.

"How was dinner last night?" Nico asked.

"So good." Harper sighed at the memory. "I've been in
Shearwater Landing for over a year, but I didn't explore much
in the way of food before I left my coven. I've been missing out."

Nico's pulse spiked at the casual mention of Harper's
abusive coven. He should have tried harder to figure out what
was going on with Harper from the moment he'd met the
nervous young man trying to sell him potions. He'd had no idea
it was anywhere near as bad as it turned out to be.

He swallowed the apology. He'd said it before, and Harper
had waved him off, claiming Nico would have spooked him if

he'd pushed, and in that case, Harper probably wouldn't have come back.

"You should check out the food trucks by the river park at lunch. Tino is always there on Fridays, and his spread is to die for."

"Okay." Harper had a hearty sip of coffee. "Want me to bring you back something?"

"Na, that's all right. I'll walk over on my break and say hi."

Harper shook his head. "You're friends with everyone."

"I've been around this neighborhood a long time." Nico didn't have many humans in his social circle, but he liked to be on friendly terms with the locals regardless.

After finishing his coffee, Harper got started on the custom potions that had been ordered that week. Some might say an apothecary shop owner should be able to brew their own potions, but Nico never begrudged having to hire a brewer. Running and manning the shop was enough work.

Nico's father had opened The Herb Emporium well before Nico was born, running it with Nico's mother, who had the potion brewing ability. Nico had grown up in the shop as much as he had in the little apartment his parents had rented in the South Banks.

Nico's parents had been on the older side, and Nico's father had passed away when Nico was in high school. From then on, he'd helped his mother keep the shop open, and when she'd fallen ill a year later, he'd taken it over completely.

Caring for his mother, running the shop, and finishing school all at once had changed Nico's life. Onyx was right. He'd never really been young. Even before taking over the shop, he was too busy working after school to get up to the kind of youthful mischief his peers had. But Nico didn't resent it. He'd had loving parents and made a solid living, and that was more than a lot of people had.

The bell above the front door chimed, and a familiar woman walked in.

"Hi, Evelyn." Nico set down the cooling dregs of his coffee. "How are you?"

She glanced over her shoulder, moving closer to the counter. "I've been better, if I'm honest."

Nico's heart sank. "What's up?"

"I hate to bother you again." She paused, tucking a lock of brown hair behind her ear.

"You aren't bothering me," Nico said sternly, but not without kindness.

"Thanks." She sighed. "I heard Michael might be back in town."

Nico cursed internally. "I'm sorry to hear that. He hasn't contacted you, has he?"

"No." She shook her head vehemently. "Nothing like that, and I can't kick him out of the city altogether, I get that. But one of my friends said her cousin heard he's popped up again, and I don't like it."

"Does your friend's cousin know where you're living now?"

Nico and Evelyn had gone to high school together. She was a witch and wasn't associated with a coven, like Nico wasn't. They hadn't kept in touch over the years, but she'd come to him about six months ago, asking for help getting away from an abusive relationship after hearing around the neighborhood that he was trustworthy.

Michael was a powerful witch, and though he was also unassociated with a coven, he'd gotten the idea to start his own, gathering friends he'd met through various less-than-legal business ventures he'd dipped his toes in over the years.

In the end, everything had worked out as best it could. Rowan had crushed the new coven's attempt to claim territory—the Valeros didn't tolerate covens involved in the drug or weapons trade, or who took advantage of unsuspecting humans —and Nico had helped Evelyn move and get a new job. Michael had left, presumably to try his shit somewhere else.

Evenly stepped closer. "No, my friend, Clare—her cousin Ty doesn't know where my new place is. He wouldn't tell Michael even if he did. He never trusted him."

"That's good. Do you have any idea where Michael is staying?"

Evelyn shook her head. "I'm not even one hundred percent sure he's here. Ty said it was a rumor he'd heard."

"I appreciate you telling me. Michael better not be trying to set up here again, but either way, if you need somewhere else to stay, I can find something."

"Thanks." Evelyn looked relieved. "I think I'll be okay with my roommates for now, but it's good to remember I have options."

"Of course. You still have my number?"

She nodded.

"Call anytime, and even if I can't get there, I'll send someone."

"I will. Hopefully, him being back isn't about me, but when I heard..."

"I totally understand. Is your security all up to date?"

"Yeah, it's solid. My roommate is dating a seriously powerful woman who cast all sorts of stuff on our place."

"Perfect. I'll call if I hear anything, and if it turns out to be a rumor and Michael's not here, I'll make sure to pass that along too."

"Thanks, Nico." She smiled. "Hope you're doing well. It was nice to see you, even like this."

"Same to you."

She left, and Harper drifted out of the back room. "I can

make her a magic suppressant so she can't be tracked. Do you think that would help?"

Nico appreciated it. He clapped Harper on the shoulder. "We checked that Michael didn't have blood or anything of hers he could use to track her before he was asked to leave the city. She should be safe from tracking, but if that changes, we'll do whatever we have to."

Harper seemed relieved. "Okay, good. How did you get her ex to leave town?"

Nico summarized the issues with Michael's new coven and how Rowan had put his foot down. "The Valeros have a strong presence here and work hard to keep criminal-minded covens out, both witch and vampire. Last year, there was a serious issue with the Orlov Coven trying to move in and get access to the port, but Rowan shut it down. Made the issue with Michael feel like a breeze."

"Why did they want access to the port?"

"Trafficking, most likely. The Orlovs had a reputation for mistreating humans, to say the least, but their leader was killed, along with most of the members, and their operations shut down." There were hardly any Orlov vampires left as far as Nico knew, and none were in Shearwater Landing.

Harper seemed to hang on Nico's words. "Oh, man. That's a lot."

Nico smiled ruefully. "Rowan's used to it."

Harper's eyes widened. "If you say so." He returned to the back room and his potions.

Could Michael have had anything to do with the break-in? Trashing Nico's place seemed like the kind of petty thing he'd do, even if he wasn't willing to risk attacking Nico outright and having Rowan's wrath come down on him a second time.

If he had been the one to break in, he wouldn't be able to get in now. Nico would have to track him down to figure out if he'd been involved.

He shot off a text, telling Rowan the guy might be back, in case he tried anything.

As he closed out of his text conversation with Rowan, his finger seemed drawn to his message thread with Onyx. He clicked it, even though he had nothing to say. Nico had already thanked Onyx for protecting his apartment, and it was too soon to ask him to come over to game again.

Still, he didn't close out of the thread.

As Nico stared at the screen, three little dots appeared, indicating Onyx was typing. Nico's heart leapt like he was a kid with his first crush. Ridiculous, but he waited with eager antici-pation as the dots popped up and disappeared.

No message came through. After a while, the dots didn't reappear. Onyx must have changed his mind.

What had he been about to say?

Nico put the phone away and returned to work, more disap-pointed than he should be.

11

ONYX

Onyx tossed his phone onto his desk. Why was he obsessing over Nico? He was the last person Onyx needed right now.

He had to call his brothers and tell them Luc had snuck up on him, but couldn't bring himself to do it. What good would it do? Luc was gone, and he didn't want to argue with Ash and Dante. Not today.

Onyx paced the office. His tattooed wings itched, his skin crawling. All he wanted was to fly, the spacious room suddenly feeling as confining as a locked cell. Onyx flexed his fingers, cracking his knuckles. Everything in him pulled tight like he was about to snap.

What was Lucifer trying to do, coming to him like he needed help? How dare he, after everything. Onyx owed him less than nothing, yet a sliver of guilt persisted. What if this time, Luc was being genuine?

No. Onyx was a fool. No wonder Luc had spent eternity hurting him. Onyx made it too easy.

He wrenched his office door open and marched down the hall, forcing himself to calm his movements by the time he reached the upstairs gallery space. He had an appointment with a buyer in twenty minutes and needed to get out of his funk. The artist deserved this sale. Onyx needed his head in the game.

"We've had a request for a last-minute appointment this evening," Scott said as Onyx came downstairs, his familiar voice as refreshing as a cool breeze on Onyx's overheated skin.

"Oh?"

Scott turned away from the computer. "They can be here by five, so I said yes. Apparently, the lead from that action movie everyone is talking about is moving to the city, and her decorator just found out that the penthouse needs to be photo-shoot ready in two weeks."

Onyx paused in front of the desk. "I have no idea what movie you're talking about, but that sounds perfect for us."

Scott stroked his chin, swiveling in his chair. "*Mmhmm.* Bet I can sell at least three pieces. They want a cohesive theme for all the art in the house. All I need to figure out is which artist they want to go with, and they might take a whole series."

Onyx turned toward a row of paintings along the back wall. "Cam does sculpture and oil on canvas. If the designer likes their work, they would be perfect. Unless the designer is only trying to fill the walls?"

"No, I was thinking Cam. Though I'm always thinking about their work." Scott paused, looking more closely at Onyx. "Are you all right?"

Onyx resisted running his hand through his hair. He'd mess it up. "Didn't sleep well. Is it that obvious?"

Scott cocked his head. "Not overly. You look impeccable as always, but I can feel the tension pouring off you."

"There goes my attempt to claim it was a fun kind of not sleeping," Onyx joked.

"I wouldn't have bought it. It's almost creepy how well I can spot when you've gotten laid."

Onyx laughed, and Scott smiled. "Don't remind me how long it's been."

"Wouldn't dream of it." Scott turned back to the computer, nose ever so slightly elevated. "I'm glad the recently-laid sense between us only works one way."

Onyx had to agree. "I prefer to keep a little mystery in our friendship, even if I'm not the mysterious one."

Even with his mood lifted, the day dragged. Onyx wasn't exactly worried. Luc wouldn't burst into the gallery. He'd sought Onyx out in the middle of the night on a deserted bridge for a reason, but that was hardly comforting.

If Onyx could figure out his brother's new angle, he could stay ahead of whatever new hurt the Devil had in store for him.

The interior designer ended up buying four of Cam's pieces, three paintings and a sculpture. She also hinted heavily that her client would love to come to Cam's next showing at Gallery Four.

It was a ridiculously successful day. Onyx should have been over the moon. He hated Luc for ruining it. Hated that his brother could affect him, even after so long. But most of all, Onyx hated that a silly, desperate part of him wanted to heal things with Luc, and still craved his brother's love.

The hollow feeling in his chest opened unbearably wide.

He needed an escape. To not think.

After wishing a very pleased Scott good night, Onyx closed the gallery. Walking through the city wouldn't help tonight, so he went to the roof and freed his wings.

The relief was only momentary, chased away by an oppressive sense of obligation. He had to see Dante, but couldn't stomach the inevitable argument with his brothers any more now than he could that morning.

Onyx launched into the air, wings singing as he caught an updraft. He longed to jump from the tallest cliff in the Eternal

Realm, let himself fall, tumbling through the air until he almost hit the ground.

Onyx hadn't thought about that kind of reckless flying in centuries, let alone done it.

He climbed into the sky, higher and higher until a chill shocked his overheated skin, and his lungs strained against the thin air. Then he plunged, wings folded in tight to his back.

Onyx hurtled toward Earth. Everything twisted inside him, the hollowness growing until he gave in and screamed. The sound tore from his throat and was whipped away on the wind, taking none of his anger with it.

Onyx spread his wings and pulled up, shooting back into the sky and narrowly missing a building. He slowed and flew aimlessly until he ended up near the river, following it all the way to the Banks.

He cut inland and landed on top of Nico's apartment building.

Why was he here?

Nico would think Onyx was clingy if he showed up unannounced, but Onyx didn't care. He hadn't been this settled since he'd looked into Luc's eyes.

The adrenaline rush from his flight must have leveled him out. It wasn't Nico.

That didn't explain why he put his wings away, pulled on his shirt, shed his invisibility illusion, and climbed down the fire escape.

Inside his apartment, Nico stood at the counter in his little kitchen, his back to the room.

Onyx crouched outside the window and inspected Nico's broad shoulders and firm ass. It wasn't fair how attractive the man was. Onyx could look at him all night. It didn't seem like a bad way to spend his time, which was absurd. He usually had better things to do.

Except tonight, it seemed he didn't have anywhere else he wanted to be. Was he going to knock on the glass like a stalker or lurk like a stalker?

He was saved from deciding when Nico turned around and spotted him. He froze, dark eyes going wide. After a moment, he shook his head.

Nico walked to the window and opened it. "What the hell are you doing?"

"Checking for cats." Onyx did his best to look indignant while crouched in an undignified position. He tossed his hair. "Didn't spot any, so you should be safe for now."

"It's a good thing you came by. However would I have relaxed not knowing?"

"Shut up and move." Onyx shooed Nico out of the way so he could climb through the window. He stood straight and readjusted his shirt, another designer piece with a V-neck. "What are you making?"

Nico closed the window. "Nothing. I'm reheating some pozole."

There was an awkward silence.

Maybe Onyx should have let himself smash into that building. Then, he'd be dead to the world, waiting for his body to heal, instead of here feeling like his cheeks might actually burst into flames.

"Well, don't let me keep you from dinner," he snapped.

Nico opened his mouth, apparently reconsidered, and closed it. He returned to the kitchen and retrieved a bowl from the microwave. Maybe he'd be polite and pretend that Onyx showing up like this wasn't weird.

"Would you like some?"

Onyx shifted his weight. "No, thank you."

Nico snorted a sharp laugh, and Onyx's embarrassment intensified. He shouldn't have come, but standing in the apartment was so much better than being anywhere else. Just looking at Nico soothed the tangled mess in Onyx's chest.

He watched as Nico ate his dinner, then washed and put away the bowl and spoon.

Nico leaned against the counter. "So, what brings you here, besides cats?"

Fuck, what could he say? Best not to make it about him at all. "I figured you had nothing better to do."

"Oh?" Nico smirked, not even pretending to believe him, damn it. "You sure you didn't miss me?"

Onyx shot forward at an inhuman speed, halting a couple of feet from Nico. The witch didn't even flinch. "I didn't miss you."

"I think you did. I think you've been daydreaming about me since you left," Nico taunted.

Onyx blushed. Why wasn't there a spell to prevent the stupid bodily reaction? "I have not. I don't even like you. If anything, I was thinking about how annoying you are."

Nico bit his lip. "So you came over to tell me you don't like me and that I'm annoying?"

"Yes." That sounded like something Onyx would do.

Nico nodded, the motion clearly mocking. "I see. And all the times you told me to leave you alone and go away, you meant that too?"

"Yes." He was making fun of him, and Onyx shouldn't care, but the scene on the bridge filled his mind—demanding Luc *go away*—and Onyx's eyes burned. He snarled, "I want everyone to stop bothering me."

Nico took a step closer, his brow furrowing in something like concern. "I don't think that's true. Come on, you didn't show up at my window to remind me how annoying I am."

Words stuck in Onyx's throat.

Nico went on. "I think you want me to bother you, and that's okay. You can tell me why you're really here. I'll listen."

He'd listen? No, he fucking wouldn't.

All the tension inside Onyx pulled to a point, and he snapped like a thousand-year-old string, longing and hot fire exploding inside him so powerfully he couldn't take it. "Yeah, well, you listen to everyone's problems. Pretending to care is so pathetic. So desperate. Your good-guy act makes me want to hurl."

Nico stepped closer. "It's not an act."

But it was. Onyx hated lies like this. Fake concern was worse than dismissal.

"Yes, it is. Just stop. Leave me alone. It's stupid how much you pretend to care. Everything about you is stupid." Onyx heaved, breath rushing in and out.

He was losing it. No one ever got to him like this. He didn't understand. There was no reason to be embarrassed that he'd come over. Other people's opinions didn't matter. He owned his desires. Did what he wanted.

Nico shook his head, huffing like he was disappointed. "Don't call me stupid, Onyx. It's rude."

Onyx's eyes burned. "Like I care." He didn't. Nico's disappointment was nothing. It didn't make the burning in his chest worse. Didn't make it harder to breathe.

"I think you do." Nico stepped closer until they were almost touching. "I think you care a lot. You're just being a brat about it."

Onyx tensed, fists balling up. "Fuck you."

Nico shrugged a shoulder. "Fine, fuck me, but I'm not wrong. You want me to challenge you. That's why you act like this."

"You think you know anything about me, you arrogant

asshole? Hell, I can't stand you!" Onyx was close to screaming, but he couldn't stop. His fury rose like a tidal wave.

Nico remained maddeningly calm. "*Mmm*, more vague insults. Is that all you've got? Nothing real to say? You want me angry so you'll get a reaction. So you can figure out what I'll do to you when I'm mad. You're practically begging me to teach you a lesson."

It was true on so many levels. Onyx spluttered, blood heating with something other than rage. He imagined Nico disciplining him like he deserved, and his core tightened even as he tried to deny the pleasure coursing through him.

But Nico wouldn't teach him a lesson. Not the way Onyx wanted. In a way that showed he cared. Nico didn't mean it like that. He'd write Onyx off and forget about him, proving his concern was as fake as everyone else's.

Nico loomed over Onyx. "You can't come into my house and insult me, Onyx. I won't allow it."

Onyx found his voice, but it came out breathy and strained. "Y-you can't stop me. I'm a demon."

"That's true." Nico gripped Onyx's chin between his thumb and forefinger and tilted it, forcing their eyes to meet. "But I think you want me to punish you all the same. Spank you for being such a brat."

Onyx whimpered. It slipped out before he could get a handle on himself. *Fuck*, he was so lost. How had he gotten here? He'd never wanted anything more than for Nico to bend him over and punish him. To care enough to not walk away.

Nico stroked his thumb along Onyx's jaw. "That's what I thought. Your eyes are so wide and hungry. You don't want to be left alone at all."

"No," Onyx whispered. He didn't want to be left alone. He wanted to be here. He wanted Nico to make it all better.

Onyx liked to submit. He'd been disciplined countless

times, in all imaginable ways, but he'd never needed it like this. It was terrifying. "You can't spank me. You wouldn't dare."

"Wouldn't I?" Nico grinned like he was the predator out of the two of them. The one with all the power.

In a sudden movement, he grabbed Onyx around the middle and hoisted him over his shoulder.

Onyx yelped. "What the fuck! Put me down."

Nico chuckled and carried Onyx across the small room and dumped him on the couch.

The indignity! Onyx fumed. He tasted smoke, pulse thumping and cock hardening behind his jeans. "What the hell do you think you're doing?"

"Teaching you a lesson about coming in here unannounced and taking shots at me. I don't care if you're a demon. That shit doesn't fly." Nico sat on the couch, grabbed Onyx's hand, and pulled.

Onyx struggled. He could get away if he really wanted to. He was far faster, stronger, so much older it wasn't even funny, and had more magic than any witch. The power imbalance between them was vastly in Onyx's favor, but that wasn't what this was about. Not what was important. Nico drew Onyx close like he had every right to. Like Onyx belonged to him, and Onyx gave himself over.

In a few quick motions, Nico had Onyx laid over his lap. Nico's harsh breaths filled the air and Onyx could hardly think past his aching cock.

Nico placed a hand between Onyx's shoulder blades, the other on his ass. He had to feel how hard Onyx was. Nico's own arousal pressed firmly into Onyx's hip. Nico's hold on him tightened. "Do you know the traffic light system?"

"W-what?" Onyx's brain struggled to catch up. He was a ball of crackling need.

"Red, yellow, green. For—"

"Please," Onyx cut him off, bucking his hips. Nico held him firm. "I've been playing like this so long the reality would boggle your mind."

Nico chuckled, the condescending prick. "All right then. Color?"

"Fucking green, witch." Onyx glared over his shoulder, eyes burning so fiercely the whites had to be completely obscured with blue flame. "Try me."

He couldn't believe he was here, that this was happening. Nico should have thrown his rude ass out and told him never to come near him again.

But Nico looked wrecked in the best way, his dark cheeks flushed, eyes sharp with determined focus. His gaze drilled into Onyx like nothing else mattered. It wasn't true, but the illusion broke Onyx. Fuck, he wanted to matter to someone.

Nico brought a firm hand down on Onyx's covered ass, the slap muffled by denim. "Don't tell me what to do."

Onyx's breath whooshed out. The sting wasn't enough, but it promised *more* in a way he couldn't let go of. He buried his face in the couch cushion and squirmed, rubbing his erection against Nico in a half-hearted attempt to get away.

Nico's hand slid from between his shoulder blades to the back of his neck and gripped, holding tight. Onyx whimpered, unable to hold the sound in. "No, I don't think so. You aren't going anywhere. Pull your pants down."

Nico was making him do it? Fucking dick. Somehow, that was so much more humiliating. Onyx shouldn't obey. He should snap back. Nico probably expected him to, but all Onyx could do was lift his hips and undo his jeans. He pushed, struggling to get them over his hips.

Nico helped him, dragging his jeans and boxer briefs down to mid-thigh, leaving Onyx's legs trapped in the fabric. Onyx settled back onto Nico's lap, bare cock pressed between them.

"That's better." Nico patted Onyx's exposed ass.

Onyx shivered. The touch was too gentle, making him aware of how vulnerable he must look, spread over Nico, clothes disheveled, his hard dick leaking onto Nico's jeans.

Nico ran his hand over Onyx's lower back, pushing his shirt up and exposing him almost to his shoulders. Nico sucked in a breath, then his fingers trailed over Onyx's tattoos. His back was almost completely covered by his inked wings, and Nico seemed fascinated, tracing the feathers and sending sparks across Onyx's skin.

Nico's fingers found Onyx's other visible tattoo, his tail wrapped around his hips. Nico traced the lines of the base, where it connected to Onyx's spine.

"*Fuck!*" Onyx bucked his hips, pleasure flaring, and almost threw Nico off without meaning to. "I thought you were spanking my naughty ass, not giving me a massage."

Nico's open hand landed on Onyx's ass with a satisfying smack. Heat flared and quickly faded. "What did I say about telling me what to do?"

"Seems to work out all right," Onyx grumbled into the cushion, wiggling his ass. Immortal healing was a bummer at times like this, making every slap not quite enough, his magic soothing the sting away.

"Brat," Nico growled, tone disorientingly affectionate. "You like pushing me, but I think you'll like being good even better."

"Not fucking likely."

A second smack landed on Onyx's other ass cheek. He hissed, pushing into the burn before it faded.

"It's going to take some work to get this bottom nice and pink, but I think I can manage," Nico rumbled, voice dropping low with lust.

Yes, please. Onyx squeezed his burning eyes shut as another wave of embarrassment hit him. He couldn't help rubbing against Nico, his cock so hard it hurt.

Nico leaned closer, whispering, "I'll do whatever it takes to make you be good for me."

Onyx let out another pathetic whimper, rolling his hips.

Nico muttered a spell, and Onyx's attention sharpened. It had been a while since he'd done anything like this with someone from the magic world.

Nico's open palm landed on his ass with a loud crack, harder than his previous blows. Onyx moaned into the couch, rubbing his cock against Nico's lap as his skin stung, heat rising. The burn lingered, and the air in the apartment was suddenly cool on his exposed rear.

Before the sting faded, Nico's hand struck again in the same spot. Onyx yelped. Nico's spell must affect his blows, counteracting some of Onyx's healing and allowing him to enjoy this as if he were a witch or a human.

"Fuck," Onyx panted, muscles going lax from head to toe.

"You like that?" Nico teased, rubbing Onyx's stinging ass cheek.

"What do you think? Don't make me say green ag—*ugh*." A smack landed on his other cheek.

"This is a punishment. You aren't supposed to like it, so stop rubbing off on me. Sit still and take it."

Onyx's cock throbbed but he did exactly what he was told.

Right now, Onyx believed that nothing mattered to Nico but punishing him for being a rude little shit. Onyx was Nico's whole world, even if only until the spanking was over and they got off the couch.

This was what Onyx needed, what he'd been craving. He was grounded, spread like an obnoxious brat across Nico's lap, and could almost believe the hollow, lost feeling inside him had been banished forever.

Nico's hand came down again, cracking against Onyx's flesh. He smacked him three times in quick succession, the burn building, leaving no time for Onyx to relax between blows. Onyx's eyes stung. He hadn't been hurt this good in so long.

Nico rubbed his stinging ass and hummed. As Onyx's muscles unclenched, he smacked him again.

A moan tore from Onyx's throat, but he didn't grind his hips. No matter how much he wanted to.

"You're doing so well," Nico crooned, rubbing Onyx's ass, then squeezing. "I knew you could do it. You want to rub that needy cock against me, but you want to be my good boy more, don't you?"

"No." Onyx shook his head, pressing his face harder into the cushion. He couldn't admit it. Nico saw through him. His heart skittered, and his wings tingled. He wanted to run. Fly far away and not think about anything.

Nico spanked him twice, once on each cheek. "Don't lie."

"No," Onyx moaned, eyes burning with fire and something a lot harder to accept. He was on the verge of crying, and they'd hardly even started. What the fuck was wrong with him? "I'm never good. Not for you. Not for anyone. Just fuck off, Nico."

Nico growled and smacked Onyx's ass. "You don't get to come into my house and tell me to fuck off." Smack. "You came to me for a reason, and I'm not going anywhere." Smack. "I'm not leaving." Smack. "And I'm not sending you away."

Tears broke free from Onyx's eyes, leaking past his tightly shut lids. His shoulders tensed and he balled his fists, but he didn't make a sound.

Nico spanked him again, the burn getting hotter now. "I'm here. I'm not going anywhere. You can't push me away."

He punctuated each stupid promise with a smack, and Onyx couldn't hold himself together. A sob broke free.

"Nico," he groaned. Pleaded. The infuriating man was

saying exactly what Onyx wanted to hear, and the scary thing was, Onyx almost believed he was telling the truth, despite knowing better.

None of it was true. Nico would leave him behind eventually. Everyone else had. But Onyx wanted to hold on.

He trembled as Nico spanked him again and again, his whole body coming alive with pain and pleasure. His cock ached, his ass burned, his hole clenched tight with every smack, jolting his core. Onyx's face was wet with tears, his moans unmuffled as he turned his head to the side, sucking in deep sobbing breaths.

"Please," he begged, hating that he was letting Nico see any of this, yet loving it. Wanting it. Wanting Nico to hold him down forever and never let go.

"I'm here," Nico murmured. "I've got you. You're being so good, taking your punishment. Being so good for me."

"No." Onyx shook his head.

"Yes." Nico spanked him once on each cheek. "But it's okay. I can make you be good if that's what you need. I'm not letting you run away. Not letting you get away with being a brat when I know what you need."

"Fuck." How did Nico see right through him? Was Onyx the most obvious sap on the planet? "Please, Nico." Onyx's cock throbbed, leaking everywhere, the denim of Nico's jeans harsh against his skin. "Please."

Nico laid into him, smacking his ass and driving Onyx's cock into his lap. Onyx shuddered, and his hidden tail tingled, the heat from his ass throbbing. He choked on ecstasy, each blow pushing him higher.

"I've got you. That's it," Nico murmured, his voice gravely and low, almost slurred with pleasure.

Nico's hand came down again, and Onyx's balls drew up. He came so suddenly, he could do nothing but shout, hot release spilling into Nico's lap. Nico's hand came down on Onyx's burning ass once more and Onyx shuddered, aftershocks pulling more cum from him, his tattooed tail on fire.

"I'm sorry," Onyx sobbed, trembling, mind scattered, as his orgasm faded. "I'm sorry. I didn't mean to. Oh, fuck." His face burned hot. He was a mess of tears and humiliation.

"Shh," Nico soothed, gripping the back of his neck in a firm, gentle hold. "Don't be sorry. It's okay. I never said you couldn't come. I said not to rub off on me. Which you didn't. You were so good." He caressed Onyx's flaming ass cheeks in slow circles.

Tension dissolved from Onyx's shoulders, and he unclenched his fists. He tried to breathe. He was in pieces like never before. All because Nico said he wouldn't leave. It was so stupid. Onyx was such a fool. He was so desperate to be loved, it was pathetic.

Nico rubbed Onyx's back in steady motions, migrating from his ass to shoulders, and eventually Onyx's mind quieted.

It was all talk. Nothing more than the shit you say during sex. Admittedly, not all of it was dirty talk, but Nico seemed like the type to dominate in a supportive, I-care-about-you way. Nico wasn't aware how deeply Onyx wanted his promises to be real, so there was nothing to be embarrassed about. This was nothing but a little fun. Onyx could handle it.

He opened his eyes and found Nico staring at his face. Not his exposed ass or his tattooed back, his cry-ugly face, smooshed into the couch, a crick starting in his neck from the odd angle.

Nico's gaze was hooded, his cheeks flushed even darker than before. For some ridiculous reason, Nico looked...proud?

"Feel better?" Nico asked.

Onyx should've denied it, but he nodded.

Nico's hand found its way into Onyx's hair, brushing it from his forehead and winding the strands around his fingers. "Good. I'm glad I could help."

Onyx's heart clenched. Was that what Nico got out of this? Did he have that much of a hard-on for helping people? Nico's dick still pressed insistently into Onyx's hip, so maybe.

"I can help you out, too." Onyx rubbed against him suggestively. "Tell me how you want me, and I'll get you off."

Nico's grin spread slowly over his face. "Fuck, you're perfect." His grip tightened in Onyx's hair, and Onyx glowed from the inside out. Even if Nico only liked this as much as he liked *helping* anyone else, Onyx would take it.

Onyx might be cocky, but he rarely felt perfect. Not genuinely. However, in this moment, sprawled out and spent, he almost did.

12

NICO

Wafts of orchids and sweet wine strangled Nico's senses, almost as intense as the throbbing in his cock. It must be Onyx's scent. Demon pheromones. Nico's downfall. *Fuck.* Nico breathed deep, the sound loud to his own ears.

He wanted to smell Onyx forever.

Onyx was beautiful. Nico hadn't exaggerated when he called him perfect. His round ass was pink with Nico's punishment, his skin flushed hot under Nico's possessive grip. Onyx looked boneless, like he was at peace, all spread out. Nico wanted to strip off his shirt and get him naked, see his fully tattooed back, and explore the tattoo of his tail.

Onyx blinked, dark lashes fluttering. His eyes glowed bright blue, turning his flushed cheeks lavender. His hair was soft between Nico's fingers. He was so pliant right now. So owned. Nico couldn't believe Onyx let him undo him like this.

After a long moment, Onyx tried to get up and Nico automatically pushed his head down, hand tightening on Onyx's ass.

Onyx hissed and wiggled his rear. "Hey, I have to move to get you off. Let me up."

"No." Nico wasn't ready to let him go. Not that he could stop Onyx if he really wanted to get away.

The fact that Onyx—an immortal closer to a God than a man—allowed himself to be manhandled was dizzying.

Nico massaged Onyx's scalp. "Let me take care of you."

Onyx's brow furrowed, some of the sharpness returning to his face. "In case the mess staining your pants didn't clue you in, I've been taken care of."

Nico laughed softly. "Not what I meant, brat. Now stay still. You can get me off in a minute."

Apparently mollified by the promise, Onyx relaxed, muttering, "Whatever," as he shut his eyes.

The rosy flush to Onyx's ass was already fading. The spell Nico used worked better on vampires. Maybe he could tweak it to suit Onyx and prevent his healing from erasing Nico's mark so quickly. If there was a next time. Onyx might never let him do this again.

Nico rubbed the abused flesh. He flicked one cheek and watched it bounce.

"*Umf.*" Onyx squirmed.

"Sorry." He wasn't really. Nico could play with Onyx for hours. Instead, he summoned a bottle of lotion from the bedroom. It floated toward him, and he grabbed it from the air.

At the sound of the cap clicking, Onyx's eyelids fluttered open. He craned his neck. "That doesn't look like lube."

"It's not. It's to soothe your naughty little bottom."

"*Fuck.*" Onyx's face flamed deep crimson, his neck flushing to match, eyes flickering with fire. He shook himself, and the flames went out. "Don't bother. I'll be healed completely before I get you off at this rate."

Nico frowned. "That may be, but I'm taking care of you anyway."

"Ugh, so kind it's killing me. Don't be a bore, and fuck me

instead. That lotion will do. Or skip it altogether and stick your dick in me."

Nico's heart stuttered. Onyx was such a little shit. He couldn't let anyone be nice to him. "You'd let me fuck you?"

Onyx propped his head on a hand. "Um, yeah. It wouldn't exactly be a chore."

Damn, Nico wanted to. "Not tonight." He needed more than one night with Onyx and wasn't above playing dirty to get it.

"You're no fun." Onyx pouted, but didn't say it was now or never, so that had to be good.

This was probably a mistake, but it was too late to go back now. Nico would figure it out. If things got awkward down the road, he'd manage. When Onyx moved on, Nico would have to deal with it.

His chest pinched at the idea of Onyx finding his mate and forgetting about him as he got wrapped up in fated love. But Onyx wasn't as enamored with mates as the other demons. Maybe Nico didn't have to worry.

He rubbed lotion into Onyx's pinkened ass, one cheek, then the other, as the color faded. The demon sighed, eyes falling closed once more.

When he was done, Nico patted Onyx's bottom one last time. "Good boy."

Onyx's eyes flew open. His fire didn't reignite, but his glare still burned. Nico watched as he struggled to decide how to react. "I'll be a good boy if you let me suck your cock."

"Damnation." Nico dropped his head back. "Yeah, all right. If you insist."

Onyx wiggled out of Nico's lap with some difficulty caused by the tight jeans tangling his thighs. He managed to stand and pulled up his pants and underwear, his shirt falling back into place.

Nico hated every stitch of clothing. "What if I want you to suck me naked?"

Onyx's hands stilled on his pants button. "Too bad."

It was worth a shot. Nico almost reminded Onyx he wasn't the one calling the shots, but didn't want to push too far. Onyx had let go so completely—more so than Nico expected—it was no surprise his prickliness had come rushing back.

Nico cupped his bulge, hand sticky with Onyx's drying cum, and Onyx's eyes tracked the motion. "Need me to take it out for you? You're going to have to get closer to finish what you started."

Onyx muttered something that sounded suspiciously like *fucking asshole*, his lips twitching as if he was trying not to smile. He glared for a moment longer before giving in.

Nico hummed in appreciation as Onyx got to his knees, pushing between Nico's thighs, his slight form fitting in the space as if he were made for Nico.

Onyx met his gaze like a man confident he was about to ruin Nico for anyone else, his conviction splitting Nico's heart open and laying him bare.

The vibrations of a ringing phone cut through the charged air. Onyx's smug expression wilted, and his gaze turned distant. All the crackling energy between them seemed to snuff out.

Nico cupped Onyx's worried face on reflex, stroking his cheek. "Is that your phone?" He'd left his on the kitchen counter.

Onyx pulled away. "Yeah. I don't have to answer." The buzzing stopped and started again, and Onyx extracted the phone from his pocket with a frown. "Fucking useless brothers."

Nico's cock rapidly deflated, Onyx's displeasure stealing his complete focus. He didn't want Onyx blowing him if he wasn't fully in the mood and enjoying it. "It's okay if you need to get that."

"*Ugh*, fine, but I hate them." Onyx stood and answered the call, pressing the phone to his ear. "What? I'm in the middle of something." He winced. "No." He paced the length of the room, then turned toward the couch. "I didn't. Dante—I'm busy. Can I call you later?"

Onyx sounded pained, and Nico wanted to wrap his arms around him. He would have if he hadn't been ninety-nine percent sure Onyx would shove him away.

"Why do you care where I am? No. I'm with Nico." A pause. "So? What does that matter?" Onyx's words got tighter and tighter. He was more upset than Nico had ever seen him. There was no playful edge to this fight.

"None of your business," Onyx snarled into the phone. "Is that why you called? See, this is why I never pick up." He listened for a few moments. "Fine, but I'm not flying all the way to your eyesore of a house." Onyx's gaze cut to Nico, and he lifted the phone away from his ear. "I have to meet them."

Nico was shocked Onyx bothered telling him anything. He figured Onyx would storm out. "Okay. Uh... Want me to come?"

Onyx chewed his lip. "Can they meet us here?"

Nico's chest swelled. He'd fully expected Onyx to tell him to mind his own fucking business. He must be really shaken about something. "Let's meet at The Herb Emporium. I don't like having people over."

Onyx nodded as if not wanting people visiting his home was normal. "See you at the apothecary," he barked into the phone before hanging up. He closed his eyes, and his nostrils flared, breaths audible from across the room.

Nico stood and approached cautiously. "I'm going to change my pants."

Onyx blinked and glared at him. "You wouldn't...you're not..." His gaze fell to the stain on Nico's crotch. "Don't tell them what a mess I was." His cheeks flushed pink, and he didn't look up.

Nico clasped his shoulder. "I don't blab about who I fuck around with. Hell, Onyx."

"That's not..." He stiffened under Nico's grip and pulled away. "Don't tell them I was upset when I showed up here."

Nico rubbed the back of his neck. Onyx actually admitted he'd been upset? Wow. "I won't say anything. Not about any of it. Let me change, all right?"

Onyx flopped onto the couch and waved him away.

Nico hurried to his room. He pulled off his ruined jeans and precum-soaked boxer briefs, then grabbed new clothes from the dresser and threw them on.

Onyx didn't want his brothers knowing he was upset— beyond the anger Onyx directed at them anyway. Why was anyone's guess. There was clearly more going on here. But Onyx had come to Nico when he'd needed someone, even if he wouldn't admit it to Nico or maybe even himself, and Nico would guard that kernel of Onyx's trust with everything he had.

Back in the living room, Onyx ran his fingers through his hair. He muttered, "Fuck it," and with a flash of light, his hair was styled, and the last remnants of tears were wiped from his face.

Onyx rose from the couch. "Come on. I don't want them beating us there."

Nico followed Onyx to the front door. "What's going on?"

Onyx paused, giving Nico a look that said he'd forgotten Nico had no clue what this was about. Was he going to change his mind and tell Nico to stay behind?

"It's..." Onyx seemed to war with himself, chewing on his bottom lip once more. "It will take too long to explain. You'll never get it."

"Try me?" Nico did his best not to sound pleading.

He wanted to help Onyx more than he ever had with anyone. If Onyx pushed him away now, Nico would fight, dammit. He'd said he wasn't leaving, and he meant it. Especially after Onyx had gone to pieces at the mere mention of Nico being there for him.

"Luc showed up last night out of the blue, but he fucked off pretty quickly." Onyx turned and opened the door, marching out into the hall.

Nico quickly shut and locked his door. "Lucifer tracked you down?"

Onyx continued down the hall. "Yes, keep up or I'll leave you behind. I don't even know why I'm bothering to bring you."

Nico caught up with him. He'd let Onyx get away with that lie for now. He had enough going on with his brothers. Now wasn't the time to confront anything else.

Onyx cut him an indecipherable look. "Are we going to have to fly to your shop to beat them? I can't remember where the apothecary is from here. My brain is still back on your couch."

Nico couldn't help his satisfied smile. "Don't worry. It's around the corner."

Onyx followed him there. He seemed relieved when they got to the apothecary, and his brothers were nowhere to be found. Nico opened the shop and turned on the lights, and Onyx hopped onto the counter, sitting with his legs dangling over the edge. He didn't even wince as his ass landed on the hard wood.

Nico scrubbed at the scruff covering his chin. Desire for Onyx to squirm, bottom sore from his spanking, made everything else fade away. Onyx shouldn't forget Nico or his lesson as easily.

Onyx gripped the edge of the counter and tipped his head back, exposing his pale throat and arching his back. He was more than gorgeous. Nico was mesmerized. Nothing could have pulled him away.

Onyx straightened and rolled his shoulders, shaking out his limbs. It was almost like watching a performer get into the zone before going on stage. Onyx cracked his neck to either side, then fixed his attention on Nico. "Don't make me regret bringing you."

Before Nico could promise not to, or scold Onyx for assuming the worst, the bell on the front door clanged. Nico turned to face the other demons.

Dante entered first, shirtless, and with dark gray horns protruding from his hair. "Thank you for letting us meet here," he said as if Nico had done him a great favor.

"Not sure why *you're* meeting us at all," Ash grumbled as he closed and locked the shop door. He, too, had his horns out, and Nico caught a glimpse of the wing tattoos on his back. "This isn't any of your business."

Nico crossed his arms, staring the big demon down. "Maybe not, but Onyx asked me to be here and I hope you'll respect that."

Ash stopped short, his gaze flitting over Nico's shoulder to Onyx. "What are you two doing together?"

"*Ash*," Dante hissed in warning.

He was ignored. Ash stalked closer, muscles bulging as he flexed

Nico didn't let himself react to the obvious intimidation. "It's none of your business what we're doing. I don't have to explain myself. Weren't you the one who wanted me and Onyx dealing with Rowan? *Together*."

"No, Dante—" Ash began.

"*Ugh*. Who cares." Onyx hopped off the counter. "I swear, an immortal life is too long to have to put up with you, Ash."

"All I'm saying is we didn't have to meet here," Ash muttered. "We could have gone to your place."

Onyx tensed like Ash's suggestion was offensive. "I'm not telling you where I live."

Did the others not know? Nico tried not to let his smugness show. He might not have Onyx's address, but Onyx had trusted him with a piece of himself he apparently kept close.

Ash rolled his eyes. "I could track you if I really wanted."

Dante clapped a hand over his face, muttering something to himself before removing it. "I thought we were starting to get along better than this, Onyx."

The sadness in his eyes tugged on Nico's heart. What the hell had happened between these three?

Onyx wasn't so moved. He huffed, face turning splotchy red. Nico half expected fire to erupt from his fingertips. "I thought so, too, Dante. Then someone learned our identities, and you didn't even bother to *tell me*."

Nico's heart sank. He didn't want to be the cause of any animosity between Onyx and his brothers.

"It wasn't a big deal." Dante pointed at Nico. "You're inviting him along now, so what's the harm? You said you weren't mad at Ollie for letting things slip."

Onyx marched forward, and Nico could practically feel the air vibrating with his fury. "You're missing the fucking point. I'm not mad about who said what, or the fact that our secret got out. You didn't tell me. All the time we spent together guarding your birds, you never thought—hey, I better update Onyx. I had to ask who the hell Nico was, and why you were trusting him with your mates."

They'd forgotten him.

Nico's chest ached at the pain in Onyx's tone. He hadn't found out that Nico had discovered demons until the night they'd met. No wonder Onyx had taken out his anger on Nico. Of course he'd lashed out.

Onyx pushed people to test whether they cared, and his brothers had failed.

"I'm sorry we didn't tell you the second it happened," Dante said, seeming blind to the depth of the problem, like he wanted to push past forgetting to keep Onyx in the loop and be done with it.

But surely dismissing Onyx now would make things worse.

Dante sighed as if he was exhausted. "Is that why you didn't tell us Luc found you?"

Onyx seethed. "Oh, right, because I'm nothing but petty. Tit for tat. How did you even find out about Luc?"

"My birds. I told you they were keeping an eye on who turned up. They saw Luc on the bridge."

"That was last night. If you saw Luc, why didn't you call me immediately?"

"You can't be serious?" Ash groaned. "You didn't need to be told. You. Saw. Him. Too."

Onyx threw up his hands. "Just as you *saw* him disappear on me after spouting thirty seconds worth of bullshit. Why are we even having this conversation?"

Ash stepped forward and loomed over Onyx. "Because you didn't try to trap him. You did nothing, and then kept it from us. Whose side are you on?"

Nico's pulse raced. The shop was dead silent for a full minute. Onyx seemed primed to blow, his body quivering. Nico longed to pull him close, run his hands through Onyx's hair, and tell him it was okay.

But Nico wasn't sure it was okay.

"I can't believe you'd ask me that." Onyx's words came out so chillingly calm that Nico's neck prickled. "I thought we were brothers, Ash."

Ash's eyes narrowed. "But you'll always be his brother first."

Dante sucked in a breath.

Onyx cocked his head, sharp as a bird of prey. "And you aren't?"

"No." Ash puffed out his chest. "Luc is no one to me. Not anymore."

"So only you and Dante can sever your ties? Even though you knew Luc centuries before I was born. Even though your bond with him was always stronger than mine. I'm forever linked to Lucifer by my blood, and there's nothing I can do about it. Is that what you're saying? I'm not my own person, able to shape my relationships. I'm just Lucifer's little brother."

Ash hesitated, hopefully realizing how much he'd fucked up. Nico didn't know the half of it, but if Ash really did think all that, it didn't sound like the kind of thing that could be taken back once it was out.

"That's not what he meant," Dante cut in.

Onyx didn't look at him. "Let Ash speak for himself."

"Fuck, Onyx." Ash deflated. "That wasn't what I meant. It's different for you. That's all. Your relationship with Luc isn't the same as mine. You're actual brothers."

Onyx's eyes flashed. "Actual brothers. How clever of you, Ash. Didn't realize you had the deductive reasoning required to make such an obvious observation."

"Prick," Ash growled.

"If all you wanted was to accuse me of betrayal, you can go." Onyx pointed to the door.

Ash didn't budge. "We need to know what Luc said."

Fuck, he was bold, there was no doubt about that. Pushing Onyx now was nothing like what Nico had done back in his apartment. Nico had called Onyx out and confronted his blatant lies, wanting him to open up, giving him the connection

Nico suspected he'd come for. Ash was pushing when the outcome might be disastrous for everyone.

"Of course. You need something from me." Onyx clenched his fists at his sides. "If I say it was nothing important, I bet you'll call me a traitor again. You love floating that possibility. Proving you wrong is the only reason I'm going to tell you what Luc said because you don't deserve shit from me right now."

Onyx took a steadying breath, but Nico wasn't sure it calmed him. "Luc asked for my help. I told him to fuck off. He asked if I believed he wanted to make things right, and I said no way in hell. He was up to his usual manipulative crap."

"Help with what?" Dante asked.

"Didn't say. Which is one more reason to call bullshit."

"I agree." Dante elbowed Ash, who grunted in apparent affirmation. "Thank you, Onyx. If the birds spot anything else, I'll call right away."

Ash turned and left the shop without another word. Onyx's gaze followed him until he disappeared from sight.

Dante waited for Onyx to look at him, but his stare remained on the front of the shop. Eventually Dante asked, "Are you sure you're safe?"

"Perfectly." Onyx still didn't look at him.

"If you'd let us protect your house like we've done with mine, I'd feel better. It'll be stronger with all three of our magics."

"Don't worry about it." Onyx turned away, still not looking at Dante, and walked behind the counter. "It's not like Luc is going to kill me. We still need to trap him, and if we can't track him, we might have to let him come to us. All I'll say is, maybe you should bother to show up when he finds me again, instead of calling me twenty-four hours later."

Dante's brow furrowed. "Yeah, okay. If you change your mind about protecting your place, we'll be there."

Onyx disappeared behind the curtain to the back of the shop without replying.

Dante glanced at Nico apologetically, shook his head, and left.

13

———

ONYX

"ARE you going to call me a brat for behaving like that?" Onyx asked as he heard Nico join him in the back room. He didn't bother turning around.

"No. Not unless you want me to."

Onyx was so tense, his back cramped. Not even Nico's perfect response helped. Onyx was rooted to the spot, staring blankly at a shelf packed with empty vials and glass jars.

He'd been right to avoid Ash and Dante. They'd managed to make seeing Luc even worse than it already was. *Whose side are you on?* Onyx wanted to scream until his throat bled.

How many thousands of years had Ash known Onyx and never seen him as an individual? Onyx was nothing but a nuisance tied to Lucifer. They wouldn't have missed Onyx if they'd left him behind. He'd been so stupid to follow them to Earth. Even now, they'd be glad to get rid of him.

A woodsy citrus scent tickled Onyx's nose.

"Hey." Nico had moved closer without Onyx realizing. He didn't touch Onyx, but he stood near enough that Onyx sensed him hovering at his back. "Tell me what you need right now."

What, Nico would give Onyx what he needed? Why would

he want to after witnessing Onyx's temper and terrible relationship with his brothers?

Not that it mattered. Onyx's needs were too humiliating to
admit.

He needed Nico to wrap his arms around him and crush
him until his joints popped. Then, Nico needed to whisper in
Onyx's ear, spouting all his stupidly sweet sex-babble about not
leaving, and fucking mean it.

Onyx cleared his throat. "I'm going home." He couldn't
move, but that was immaterial. The intent was there.

"Look at me," Nico ordered, not sounding mad but undeni-
ably stern.

Onyx's shoulders dropped, a small coil of tension leaving
him. "No."

"Yes." Nico pressed closer, his chest to Onyx's back. "Look
at me and tell me you're going home and that you want to be by
yourself, and you can go."

Onyx's pulse spiked, and a chill wound down his spine. Had
Nico guessed it would be impossible for him to leave once they
were face to face? Onyx didn't have the energy to fight right
now, but that didn't mean he'd give in.

"Onyx." Nico laid a hand on his hip, fingers curling posses-
sively around him. "Talk to me."

Tension returned with a sharp snap. "I don't want to talk to
you."

Nico's hand tightened. "Then look at me, tell me you want
to go home."

He must know Onyx was lying. Why did Nico have to make
him admit it? Could he sense that Onyx was even needier now
than he'd been when he'd shown up outside his window?

The damn witch could give Onyx what he wanted, if he
knew so much. But he wasn't. He was making Onyx earn it.

It was enough to get Onyx to turn around.

But that left Onyx chest to chest with Nico. He craned his neck and met Nico's eyes, finding soft understanding written all over his face. Fuck. Onyx choked on his next breath. Nico was easier to deal with when he was pissed off and playing along.

"I should have left you at home."

Nico's lips quirked. "But you didn't."

No, he'd been foolish. Nico was like an emotional support blanket, a beautiful and understanding presence that Onyx suddenly didn't want to live without. One little spanking and Onyx was hooked.

The stress of seeing Luc was obviously too much for him.

Onyx bared his teeth. "Didn't anyone tell you that I'm impulsive and make silly choices? Bringing you here was nothing but a whim. Don't read into it."

Nico's brow furrowed. "I can't imagine you making silly choices, and I doubt you could have founded your gallery on impulse."

"I wasn't talking about the gallery, I was talking about you, and all the other dumb shit I do in my life."

"I don't believe you." Nico cupped the back of Onyx's neck, fingers threading through his hair.

Onyx fought not to melt into the touch. "*Ugh.* It's not like you know me better than I know myself."

"Maybe not, but describing yourself as impulsive and silly sounds like someone else's words. You don't really think that." Nico's stare sharpened. "You shouldn't."

Onyx rolled his eyes even as his chest fluttered and stomach flipped. "Stop with the motivational crap. It's gross."

Nico laughed, hand tightening in Onyx's hair. "Gross or not, you're relaxed now. Aren't you?"

"No," Onyx snapped. But he was. His body had gone lax, and his raging internal fire was all but snuffed out. He was still mad at Ash and Dante, but when wasn't he?

"My mistake." Nico's eyes shone, and Onyx suspected he was laughing at him. "In that case, would you like help relaxing?"

Onyx would love it, especially if it involved Nico's cock inside him. But he shook his head. Nico was too smug about all this. He acted like he had Onyx all figured out.

"No?" Nico teased, and Onyx's fire sparked at his sheer nerve. "Then tell me you want to go home."

Fuck, back to that? Damn him. Onyx pulled away, but not far enough for Nico to have to let go. "Why are you like this?"

"Like what?" Nico pulled Onyx close again. "You mean, why do I call you on your shit? Because you don't want to go anywhere and you need to learn that it's okay to admit it."

It wasn't okay, though. Onyx was sick of hoping people would like him as much as he liked them. He was sick of staying only to find out he shouldn't have bothered.

Onyx pulled free of Nico's hold. "That's not a lesson I need to learn. Spanking me once doesn't mean you can tell me what to do. You don't know anything about me."

Nico shoved his hands in his pockets, and Onyx was disappointed he hadn't pulled him back into his possessive embrace. "I know a little about you, but you're right. I don't know you well. Yet."

"You say that like learning more is a given. I might never want to talk to you again."

Nico nodded. "Maybe not, but you still haven't left."

Onyx was making a fool of himself. All his quips were hollow, and Nico knew it. Dammit, Onyx couldn't have Nico thinking he wanted to spend time with him. That would give him the upper hand and the power to hurt Onyx when he changed his mind.

Onyx stepped closer to Nico. "I seem to remember promising you a blow job. I can't leave before I make good.

That's the only reason I'm still here. Wouldn't want you thinking I don't follow through."

Nico's expression didn't change. Not even a hint of interest flickered behind his eyes. Onyx's heart sank.

"You don't have to," Nico said.

The rejection stung like venom injected directly into Onyx's heart. He'd thought for sure Nico would want to keep screwing around. "Obviously I don't have to, but fine. Want to turn down the best head you'll ever get? Suit yourself."

He pushed past Nico, heading toward the front room, refusing to let the witch see him blush. He was too easily humiliated around him.

Nico's hand wrapped around Onyx's wrist. "Wait. I wasn't turning you down."

"Didn't sound like a yes to me."

Nico pulled Onyx back in, turning him around until they faced each other. "I want you to suck me off, Onyx. Hell, of course I want that. All I said was, you don't have to do it because you offered earlier."

But Onyx wanted to, even more so than he had back in Nico's apartment. Onyx needed an excuse to stay. It wasn't just that he couldn't bring himself to walk away. He needed to feel like someone cared after the way his brothers had spoken to him. He needed some form of connection.

He needed Nico.

Onyx pressed closer and gripped Nico's hips. "I haven't changed my mind." To prove his point, he got on his knees.

Nico ran a hand through Onyx's hair, sending tingles cascading over his head and down his spine like a waterfall. "Don't be annoyed that I wanted to double-check."

Onyx sniffed. "I'll be annoyed whenever I want."

Nico tugged Onyx's hair, tilting his head back. "And I'll

always check in with you. So I guess we'll both have to deal, won't we?"

Onyx's lips parted, arousal pooling inside him as his scalp prickled. Nico held him tight and he fucking loved it. He swallowed. "I haven't decided if I want to keep dealing with you after this. Why don't you convince me?"

Nico chuckled. "Weren't you going to give me the best head of my life? Sounds like you convincing me, not the other way around."

Onyx reached for Nico's jeans button. "It *will* be the best you've ever had. But it's your job to make me want to do it again. I can get laid anytime. I don't need it to be with you."

"Liar." Nico released Onyx's hair and pushed his hands out of the way.

He opened his pants and pulled them down, freeing his half-hard cock from his underwear. Nico wrapped a hand around it and pumped until he was hard. With his other hand, Nico took hold of Onyx's hair and held him in place, rubbing the thick head of his cock along Onyx's lips.

Onyx opened his mouth on instinct, and Nico guided him forward, pushing him onto his cock. Onyx groaned as his lips stretched around Nico's girth. Musky citrus filled his nose, and his mouth watered.

"This is the cock you want." Nico pushed Onyx onto him until his mouth met Nico's hand at the base. "You couldn't leave without a taste. Don't pretend it isn't me you want filling you up."

Onyx groaned and batted Nico's hand out of the way so he could sink all the way down and bury his nose in Nico's pubes. Nico gasped, and a satisfied thrill coursed through Onyx. He worked his throat, taking advantage of the fact he'd banished his gag reflex before falling to Earth and didn't possess the human instinct to gasp for air.

"*Fuck.*" Nico's grip on Onyx's hair tightened until it stung. He thrust, trying to get deeper, but there was nowhere to go. "Fuck. Oh, hell."

Onyx slowly pulled back, satisfied that Nico finally knew what he was getting himself into. He worked his tongue as he sucked, exploring Nico until he reached his cockhead, and sucked his tip, playing with his slit as his hands cupped and squeezed Nico's balls.

Nico brought his other hand to join the one on the back of Onyx's head, and Onyx's eyes fluttered closed.

Nico pulled his hair. "Hey. Look at me. I want you to know who you've got in your mouth."

Onyx opened his eyes. Like he could forget.

He pressed forward and swallowed Nico down, impaling himself on Nico's cock. Onyx's eyes watered as desire burned through him. He was hard in his too-tight jeans, Nico's thick length perfect to choke on.

"You like that?" Nico bit his lip and thrust his hips. Onyx moaned. "Your glowing eyes are so fucking pretty, turning your red cheeks purple. You love drowning on my cock."

Onyx whimpered, face flaming hotter. Nico's description set his heart thumping. Onyx pulled back only for Nico to thrust forward, and he whimpered again.

"You're getting desperate." Nico thrust again. "Was it what I said or how good my cock is?"

Onyx wasn't sure. Probably both.

"I want to see all of you." Nico's thrusts turned steady, pulling little choked moans from Onyx each time he hit the back of his throat. "I want you naked in your demon form so I can hold you down by the horns and fuck your face. I bet you'd love that. I want to see everything you're hiding from me."

Onyx whined and tried to pull back, but Nico didn't let him. Good. Escaping wasn't the aim. He didn't truly want to get away from anything except the idea of Nico seeing him. He hadn't shown his horns and tail to anyone in centuries.

"Yeah, you don't like me seeing what you're hiding, do you?" Nico thrust deep and swirled his hips as Onyx's throat spasmed. Nico's eyes rolled back. "*Fuck...* You're so good. How can I not want all of you?"

Onyx let out a shrill sound. His whole body burned. It was a good thing he was clothed, or Nico would see him blush all over. Onyx's emotions made a spectacle of themselves all over his body, especially in his demon form. Nico couldn't see that. It was too much.

"*Uhh*, hell...you're killing me." Nico's eyes fell closed, and his hold loosened.

Onyx growled and took over, working his head up and down.

Nico opened his eyes and smiled. "You don't like me looking away either. That's fair. I won't do it again. Oh, *fuuuck*."

Yeah, Onyx was blowing the witch's damn mind. Excellent. He had to destroy Nico as much as Nico was destroying him. It was the only way he'd survive this.

"*Oh.*" Nico's breathing grew heavier. "Onyx, take your dick out. Be a good boy and show me how much you like this. Come for me. Please. Oh, shit, I'm close. Please."

Onyx hurried to undo his pants and pulled out his straining cock.

Nico's attention didn't stray. Sweat prickled his brow, and his cheeks flushed dark. He pulled back until his cock almost slipped from Onyx's lips. Onyx fisted his own cock and began stroking.

Nico hummed and thrust forward. He fucked Onyx hard, bringing tears to Onyx's burning eyes.

"Onyx, yeah, so good for me. *Ugh.*" Nico released a strangled sound as his cock began to pulse, filling Onyx's throat.

Onyx hollowed his cheeks, pulling back so he could taste Nico's citrusy release on his tongue. Onyx jerked himself hard and rough, pleasure sparking down his spine and through his hidden tail. He swallowed all of Nico's cum, drinking in his moans and labored breathing.

Onyx was nearly there. He worked himself harder.

Nico pulled his spent cock from Onyx's lips, his grip on Onyx's hair unfaltering. "Look at you, right where you're meant to be. On your knees for me."

Onyx's whole body trembled as his orgasm tore through him, unable to break Nico's stare. It was too much. Too good. He was giving too much away, even clothed in his human form.

Pleasure faded. Onyx gasped for breath. He dropped forward, resting his forehead on Nico's thigh.

Nico's grip turned soft, stroking his hair so gently, Onyx almost burst into sobbing tears. Good tears or bad, he couldn't tell. Maybe both.

Onyx needed to sleep for a week after this much emotion. His body was relaxed, but his mind was wrung out. Sex with Nico shouldn't be any different than the countless times he'd fucked around at the club, or the endless times he'd fucked around over the centuries, but it was.

"That was fucking incredible," Nico groaned, still out of breath.

Onyx was glad there was something to be smug about. Smug was safe.

"I know, I'm incredible." He was too winded to sound arrogant, but it would have to do.

Nico chuckled and patted Onyx's head. "Yeah, figured I'd tell you anyway."

"As you should." Onyx nestled into Nico's thigh.

After a long moment, Nico tugged his hair gently. "Come on, get up."

Onyx groaned. He didn't want to move. Dammit, he'd have to go home now.

"Up." Nico tugged harder.

"Ow." Onyx unstuck his face from Nico's thigh and glared at him.

"Don't complain. You like it when I pull your hair."

"Doesn't mean you can do it whenever you want."

"My mistake." Nico released him, then smiled at the look of disappointment that must have been obvious on Onyx's face.

Onyx looked away, busying himself cleaning the sticky mess he'd made with a spell, and tucking his cock away. He stood and buttoned his jeans, turning away as Nico righted his clothes.

"I'm off home. Think I'll fly unless you need an escort back to your place."

"I can manage."

Onyx shot Nico what was hopefully a condescending look. "Good."

He followed Nico out of the shop. Nico locked up, pulling the metal grate down over the door and windows. They both hesitated, neither making a move to leave.

Nico glanced in the direction of his apartment, then back at Onyx. "Can I see your wings?"

Renewed heat flooded Onyx's traitorous face.

"You don't have to show me," Nico hurried to add. "I, uh, wasn't kidding about wanting to see you. But I'm sorry if it's presumptuous to ask."

Onyx's chest warmed.

He should shut Nico down. It was the smart thing to do, so why couldn't he successfully push Nico away? Nico was being so genuine and respectful, it was sickening. Onyx hated it. Or at least he tried to convince himself he hated it because really, he loved Nico's interest.

He wanted to enjoy it before Nico got bored.

Onyx silently cast an invisibility illusion over himself, allowing Nico to see through it. "You're not being presumptuous. Here, I'll show you. Since I'm going to fly anyway."

Nico grinned, and it was annoyingly wholesome. Then he looked quickly up and down the quiet street. "Wait, you can't show me here. Someone could see."

Onyx waved a careless hand. "It's fine. I'm invisible to everyone but you right now."

Nico gaped. "You can be invisible?"

"Did no one tell you invisibility was another demon trick? I can also let select people see through the illusion, like you, Dante, Ash, unfortunately, and of course, the little mates."

Nico blinked like this surprised him.

Onyx didn't ask why. He rolled his shoulders and whipped off his shirt.

Nico's gaze turned hungry as he took in Onyx's bare chest. "Your nipples are pierced."

"Oh, shit, really?" Onyx looked down at himself in mock surprise.

Nico laughed. "How did I not notice that through your shirt?"

Onyx braced a hand on his hip. "Have you been checking out my nipples?"

"I've been checking you out in general." Nico's gaze dropped back to Onyx's chest. "You've worn shirts tight enough that I should have noticed."

Onyx suppressed the smile threatening to break free. "It's called magic. Thought you'd be familiar."

Nico cracked up, shaking his head. "Little shit. I didn't realize piercings were worth hiding with magic."

Onyx wouldn't explain why he hid them. He didn't care if people saw his piercings beneath a tight shirt. This wasn't some embarrassing thing. It was more that he'd gotten the piercings for himself. They weren't for other people to notice unless he wanted them to. Like everything else about Onyx, he chose when to reveal them.

Nico's reaction had been worth it. The longer Nico looked, the more Onyx's skin prickled.

"Ready for my wings?"

Nico's gaze shot to his face. "Definitely."

In a flash, Onyx released his midnight blue wings. He unfolded them and shook them out, keeping his other demon features hidden.

"Oh, wow." Nico took a step forward, eyes wide.

"I'm very pretty." Onyx ruffled his feathers.

The tips of his wings were much lighter than the feathers at his shoulders, creating a fading blue ombre. The effect was pleasing, even if it was due to a lack of pigment.

Nico's eyes shone as they swept over Onyx. "You're more than pretty. You're amazing, Onyx. Thank you for showing me."

Onyx couldn't speak. Why was Nico thanking him? It was so weird. Onyx wasn't amazing. Wings were an appendage like any other.

But Nico's words had Onyx melting into a pile of blue mush.

"G'night," he choked out and shot into the air, leaving Nico behind.

14

——

NICO

"What's up with you?" Harper asked the next afternoon as they worked together at The Herb Emporium.

"Hmm?" Nico glanced away from the notebook he'd been pretending to study.

Harper let the curtain fall closed behind him and came closer. "You seem...off."

"Off? No, I'm fine." Nico tucked the notebook in a drawer. He'd been thinking about Onyx, and as much as his talented mouth and gorgeous wings were on Nico's mind, they weren't what plagued him. "Did you see Ash last night?"

Harper nodded. "He mentioned that you were with Onyx, and I get it. If you're worried about Lucifer, we can make sure you're protected at home, and even here at the shop. Actually, I'm surprised Ash hasn't demanded to protect this place yet."

It was a good thing Ash hadn't insisted on overstepping like that. After last night, Nico was inclined to push Ash away, even if the impulse was probably off base. Ash wasn't a bad guy over-all. Not that Nico wanted to get into any of that with Harper.

"I'm not worried about Lucifer."

Harper arched a brow.

"Okay, I'd be a fool not to have concerns about the Devil, but that wasn't why I brought up the meeting last night." Nico wasn't sure he should ask Harper for details, but he wanted to know if the fight between Ash and Onyx last night was typical. "Ash and Onyx don't get along, do they?"

Harper leaned his hip against the counter. "No, bickering is the best I've seen between them. Ash made it seem like Onyx had a bad attitude back when I first met him, but I don't think that's the whole story. Onyx and I had a rocky start, but he's honestly the loveliest guy. He and Ash just rub each other the wrong way."

It seemed deeper than that, but Harper hadn't been there last night, and Ash might not have shared what happened word for word. Maybe the accusations tossed around weren't typical.

At least Nico had been there as some form of moral support, even if Onyx hadn't talked to him about it. "It's great you and Onyx get along, even if Ash doesn't."

Harper smiled. "Yeah, Ollie likes him too." He paused, clearly wanting to say something more.

"What?"

Harper dropped his gaze. "I'm glad you and Onyx are, um, getting to know each other. Kinda surprised, but maybe I shouldn't be. I don't know why Onyx gives such a bad impression when he meets people."

It was most likely a defense mechanism. Onyx seemed to push people away to test them, and didn't seem to want anyone knowing he liked them. At least it appeared he'd dropped those pretenses with Harper and Ollie.

Did that mean Onyx trusted the boys not to reject his friendship? Onyx still pushed Nico away. Did he not trust Nico, even after everything they'd shared?

Nico's heart ached in protest. He'd have to work on that.

"It's so much easier not hiding demon stuff from you,"

Harper went on. "It'll be better for you to know what's happening with Lucifer, too. Safer, so you aren't dragged into things blindly. You'll be prepared if anything's coming. Not that Lucifer would have any reason to come after you, unless..."

Nico waited a beat. "Unless what? Don't leave me hanging."

"Sorry." Harper hesitated again. "I wonder... Lucifer came after me and Ollie because we were hanging around the other demons. He could potentially target you if you're spending more time with Onyx."

"But that was different." Nico and Onyx weren't the same as Harper and Ash, or Ollie and Dante.

"True. Our attacks were before Lucifer believed we were real mates. Now that he knows, he probably won't attack you if he thinks you're Onyx's mate. At least that's what Ash and Dante believe. But there's always a slim chance. We don't really know what's going through Lucifer's mind."

"Wait. Why would Lucifer think I'm Onyx's *mate?*" Nico's body flashed hot, and sweat broke out on the back of his neck. Did Harper think he was Onyx's mate?

Nico's reservations about the mating bond were general. He'd never considered that the situation would apply to him. If it did, what would he think? Would he change his mind about immortality? Would he accept being bound permanently to another soul even when he'd sworn never to put himself in that position, no matter how much he trusted someone?

Harper shuffled his feet, breaking eye contact for a second. "If Lucifer is spying on us again, and notices the two of you spending time together—even if it's platonic—he might assume Onyx is being drawn to you, like Ash and Dante were drawn to me and Ollie."

"But Onyx isn't drawn to me." Nico could have laughed. He wasn't special to the demon.

The image of Onyx outside his window filled his mind.

Nico shook it off. Onyx had needed someone. He liked Nico, and Nico had already proven he couldn't easily be pushed away. Of course Onyx had shown up. It was no more than one friend seeking support from another.

Nico was like any other friend-with-benefits in Onyx's life. But why did acknowledging that stab him in the heart?

"Onyx certainly didn't want to help you with Rowan. I guess he would have if he'd been drawn to you." Harper seemed to mull this over, except he looked less convinced by his own logic the longer he was quiet. "Anyway, you'd know more than me. I don't mean to tell you what's going on with you two. Onyx is a good guy, and I think he wants friends more than he admits. That's all."

"You're right about that." Nico wanted Onyx to be open to positive relationships, especially in his case.

He was pretty damn drawn to the prickly demon. To some extent, it had to be mutual. That didn't mean it was magic. People were drawn together all the time, and it had nothing to do with mates.

ROWAN:

I need to speak to Onyx.

Nico stared at the ominous text.

He'd closed the shop for the day. Harper was long gone, meeting Ollie and their human friend, Dex, to go to a concert. An event that Harper had said the demons wouldn't be attending.

Nico was glad to hear that the boys did things on their own. Maybe there wasn't as much to worry about with the mating bond as he'd assumed. His reservations were still valid, but the longer he spent around the mated pairs, the more he realized being mated wasn't overriding the boys' lives. The bond was potentially problematic, but, in their cases, didn't seem to be in practice.

Perhaps Nico was going soft on the idea. He couldn't lie, the possibility of being Onyx's mate had nagged at him all day.

He replied to Rowan.

NICO:

I'll let him know. Want us to come by tonight?"

ROWAN:

Yes. This can't wait.

NICO:

What's going on? Can I get a heads up?

ROWAN:

Sorry, Nico. I've got to pass this on to the demons before I tell anyone else.

Shit. Nico scrubbed a hand over his face.

NICO:

Got it. No worries. I'll text when we're on our way over.

After double-checking that everything was in order, Nico left the shop and closed the metal grate.

He'd wanted to invite Onyx over to game this weekend, and was uneasy having to contact him about Rowan. Onyx probably wouldn't like it and might use it as an excuse to convince himself that Rowan and demon business were the only reasons Nico kept him around.

It wasn't true, but Onyx was sensitive about people only getting in touch when they needed something. The argument with Ash and Dante was enough to make that clear.

Fuck, Nico was overthinking. It wasn't like he was dating Onyx. He only wished he were. That way, this thing between them could grow until it was solid and undeniable.

As he walked home, Nico brought up Onyx's contact and hit call. The phone rang, but Onyx didn't pick up. Instead of leaving a message, Nico sent a quick text asking Onyx to call him back.

Nico stopped in the coffee shop on the corner of his block and ordered a double espresso. However the evening played out, he had a feeling he would need the caffeine.

As he sipped his coffee out on the sidewalk, Nico contemplated calling Onyx again. He didn't care about coming across as needy. He wasn't letting Onyx push him away, regardless of how urgent Rowan's request was.

A car backfired, and Nico's head whipped around. Across the street, a man spoke animatedly with two others, gesturing wildly with his arms. Nico's eyes narrowed. That looked a hell of a lot like Michael.

So, he *was* back in the city. What in damnation was he doing on Nico's block? Fuck, maybe he had been the one to break in. Nico didn't recognize the man Michael was with, but the woman seemed familiar. Nico wasn't sure from where.

Before he could decide how risky it was to confront Michael when he wasn't alone, an SUV pulled up, and the three climbed in. Perhaps one of the others lived on the block, and Michael's presence was a coincidence. It was possible, but Nico wasn't about to assume all was well.

He strode over to his building and went inside. The gate and front door could easily be unlocked with magic. Witches didn't usually protect shared entrances unless everyone in the building was magical and part of the same coven.

Inside, everything seemed fine. Nico hurried up the stairs to his floor. As he approached his apartment, he noticed Lucia's door was open.

"Nico," she called from the doorway. "Are you just getting back from work now?"

He stopped in front of her. "Yeah, why?"

"There were these people yelling in the hall." She glanced disapprovingly up and down the corridor.

Nico's heart skipped. "Yelling? About what?"

"I didn't quite catch it. I had the music on. You know me. But the commotion went on for a minute, and I turned it off. By the time I pressed my ear to the door, all I heard was a string of bad language."

"How long ago was that?"

She frowned. "Maybe five minutes. Any idea what it was about?"

Nico's grip tightened on the to-go coffee cup. "I saw a guy out front who's been involved in some shady witch dealings in the past."

Lucia tutted. "Someone like that wasn't in the hall yelling for me, so why's he poking around your front door? Everyone knows you don't tolerate nonsense."

"If I had to guess, he wants payback for not turning a blind eye to his business, or for tipping off Rowan to what he was up to." Nico didn't mention Evelyn, though Michael could be angry that he'd helped her. It was probably a combination of all three.

Lucia gripped his hand. "You're such a good man, always doing the right thing, but you never remember there's a risk to you too."

"Can't let that stop me."

She squeezed. "I know. But be careful."

"I am." Nico's phone began vibrating in his pocket. "I've got my place protected. No one's getting in. Want me to see about getting your security enhanced?"

Lucia's eyes widened. "If you really think it's necessary. I'm not defenseless, but I'm not stupid either. If I hear anything more, I'll call you and pretend I'm not home."

"Thanks." Nico rested a hand on her shoulder. "I'll take care of it and tell you when things are resolved so you won't have to worry."

"Who's worrying?" Lucia gave him a stern look. "Don't go taking care of it by yourself. Get that vampire to sort it out for you."

Rowan would always help, but he might have too much on his plate. Who knew what he needed with Onyx? "I've mentioned it to him." At least he'd mentioned Michael was back, even if he hadn't brought up the break-in to his apartment.

Lucia nodded. "Good. Come by tomorrow. I'm making empanadas de mole amarillo."

Nico's mouth watered. "I'll be over. That's a promise."

She smiled.

By the time Nico got inside his apartment, his phone had stopped ringing. Pulling it from his pocket, he saw Onyx had called. A grin tugged on his lips.

Fuck, he was a fool.

He called Onyx back.

"Oh, good. You aren't ignoring me," Onyx said as he picked up.

Nico chuckled. "I called you first, so how could I be ignoring you?"

Unsurprisingly, Onyx didn't acknowledge the flaw in his logic. "What do you want? I'm busy."

Nico paced the apartment. "I know you're busy. I was going to call later and see if you wanted to game, but something came up."

There was a beat of silence. "You called to say you can't hang out with me because something came up? Even though we didn't have plans?"

"No. That's why I wanted to call, and I would have, but Rowan asked to meet with you."

"Oh." Onyx's disappointment was unmistakable.

"We can still game after meeting him. If you don't have anything else lined up."

"I don't know, Nico. I don't want to see the vampire. I'm not in the mood."

"I get that." There was no way Onyx was over what had happened with Ash and Dante, and Nico didn't doubt he wanted to avoid magic world problems. "But it sounds urgent, and Rowan wouldn't tell me what it was about. I'd deal with it if I could, except he said he needs to tell you before anyone."

Onyx let out a long, dramatic sigh. "Fine. Whatever. But if it's some bullshit and Rowan is wasting my time, he's going to hear about it. Meet me at the club." Onyx hung up without waiting for Nico's reply.

He hadn't put up as much of a fight as Nico had anticipated. That had to be good. Nico was making progress. He just didn't know where it was leading.

15

———

ONYX

O_{NYX} _{WAVED} to Jade as he entered the strip club. "I promise I'm not stalking you."

She sashayed toward him. "If you say so."

That morning, Jade had called Onyx. He'd been glad to hear from her and had set up a meeting for the two of them at the gallery next week. Ideally, he wouldn't have shown up at the club before then. It was just his luck that she was working tonight.

"I'm meeting Nico and figured it was rude not to stop in before heading upstairs."

To her credit, Jade didn't seem bothered. "Star will be sad she missed you."

"As am I." Onyx handed Jade several crisp twenties. "Would you mind sharing this with the bartender and bringing me a bourbon?"

"Not at all." She grinned and walked off with the money.

Onyx killed time showering the dancer on stage with the rest of his cash, too fidgety to enjoy it. Seeing Nico again so soon wasn't good. He should have blown this off. Who cared if the vampire wanted to see him? He didn't come when called.

But Onyx *wanted* to see Nico. That was the whole problem. He was a Nico addict. Onyx had spent the afternoon daydreaming, imagining showing up at the witch's apartment and harassing him until he bent Onyx over and fucked him.

"Here's your drink." Jade appeared and handed him a glass. "I've got to get ready to go on stage, but it was good to see you."

"Likewise. I can't wait to check out your portfolio next week."

Her cheeks flushed. "I'll try not to hyperventilate in the meantime."

"There's no need. I swear, I'm not worth worrying over. Have a good night. I'll probably be gone by the time you get on stage."

She nodded and hurried off.

Onyx turned toward the door and came face to face with Nico.

"Good. Right on time. Here." Onyx handed him the bourbon.

"Thanks." Nico's brow furrowed. "This is exactly what I needed."

Onyx's heart swelled. Fuck, he was hopeless. "Let's get out of here. I don't want to make Jade uncomfortable if I'm going to meet her at the gallery."

"Jade?" Nico looked around. "What are you talking about?"

Oh, right. Onyx pulled Nico toward the door. "She's an artist. I like her paintings, especially the sapphic ones. I gave her my card last time I was here and wasn't planning to see her again until we met at the gallery, but then Rowan had to be a pain in the ass, and I'm concerned about giving off creeper vibes."

"You met an artist that you want in your gallery here?" Nico sounded surprised.

Onyx paused to stare, nose lifted. "Yeah, so?"

"So, nothing. That's cool." Nico knocked his drink back and handed the empty glass to a bouncer at the door.

They headed out of the club and up the stairs.

"Rough day?" Onyx asked.

Nico waved him off. "Na, nothing like that."

Onyx didn't believe him. Nico liked to call Onyx a liar, but he wasn't the only one hiding things. Nico usually sipped his drinks slowly. Surely the bouncer wouldn't have minded them taking something upstairs.

But if Nico didn't want to tell him what was up, it wasn't Onyx's job to get it out of him. Under no circumstances was Nico allowed to catch on to how much Onyx cared.

They bypassed the casino and headed to Rowan's office, where the door stood open. Nico walked right in, and Onyx followed.

Rowan rose from his desk. "Thank you for coming on such short notice. Shut that, will you, Nico?"

Nico closed the door.

Rowan approached, a grim expression lining his fine face. Onyx would have taken a jab at the dramatic atmosphere if the suspicion that this was actually serious hadn't crept up on him.

"Are you happy to discuss everything with Nico present?" Rowan asked him.

"Since I don't know why I'm here, how can I decide?" Serious or not, Onyx wouldn't completely change his attitude. "You're lucky I showed up. So, spit it out. I'm busy tonight."

Rowan slid his hands into the pockets of his suit pants. "There's a bounty out on the Hounds."

Shit, not what Onyx expected. He let the use of the offensive term go. "Who's dumb enough to put a price on our heads?"

"I'm not sure, beyond the fact that it was demons, not witches or vampires. My coven got wind of it through our intelligence network."

Onyx fumed, for some reason cutting a sideways glance at Nico. Not for reassurance. Though his steady presence kept Onyx's fire in check.

He forced his attention back to Rowan. "What's the bounty for? Our deaths? Demons would have a better chance of offing us than hiring someone less powerful."

"They want information. Anyone whose tip leads to your capture will be paid."

"When did you find out?" Nico asked.

"Late this afternoon. I messaged you right away." Rowan turned to Onyx. "I'd have called directly, but I don't have your number."

Under no circumstances did Onyx want to take the vampire's calls, but it seemed rude to make Nico play secretary. It would, however, give Onyx an excuse to keep in touch with Nico. Whatever. Now wasn't the time to talk phone logistics.

He studied Rowan. "Are you sure no one in your coven will sell me out?"

"Yes." Rowan's eyes glowed faintly. Vampires had no internal fire, but their magic was embedded in their gaze, and they sometimes got a glow to them. Rowan was likely trying to convey his sincerity.

"You better hope you're right." Onyx stepped closer. "If any of your people aren't loyal, I'm going to make it your problem."

"I'd expect nothing less." Rowan didn't seem the least bit worried. His unflappability was infuriating.

Onyx ran a hand through his hair. "I've got to see my brothers. Get my number from Nico and call me with any urgent news about this, but *do not* contact me for any other reason."

Rowan smiled. "I wouldn't dream of disturbing you with anything that didn't revolve around you."

"All right, smart guy." Onyx thinned his lips. "I appreciate the warning." He turned to Nico. "Come to the roof with me."

"Sure." To Rowan, Nico said, "I'll send you Onyx's contact."

Onyx headed for the door, saying over his shoulder. "Keep Nico in the loop too. No need to be all mysterious."

"Noted." Rowan sounded surprised, but Onyx didn't stop to analyze why that might be.

He opened the door, and Nico followed him out. "I can't believe I have to see Dante and Ash. For that alone, these bounty-placing demons need to pay."

"I'm sorry."

Onyx paused. "Don't be. It's fine. I'm being a whiny little brat."

Nico grabbed him before he could turn away. "No, you're not. Ash said some serious shit last night."

Nico's fingers seemed to burn Onyx's wrist. He longed to lean into the touch, his chest warming as his ever-present rage softened. Was he really so easily comforted?

"I shouldn't let it get to me." He pulled from Nico's hold and headed up the stairs.

Nico followed him silently to the roof. Once they were outside, they faced each other. Onyx's stomach flipped.

Nico shifted closer. "Want me to come with you?"

Yes. Onyx wanted that so much. "No, it'll be better if you stay."

"Are you sure?"

No, Onyx wanted his Nico support blanket. "Yeah, it's fine. I'm not so fragile that I'll go to pieces seeing big, scary Ash. Yesterday was a fluke. I don't know what my problem was, so why don't we forget it?"

Nico frowned. "Don't dismiss yourself like that."

"Don't tell me what to do," Onyx snapped, then sighed. "I want to get this over with."

"All right. It's your call." Nico turned to go.

"Wait. You're going to miss another chance to see my wings?" Onyx called before he could stop himself.

Nico turned, a wide smile on his face. "Not if you're offering to show me again."

Wrong move. Onyx should have played it cool. He'd succeeded in getting rid of Nico, only to pull him back in.

Why was he so obsessed?

He'd think about that later. "I wouldn't want to deprive you of my beauty. I'm not that cruel."

Nico chuckled, and Onyx's heart swelled. He made himself invisible to everyone but Nico, whipped off his shirt, and freed his wings.

Nico whistled. "Don't think I'll ever get tired of seeing that."

Onyx preened. Fuck, he was so easy, but right now he didn't care.

"Do a spin for me, little butterfly."

Onyx's heart leapt, and his face flushed. There was so much affection in Nico's gaze, it was ridiculous. Onyx swallowed past the sudden ache in his throat and put his hands on his hips. "Butterfly? These aren't butterfly wings? What the hell are you talking about?"

Nico smiled wider. "I don't know, you're like a pretty little butterfly. I don't care that you have feathers, you've got butterfly energy."

Onyx laughed, clapping a hand over his mouth. "You're a menace."

Nico's eyes roved over him. "And you're so fucking gorgeous it's devastating."

It was a good thing Onyx couldn't die because he swore his heart stopped.

"What the hell am I going to do with you?" Onyx rose off the roof, flapping his wings enough to hover, and did a little spin. He was showing off, so sue him.

Nico was more than an emotional support blanket. He was a drug that got Onyx so high he didn't ever want to come down.

Nico took a step closer. "I've got a few ideas about what you can do with me. But you'll have to fly back over here later to find out."

"*Hmphf.*" Onyx snorted. "I don't think butterflies come when called."

"Then I'll wait." Nico reached out and brushed a finger along the back of Onyx's hand. "Let me know how it goes with your brothers."

Onyx's fluttering heart crashed back to Earth. "Okay. I should go."

He shot higher into the sky and headed across the city even though all he wanted to do was stay on the rooftop with Nico. Possibly forever.

16

ONYX

"I've told you everything, Ash. How am I supposed to know how the bounty was set up?" Onyx wanted to pummel Ash's over-large muscles until something popped.

Ash had the audacity to look offended. "I'm just wondering. Did the demons reveal themselves to a group of vampires or witches when they set the bounty? How'd they get the word out?"

"While that might be nice to figure it out, it doesn't really matter," Dante said.

They stood in Dante's kitchen, where it appeared Onyx had interrupted Ash baking cupcakes. Naturally, Dante wasn't far from the sweets.

No one had mentioned last night, at least not yet. Onyx wouldn't be the one to bring it up. He planned to dump the necessary info and get the fuck out, fly to Nico's, and claw all those soft, mushy feelings back into his chest.

Ash set down a spatula. "We said we'd face Luc in Shear-water Landing, but are we going to stay if we're being hunted from all angles?"

Dante's feathers ruffled. Maybe Onyx wasn't the only one getting agitated. "It's no different than before."

Ash pointedly moved a bowl of frosting away from Dante. "Luc and a couple of random escaped demons hunting us is very different than a bounty on our heads and the magic world on alert. Even Harper's coven's hunt wasn't a threat like this."

Onyx hated to agree, but Ash had a point. "It's not great. Though I don't see why demons care about us now that they're free." The escapees hunting them before had been worried about being dragged back to Hell. That wasn't such a concern now.

Dante tore his eyes from the frosting. "Our fight with Luc in the Realm of the Damned was pretty public. Maybe they think we were trying to prevent him from opening the gateway."

"That's stupid. We'll have to set the record straight." Onyx grabbed a spoon, scooped a glob of frosting, and stuck it in his mouth.

"Hands off." Ash snatched the bowl away.

It was infuriating that Ash was acting like nothing had changed, even after calling Onyx a traitor. Did he honestly believe the accusation hadn't mattered? Or was this a sign that Ash hadn't meant to be so harsh?

Onyx caught himself. If Ash hadn't meant it, he could apologize properly. Onyx wasn't making excuses or putting any more hope into this doomed relationship.

He set the bowl of frosting on fire. It flared blue and melted over Ash's hand.

"Asshole," Ash growled, his eyes glowing orange.

Onyx tossed the spoon on the counter. "Harper will forgive me for ruining his cupcakes."

"What I was saying before," Dante interrupted, "was, even though the bounty isn't a great development, it's not that different than anything we've faced. They want us captured, obviously not killed, and no one in the magic community knows our identities except the people we trust. Our mates and Nico. Random witches and vampires aren't going to be any help to the demons searching for us."

"True." Ash burned the mess from his hand with orange fire, leaving it clean. "Nico won't sell us out."

Onyx's fire sparked. "Are you forgetting that the whole Valero Coven knows who I am?"

Ash shrugged like this wasn't a problem. He probably didn't care, seeing as the Valeros didn't know his identity.

"We trust them, don't we?" Dante asked.

"I guess. But not in the way we trust the mates and Nico."

Dante moved around the counter and lined up ingredients for Ash to whip up a new batch of frosting. "Still. If we aren't seriously worried they'll sell us out, this bounty changes nothing. Well, almost nothing. Onyx, it may be best not to be seen around Rowan, in case anyone gets suspicious of your connection to him."

That wouldn't be a problem. Any excuse not to see the vampire was ideal.

"You trust Nico?"

Onyx jolted and glared at Ash. "Yeah, so? Don't you?"

"Of course. Harper trusts him, and he'd never betray Harper. He seems noble." Ash narrowed his eyes. "Why do you trust him?"

Onyx's heart pounded. Why did he? Because Nico acted like he cared? Because Onyx had a crush?

He pushed his feelings down. "Nico's never implied he'll use our secrets against us. All he wants to do is help. Why wouldn't I trust him?"

Ash nodded. "True. Harper said Nico likes to help people."

Onyx's heart clenched. That was probably all Nico saw in

him: someone to help. A brat to tame. An outlet for his caring ways.

Dante spun abruptly toward the sliding glass door off the living room. "Someone's outside the reserve."

Ash dropped the butter. "What?"

"There's a magical presence outside my shields. I increased my sensors to detect anyone poking around." Dante's eyes turned white, a sign that he was connecting to his shearwater flock.

Onyx and Ash stood frozen in silence.

"The signal is faint. Maybe they're still flying toward the hill. The birds can't see anything."

"Should we go out and hunt them down?" Ash asked.

Dante's white eyes darted back and forth. "Seems like their magic is fading."

"What does that mean?" Onyx glanced questioningly at Ash, whose expression was pinched in confusion. No surprise there.

"My counterspells must have diverted their interest, like they're supposed to. They're leaving." Dante blinked, and his black irises reappeared. "If we want to catch a glimpse of them—"

He didn't need to finish before Ash was speeding out the open door, Dante right behind him.

Onyx followed.

"Stay within the protections for now, so they won't catch any hint of us," Dante called. "I'll send some birds farther afield."

They flew along the tree line, scouring the clifftop. Onyx hadn't brushed up on detecting invisibility illusions, so he cast out for any sense of magic.

Nothing registered.

"They're gone," Dante called after they'd covered the extent of the reserve.

Onyx turned toward the house. He arrived first and waited for Dante and Ash in the kitchen. It was too bad they hadn't gotten a sense of who the intruder was.

Ash returned to the mess of baking on the countertop. "Think they'll be back?"

The enchanted flock being common knowledge meant the clifftop nests were the first logical place for demons to search for them.

Dante opened a drawer and pulled out a king-size chocolate bar. "We'll have to wait and see. Hopefully my spells convinced them nothing's here and they'll move on."

"Well, that was a whole lot of nothing." Onyx turned to go. "Have fun baking. I've got better things to do than be Ash's sous chef."

"Wait." Dante grabbed his arm. "You shouldn't leave immediately."

"But we didn't find anyone. They're gone."

"From the area around the reserve. They could be watching the clifftop or the coastline from farther away, and if they're looking for invisibility illusions like Pamala did, you'll give us away. That's why I had us stay within the protected area."

Onyx tasted smoke. Dante had a point, but fuck. "I had plans tonight."

"I'm sorry." To his credit, Dante looked it. "Please stick around for a few hours, just to be safe."

Onyx wanted to tell them both to piss off, but they had to be smart about this.

"We aren't going to hide completely," Dante went on. "We can't let demons think we're easily intimidated, but there's also no reason to give anything away for free. We need to scope out the threat before we confront it."

"Yeah, yeah. Got it. I'm not stupid." Onyx marched to the fridge and pulled out a bag of blood.

Seemed he wouldn't be finding out what Nico had on his list of things to do with him. He shouldn't have been so disappointed.

THE NEXT MORNING, Onyx flew from Dante's house directly to the gallery.

He landed on the roof and pulled out his phone, bringing up his texts with Nico from last night.

ONYX:

I'm sticking with my brothers tonight. Nothing major, but someone came poking around our protections so we're lying low. Don't miss me too much.

NICO:

Are you all right?

ONYX:

Peachy.

NICO:

Okay. Stay safe. My list is growing.

Onyx hadn't responded. Maybe he should have, but Ash had been eying him suspiciously, and Onyx hadn't wanted to give Nico the impression he was too interested in his list.

There wasn't anything he cared about more than the damn list, but that was beside the point.

Onyx shoved the phone away. He'd had a terrible night and wasn't looking forward to a day without Scott. He could have gone home, rather than to the gallery, but that would have been worse. At least here, he could answer emails and double-check things for the upcoming show.

A cat was becoming more tempting by the day.

Onyx descended the ladder and slipped through his office window, stopping short.

His senses prickled. Something wasn't right.

The office door remained closed, and he didn't hear anything beyond. Onyx reached out with his demon sense. The protections he'd placed on the gallery were intact.

It would be just his luck to have a human intruder. But there was a state-of-the-art human security system to prevent that.

Maybe it was nothing more than paranoia after last night.

Still, it was better to check. Onyx re-rendered himself invisible and carefully opened the office door. He slipped into the hall and slunk silently forward. As he stepped into the upstairs gallery space, his heart leapt into his throat.

A tall figure stood with his back to Onyx, facing the painting on the far wall.

Even from behind, Onyx could tell it was Luc. That familiar night-black hair with its recognizable wave and his unmistakable posture, at ease but with a hint of authority. He even wore the same coat from the other night.

Onyx should shock him with lightning and call Dante, but for some reason, he couldn't move.

Why was Luc here?

Abruptly, Luc turned and smiled, their eyes locking. "Onyx, it's good to see you again."

The fuck? Onyx took a step backward. He was invisible!

Luc held up his hands as if in surrender. "Would you like to know how I can see you?"

Of course he would. What an obnoxious question.

For some reason, Onyx couldn't get his voice to work. All he did was stare.

"I've always been able to see through your invisibility. Ash and Dante's too. Well, not always." Luc's expression darkened. "Ever since I took your magic."

Onyx swallowed, his throat parched. Luc had never, *ever* phrased it like that. He'd always pretended he'd borrowed their magic, acting as if it had been a mutual decision to share power. He'd never admitted it was stolen.

"Are you serious?" Onyx breathed.

Apparently, it hadn't been a trick of the tower that allowed Luc to see Onyx, Dante, and Ash in the Realm of the Damned. Why explain and give away such a huge advantage?

Luc shrugged one lazy shoulder. "Very serious. You might have figured it out. Did none of you wonder how I stalked Ash so easily?"

Shit, the Devil had a point. It wasn't as if Ash had been flying around the city without an invisibility illusion back when he'd been following Harper.

Luc took a step forward, his handsome features twisting. "I need your help. I don't want to be on opposing sides. Please, Onyx." He sounded desperate.

Damn, he was an excellent liar.

Onyx's heart hardened. "How did you get in here? My wards aren't broken."

Luc's face fell. "We're family. It's harder to ward against your own blood. You should have strengthened your spaces with all three of your magics, like Ash and Dante did."

Onyx's internal fire raged. "Don't tell me what to do."

"Sorry." Luc averted his gaze. "I'm glad you didn't ask them to help, or I wouldn't have gotten in. I have something for you."

Onyx's pulse pounded in his throat. He swallowed past it. "I don't want it. I told you to leave me alone. If you can see us flying around so easily, why don't you accost Ash? You always preferred him. Oh, right, you almost killed his mate, and now he hates you as much as I do."

"Onyx." Luc stepped forward, and Onyx encased himself in a protective shield of blue fire. Luc didn't react to the defensive display. "I don't prefer Ash. You're all my brothers."

"Shut up." Onyx heaved a breath, suddenly feeling like he'd been flying at full speed for hours. "Just stop talking. If being your brothers mattered, you'd never have hurt Ash and Dante's mates. You managed to send Dante into a murderous rage. *Dante!* Only you could betray a so-called brother that horribly."

"I didn't know they were true mates!" Luc's voice rose, giving away his frustration. "And don't forget everything that happened before. We all did horrible things to each other."

"You started it. Anything we did was in retaliation for stealing our magic. For keeping us prisoner. There is no excuse for any of that. You are not the wronged one, Lucifer."

"I'm not saying that. All I want is for you to understand that I was angry. You'd abandoned me, and when I finally found you, everyone was going on about mates. Stabbing at ancient, festering wounds."

"Oh, please. That's no excuse. I don't give a shit about your poor tortured soul. If anyone deserves damnation, it's you."

Luc's face twisted. "Maybe. But how am I supposed to convince you I'm sorry without explaining my actions?"

"There is no way to convince me. You went too far and then kept going. No one is ever going to forgive you for hurting those boys."

Luc cocked his head. "You care about them?"

Onyx's heart clenched, and his fangs ached. He wanted to make Luc bleed. "Of course I do."

Luc nodded as if he was taking this seriously. "Then know that I'm sorry. Please, Onyx."

"No." Onyx's shield burned brighter. "Not good enough."

"Then what can I do? I'd never hurt your mate. I'd—"

"My mate! What mate?" Onyx had to yell to hear his own voice above his pounding pulse. His face burned hot, eyes flaming.

"Nico." Luc smiled softly, and Onyx's boiling blood ran cold.

"He's not my mate."

"No? You protected his house."

Had Luc been to Nico's apartment? Fuck.

An inhuman growl ripped from Onyx's throat.

"Onyx, please calm down. Nico is fine. I'd never hurt him. I'm so glad for you."

"Shut the fuck up."

Nico wasn't his mate, but Luc still could have hurt him. Everything Luc said was a lie. All he did was lie. This was all some game. Some power play.

"All I want is a chance to find my mate, too." Luc had moved closer without Onyx realizing, and loomed over him. "They're trying to kill me, Onyx. Even after everything that's happened between us, I know you wouldn't wish permanent death on me. Please, I need your help, and I'll make everything right."

"Bullshit. You're here, intimidating me. Threatening Nico. You're a filthy liar, and I'm not a naïve fool anymore."

Luc grabbed Onyx by the shoulders, wincing as Onyx's protective fire burned him. "You were never a fool."

Heat sparked between them, and Onyx was overcome with a dizzying wave of power. He gasped and choked, his eyes rolling back. Everything in him seized.

Then all sensation disappeared, and Onyx crumpled to the ground. He blinked and pushed himself up with shaking arms.

Luc was gone.

Onyx's blood boiled. Rage coursed through him and burst.

His wings erupted from his back, tearing his shirt. His horns sprouted from his hair, and his tail struggled against the constraint of his jeans.

Onyx's whole body burned.

What had Luc done to him? He felt different but couldn't place why. There was no time to figure it out.

He forced his horns and tail away, pulled his phone from his pocket, and called Nico.

There was no answer. He called again. And again.

Nothing.

Onyx ran for the office window and leapt into the air. If Luc had hurt Nico, Onyx would burn the entire universe to the ground. No one was allowed to touch him.

Onyx didn't want a mate. Didn't need one. He had no desire to put his hope in someone like that. Tears streamed down his face as he flew, but no matter how fast he went, he couldn't escape his thoughts.

What if Nico was his?

The possibility was terrifying.

17

———

NICO

"Aww shit!" Nico glared at the TV. "You're not playing fair, Leo."

"You're not trying hard enough. Don't blame me." Leo's voice filled Nico's headphones, followed by laughter from the rest of the players in their band.

A crash penetrated his noise-canceling headphones, and Nico whipped his head around. Onyx was crouched, wild-eyed, outside the window.

Nico's skin prickled at the look of sheer terror on the demon's flushed face. "I've gotta go, guys."

A chorus of *no*, and *what*, filled Nico's ears. Onyx yanked the window open and scrambled inside, wings catching on the window frame.

"Sorry. I'll text later. Something's come up." Nico whipped off the headphones and exited out of a game with a click. "Onyx, what's wrong?"

"Why the fuck didn't you answer your phone?" he snarled, chest heaving, wide eyes red-rimmed, and sweat lining his brow.

Nico scrambled to take it all in. "I must have left my phone in my room."

Onyx's gaze flared with blue fire. "In your room? This apartment is tiny, couldn't you hear it ringing?"

"I was playing *World's End*." He gestured to the discarded headphones and controller, a hit of defensiveness in his tone.

Onyx blinked. His attention darted around the apartment, and he seemed to deflate.

Nico's own growing tension pulled his muscles tight. "What's going on?"

Onyx's cheeks flushed even darker. "Nothing."

Oh, come on. Nico crossed his arms. "Nothing? You stormed in here because I missed a call?"

Onyx clenched his fists, and his wings disappeared. He didn't meet Nico's eye.

Enough. Nico wasn't letting Onyx bottle everything up. Something wasn't right. Onyx's blatant fear had disappeared, but it was too jarring to forget.

Nico approached and gripped Onyx's shoulders. "What's wrong? Why were you worried when I didn't answer?"

Onyx closed his eyes.

Nico was on the verge of shaking him. "Please talk to me."

"No."

"Onyx." Nico's voice filled with warning, something deep inside him clenching in desperation.

"*No,*" Onyx said more forcefully, eyes popping open.

Nico caught his gaze and clung to it like a lifeline. "Yes. Tell me why you're acting like something terrible happened."

Onyx pulled away, but Nico tightened his grip. The demon allowed himself to be held, narrowing his eyes and lifting his nose. "Make me."

So feisty, even when he was scared. Maybe especially when he was scared. If meeting Onyx's challenge was what he needed to feel safe—to open up—then Nico could play.

"You want me to spank you, is that it? Just ask. There's no

need to cause a scene and snap at me like I've done something wrong."

Onyx spluttered. "I'm not causing a scene. It's not my fault you ignored my calls. Am I not allowed to be upset?"

"Of course you're allowed to be upset, but I don't think missing your calls is the problem. What happened?"

Onyx trembled in Nico's hold. "Nothing. I thought... Nothing."

Onyx resisted like it was the only thing keeping him together. What was he scared of?

Nico tightened his grip. He wasn't backing down. "We both know you're lying. This isn't nothing."

Onyx shook his head, his gaze darting around like a trapped animal.

"Were you worried about me? Did you think there was a reason I didn't answer?"

"No," Onyx whispered. "I don't know. It doesn't matter."

"Then what do you need? You're upset about something, and don't tell me it's that I missed a phone call."

"It wasn't one phone call," Onyx snarled.

"My mistake. But what did I tell you about barging in here and getting angry at me for no reason?"

Onyx's chin jutted out. "I'm not allowed to do that."

"No." Nico tilted Onyx's chin up. "So tell me your reason for barging in, or accept your punishment."

Onyx shivered, his eyes bloodshot like he'd been crying. His voice broke. "I'm a mess. Just make me feel better."

Nico's chest expanded, warmth flooding him. Maybe it was a small admission on Onyx's part, but it was a start. "I can do that. I've told you I'll give you what you need, if you ask."

Onyx's eyes flashed. "I did ask."

"Sounded more like a demand. Want to try again?"

Onyx pursed his lips. "I need you to help me calm down.

Can you help me? Please?" He added the last word so quietly it was almost inaudible.

Nico stroked Onyx's cheek. "Good boy."

Onyx's eyes fluttered closed, and some of the tension seemed to flee his rigid stance.

Nico released Onyx and cleared his throat. "Take off your clothes and bend over the couch."

Onyx's face flamed, even his forehead turned red, but he quietly complied. Shedding his jeans and underwear, he stepped toward the couch.

"Over the arm." Nico guided him to the right spot and Onyx bent over, offering up his bare ass.

He was beautiful naked. Nico couldn't believe he was getting to see this. Onyx arched his back, tattooed skin on full display. He folded his arms on the couch cushion and buried his face in them, then spread his legs.

Nico approached. The dark hair on Onyx's legs turned lighter on his thighs, and he either waxed or groomed with magic because his ass and balls were bare.

A shiver rocked Onyx's body, but he stayed quiet, the silence unsettling. Onyx should be goading Nico into hurrying up. He should be complaining, reminding Nico he could get someone else to satisfy him if Nico didn't get on with it.

Something had changed. Nico had no idea what, but he wouldn't let Onyx down. If this was how he wanted to be comforted, then they were a perfect match.

"I'm going to spank you for bursting in here and yelling at me. Unless you're ready to tell me what's really going on."

"There's nothing to say." Onyx's voice came out muffled, face wedged into the crook of his arm.

"All right. If that's how it's going to be." Nico brought his palm down on Onyx's ass with a satisfying crack.

Onyx tensed beneath him, jolting forward. Nico cast the

spell to counteract as much of Onyx's healing as he could and smacked him again.

Onyx tensed further.

"Relax, or this is only going to hurt more."

Onyx turned his head to the side and glared over his shoulder. "You don't think I know that?"

Nico smiled and smacked him again, heart thudding as Onyx's eyelids fluttered. "You want this to hurt? You want me to force you to relax?"

Onyx muttered something incoherent.

Nico smack him three times in a row, his palm tingling, and his cock strained against his jeans. Onyx took each hit without a sound, his body seeming to tense further with each blow.

"You can let go." Nico smacked Onyx harder. "It's okay. It's all right to be scared or upset. It's okay to come to me. But you can't show up and lie."

Each statement was marked with a slap. Onyx's ass bloomed pink and Nico swore the tattoo of his tail quivered.

"Are you ready to tell me what this is about?"

"No." Onyx reburied his face in his arms.

"Okay." Nico gripped an ass cheek in each hand and spread Onyx wide, exposing his pink hole. Onyx's pucker clenched, and Nico bit his lip.

He wanted inside this perfect ass, but Onyx was so tense he had to be about to snap, and that wasn't how Nico wanted him. There needed to be no resistance left, no more fight, only Onyx's true desires laid bare.

Nico let go and spanked Onyx, setting a punishing rhythm. Nico's palm burned as Onyx's ass reddened. It didn't matter. All Nico cared about was seeing Onyx's muscles go lax, his shoulders unbunch, his knees go weak until he stopped bracing against Nico's blows, his toes curled in the carpet.

"That's it," Nico praised, not letting up, sweat dampening

his brow. "Relax. Let it burn. This is what you needed. You have to remember it's okay to tell me that. You can tell me anything. I'm here for you. You don't have to lie."

Onyx whimpered. "Nico, please."

Nico rubbed Onyx's lower back. "Please, what? Are you ready to talk to me?"

"No. Keep...keep going. Please. I need to feel you."

Nico trailed his hand lower, grazing Onyx's tail tattoo.

"*Oh, aah,*" Onyx cried out.

"Does that feel good?" Nico brushed the tattoo again, and Onyx's whole body convulsed.

"*Nico.*" Onyx's voice was high-pitched, almost panicked. He struggled to push himself up.

Nico leaned over and pushed Onyx's head down, bracketing Onyx's body with his, and tangling his hand in Onyx's hair. "I didn't say you could get up. Tell me, does it feel good when I touch your tail?"

"Y-yes." Onyx's voice shook, and he choked on a sob. He hadn't broken into tears like last time, but he sounded on the verge of collapse.

Nico massaged Onyx's scalp. "Is it okay for me to touch your tail?"

Onyx wiggled beneath him, ass rubbing against Nico's groin, but he didn't speak.

"Stop rubbing that needy ass against me. I need an answer. Touching your tail: tell me a color."

Onyx shivered. "Green." The word came out breathy, like Onyx was releasing the last bit of air from a balloon, and at last, his tension disappeared, his body going limp beneath Nico.

Fuck. Nico's pulse pounded. "Good boy. You're doing so well."

Onyx leaned into Nico's touch, rubbing his head against Nico's hand like a cat. "Is my punishment over?"

"Are you ready to talk?"

Some of Onyx's tension returned. "Fuck off. You know that's not what I want."

Nico smiled. "No, you want me to spank you until you can't see straight. I bet your demon healing is already soothing your naughty ass."

Onyx released a strangled sound.

Nico stood, gaze raking over Onyx's prone form. The tattoo of his wings seemed to glow blue, feathers outlined so intricately they almost looked real.

He was the most wonderful thing Nico had ever seen.

Nico brought his hand down and watched Onyx's ass bounce. He spanked him until he panted with the effort. Soft pleas fell from Onyx's lips each time Nico's hand met his thoroughly pummeled rear.

Onyx lay there and took it, his ass as red as his flushed face, but he didn't let go. Tension lined his brow. He needed more.

Maybe he wouldn't ever want to talk about what brought him here, and there was nothing Nico could do.

Nico traced the tattoo of Onyx's tail, and heat flared along Onyx's skin. Not the heat of a well spanked ass. Not a blush. Something within Onyx radiated a palpable warmth. His fire? Nico's breath caught, and he did it again, mesmerized.

"*Nico*," Onyx panted. "Nico. Wait. I'm going to... Wait."

Nico couldn't stop touching, but he didn't need to unless Onyx really asked. "Color?"

"Green, but Nico...Nico." Onyx's body shuddered. "Fuck. I can't. Dammit."

He looked over his shoulder, tears streaming down his cheeks, his eyes burning and wild. Onyx's fangs dropped as his mouth opened on a moan. His body seemed to vibrate, tensing like he was trying to hold himself together, then with a guttural cry, his face changed.

Onyx's red cheeks turned lavender—not the lavender cast by the reflection of his burning blue eyes, but a true change in the skin—spreading all the way to his forehead. Two horns sprouted from his hairline, sticking straight up and curving back at the tips. They were such a pale blue, they were almost translucent. Veins were visible at the base, flushing red, then fading to lavender.

Nico forgot to breathe. So much raw emotion, so much passion lit Onyx's face. Nico couldn't move.

Before him, Onyx trembled, his burning gaze locked on Nico's. Something grazed Nico's hand, and he glanced down.

Onyx's tail unfurled from his hips. The sleek appendage was the same translucent blue as his horns, the base flushed deep lavender, fading to what Nico could only call a purple blush at the top of Onyx's ass.

"Nico, I—I'm sorry. I can't. Oh, fuck." Onyx turned his face away.

"You're gorgeous." Nico tangled a hand in Onyx's hair, turning his head until their eyes met.

Onyx blinked, and tears slid down his cheeks. "I didn't mean to show you."

"But you did, and that's okay. I'm glad. I think deep down, you know you can let me in."

Onyx's breathing shallowed. "I was scared something had happened to you. That's why I came. I have to protect you so you don't get hurt."

Nico's chest seized.

Why would Onyx think something had happened to him?

He could find out the details later. All that mattered was Onyx opening up. Showing Nico everything. Even if he hadn't meant to release his horns or tail, he must've felt safe if this was his body's reaction. And there was no getting around the fact that Onyx chose to speak at last.

"I appreciate you wanting to protect me, Onyx. I like knowing that. You don't have to hide caring about me."

"Yes, I do." Onyx's teary gaze sharpened. "I always do."

"You don't have to with me. I'm here for you, Onyx. I'm not going anywhere."

Onyx closed his eyes.

Nico braced himself for Onyx's argument, his dismissal, but it didn't come.

"Fuck me, Nico. Please. That's what I need right now. If you're here for me, please just do it. Make me feel good."

He sounded so desperate, so scared. Did he not believe Nico? Did he think Nico would leave? Nico wanted to stay in the worst way. He wanted to be Onyx's everything. Comfort him. Support him. Defend him against anyone who doubted him.

"I'm not just going to fuck you to make you feel good, Onyx. I'm going to do it because I want it as much as you do. Because you're so good, trusting me. Because I've never been more turned on than I am seeing you—all of you—laid out for me. I've never wanted anyone the way I want you."

"Fuck, Nico, please." Onyx bucked his hips.

Nico straightened and pulled his shirt over his head. "Let me get lube."

"Don't you dare leave me. Not for a second. You don't need it." Onyx scrambled to get up, and Nico gripped his hips, holding him down. He didn't throw Nico off, even though he could have.

Onyx's tail flicked back and forth, brushing Nico's stomach.

He tightened his grip on Onyx's hips. "You need lube. I don't want to hurt you that way."

"You won't." Onyx huffed and wiggled his ass. "Stick your fingers in me and see."

What? There was no way Onyx had prepped before coming

over, was there? Not if he was worried Nico had been hurt. Besides, Nico would have noticed when he'd spread him open earlier.

He released Onyx's hips and slid his fingers along Onyx's crack. He found Onyx's hole, and his eyes popped wide.

He was slick.

Nico pressed a finger inside, and Onyx groaned, pushing onto it.

"When did you...?" Nico couldn't help pumping his finger. Onyx gripped him tight, sucking him into his wet heat.

"Demon trick." Onyx shot a positively evil look over his shoulder. His cheeks and horns flushing an even darker lavender, hints of red coming through. "I can get myself wet whenever I want."

"What?" Nico's mind blanked.

Onyx pressed his ass back. "Magic. I know you've heard of it. We've covered this already. Now fuck me."

Nico growled and plunged a second finger inside Onyx.

Onyx clenched and made a satisfied sound. He draped his tail out of the way, the base forming a sensual arch from the top of his crack as the rest of it settled along his spine.

Nico gripped the lavender base and watched it flush deeper, red blooming within as color spread down Onyx's ass.

His hole flushed red, then faded to lavender around Nico's fingers.

Nico almost came in his pants.

Onyx shouted, hips bucking. His tail muscle quivered in Nico's grip, and Nico stroked on instinct. Onyx moaned like was getting the best fuck of his life. Damnation, Nico only had two fingers in him.

He pumped his fingers, watching Onyx's lavender hole suck them in as he stroked Onyx's silk-soft tail.

"Nico, fuck, Nico. Fuck!" Onyx stiffened, back arching. His

hole convulsed, and the scent of sweet wine and orchids flooded the room.

"Shit, did you come? That's so fucking hot." Nico let go and withdrew his fingers, in awe, like this was the first time he'd ever had sex.

"Don't stop." Onyx writhed, bucking his hips and hitting nothing but air. "I'll come for you again. Promise. Get your dick in me."

"*Ngh.*" Nico had never dropped his pants so fast. He spread Onyx with one hand and lined up his cock with the other.

The contrast of dark skin against lavender made his head spin.

"Nico, I need you," Onyx panted.

He pushed in, mesmerized by the sight of his cockhead breaching Onyx's tight hole.

The scent of orchids intensified as heat enveloped Nico's cock. Onyx was so wet and tight. Slick oozed out of him and slid down Nico's shaft.

"That how bad you wanted this cock? You're dripping for it?"

Onyx bit back a strangled cry. "Yes."

Nico snapped his hips forward, settling fully inside. "You're so hot. Shit, Onyx."

"Demon fire. No other hole is ever going to be good enough for you again."

"Fuck no. Not after you." Nico gripped Onyx's hips and thrust, unable to hold back.

He was possessed. Fevered. Onyx's sweet orchid scent was like a drug, spurring him higher. Nico thrust like a wild animal. Their skin slapped, and Onyx's slick ran down Nico's balls.

"Fuck me, Nico." Onyx bucked his hips, meeting Nico's thrusts. "I'll be good for you. *Ugh,* fill me with your cum and I promise I'll be good."

Nico's brain short circuited and he pounded Onyx's ass like the world was about to end.

He tore his gaze from the place they joined and found Onyx's burning eyes fixed on him, fangs down, his mouth open, allowing his loud moans to fill the room unrestrained.

Every time Nico's hips slapped Onyx's reddened ass, his fiery eyes flared. Onyx's pale horns shimmered, the blush almost reaching their pointed tips.

No one had ever looked at Nico with so much naked desire.

Nico hauled Onyx's hips back as he thrust. He reached for Onyx's dick and found him hard and dripping, even after coming once already. It nearly sent Nico over the edge. He managed to hold off and took hold of Onyx's tail, finding it girthier than the slender cock in his other hand, both equally smooth.

Onyx whimpered and squirmed, bracing against the couch as he thrust backward. Nico found his rhythm again, each jack-hammered thrust sending Onyx's tail and cock fucking into his fists.

Onyx shouted and cum spilled over Nico's fingers, his hole strangling his cock. Onyx's tail quivered, and Nico's hips stuttered as he buried himself deeper, filling Onyx with his cum.

Nico had never had a breeding kink, but he found himself reveling in pumping Onyx full of his seed, never happier that fucking immortals meant no need for condoms.

He dropped forward and buried his face in Onyx's sweaty neck, panting and sucking in deep lungfuls of Onyx's sweet scent.

Nico pressed a kiss to the soft hair behind Onyx's ear.

"Was I good?" Onyx whispered.

Nico's heart skipped. "So good. My perfect little butterfly."

18

—————

ONYX

MY PERFECT LITTLE BUTTERFLY. If Onyx hadn't already melted into goo, he would have after hearing those words. Why couldn't every moment be as blissful as this one?

He clung to the feeling, and still, it slipped away.

As Onyx's pleasure faded, the sting in his thoroughly spanked ass healing, fear crept in, turning his fire cold.

This was too much. He'd shown Nico way too much. Said too much. Fucking felt too much.

Was Nico his mate? His pulse quickened. He wished he'd never even entertained the question. If it turned out Nico wasn't, Onyx wouldn't be able to handle it.

That was why he never wanted a mate, but the seed had been planted and had already begun to grow.

Nico stirred on top of him. "What's wrong? You're tense again."

Onyx should deny it. He couldn't. It would be better to get away. "Let me up."

"Yeah, all right." Nico pulled away and his cock slipped free.

Onyx clenched around nothing, fighting an irrational urge to cry. He couldn't bring himself to stand.

Nico's hand came to rest on Onyx's lower back, above his tail. "Let's shower. I'll clean you up."

Onyx didn't move. He didn't want to figure out what came next. "You don't have to clean me."

"You want my cum dripping out of you forever, dirty boy?" Nico taunted.

"Maybe." Onyx suppressed a smile as some of his pleasure came rushing back.

Thank fuck Nico knew when to give him a break from sincerity. If he'd said he would take care of Onyx, Onyx might have lost it.

Nico pulled him off the couch and spun him around.

It was impossible to meet Nico's gaze, so Onyx focused on the dark hair covering Nico's chest. He should return his damn horns and tail to tattoos. If his blushing had seemed out of control in his human form, it had nothing on his demon form.

Dante and Ash probably assumed he hid his horns and tail because his lack of pigment was irregular. That wasn't it at all. The translucent blue skin wouldn't be a big deal if it weren't for the flushing. Even Onyx's forehead and cheeks turning lavender would have been fine if it were always like that when he had his horns out.

But no, the color only showed when Onyx's fire burned. Like his eyes, but much more sensitive to any incremental change in his mood. And unlike his eyes, it was near impossible to control.

It wasn't fair that he had to walk around like a neon sign broadcasting when he was upset, or had a crush, or was lying, or feeling anything other than neutral boredom. It made it so much harder to pretend he didn't care.

"Take a shower with me." Nico's hands roamed Onyx's

body like he couldn't help touching him, and it went some way to soothing him.

"Fine. If you're going to keep asking." Onyx still couldn't look at Nico, his insides twisting.

Humiliation increased his pleasure in the heat of the moment, but now Onyx wanted to crawl out of his stupid translucent skin.

Infuriatingly, Nico tilted Onyx's chin until their eyes met. "You're not turning bashful on me, are you?"

Outrage had Onyx flushing to the tips of his horns. "Bashful? Not fucking likely. I'm a work of art, and you're lucky to see me naked."

"*Mmhmm.*" Nico pumped his eyebrows. "So true. No one does naked like you. Thank you for allowing me to see such beauty." He even said it without sarcasm.

Onyx's skin burned. His cheeks were bound to be purple. Face and ass. Fuck.

"Come." Nico tugged him out of the living room. "You're lucky the bathroom was renovated recently, or we wouldn't both fit in the shower."

Onyx zoned out as Nico turned on the water and guided him into the—still small—shower. Nico seemed happy to quietly pamper Onyx, gently washing his body as Onyx stood there like a rag doll.

Letting someone take care of him was divine. Onyx wanted Nico to look after him forever, which was idiotic. He was a demon. He didn't need looking after. If anything, Onyx had to take care of Nico and ensure nothing bad happened to *him*.

"What was that heavy sigh for?" Nico asked, jarring Onyx out of his daze. They were scrubbed clean, and Nico turned the shower off.

Onyx pretended to be interested in the loofah hanging from the basket holding the shampoos. "Tired," he lied.

"Then let's lie in bed."

Onyx didn't protest as Nico guided him out of the shower and toweled him off like a helpless child. He didn't object when Nico dragged him to the bed and curled up with him under the comforter, despite it being the middle of the day.

Nico turned Onyx on his side and pulled him in close, his back pressed against Nico's hairy chest, his tail nestled alongside Nico's cock.

Nico's lips brushed along the shell of Onyx's ear. "Will you tell me what you were protecting me from when you came over?"

Onyx white-knuckled the arm wrapped around him. He didn't want to. Talking was the worst, especially after he'd already revealed too much. But Nico deserved to know if he was in danger.

Onyx nestled as far back into Nico's embrace as possible. "I went to the gallery this morning and found Luc there. He got in without breaking my protective spells. Said it was because we share blood."

"Have you sworn blood loyalty to him?"

"No. Forced loyalty isn't a thing in the Eternal Realm. Being Luc's brother by blood must have made it harder for my protections to sense the difference between us. He obviously found a way to exploit our connection."

Nico nuzzled behind Onyx's ear. "Finding him in the gallery must have been a shock. It's your space. He shouldn't have invaded it like that."

"Yeah, well, he *is* the Devil." Onyx hesitated, gripping Nico tighter. He'd probably leave bruises, but Nico didn't complain.

"Luc mentioned you and"—Onyx took a breath—"I was scared he'd hurt you. Seeing how easily he got into the gallery meant he could break into your apartment without me knowing.

He could have done anything to you. I need to call Dante and Ash and have them protect you better."

He should have done that already, before Luc showed up, but he hadn't thought past whatever had made Nico jumpy that evening. Onyx had assumed the danger was minimal—Nico hadn't acted like it was serious—and had no reason to think Luc would target him.

But if they were mates... No. Now that Luc *believed* they were mates, things were different. Onyx had to be prepared for Luc to act on that belief.

"Why would Lucifer mention me?" Alarm laced Nico's tone.

Of course it did. But knowledge of Luc's vicious side wasn't what caused Onyx's pulse to pound. He couldn't admit why Luc had brought Nico up.

"Luc must be spying on us again. He saw through my invisibility and said he could see through Ash and Dante's too. It was how he tracked Ash and found Harper—" *No, don't mention mates.* "He's obviously seen me with you. Luc was taunting me. Trying to trick me into thinking he was sorry. But the only reason he'd mention you is to remind me he could hurt you. It was a threat. I won't believe any of his lies. Not again."

"Hey." Nico squeezed him. "Slow down. How did Lucifer threaten me? What did he say?"

"He said he wouldn't hurt you, but it was a lie, I know it. That's how he works."

There was a long silence.

True, it turned out Luc hadn't hurt Nico. That didn't mean he wasn't planning to. Luc wouldn't change overnight. He was up to something.

"What else did Lucifer say?" Nico asked at last.

"He kept saying he's sorry for hurting Harper and Ollie. He claims not believing they were real mates excuses his actions.

He asked for help, and this time said something about demons wanting to kill him. But why would they? He freed them."

"Retaliation?" Nico suggested. "Eliminating Lucifer would ensure he can't reimprison them. How did he manage to trap everyone in the first place?"

Onyx had put those potential motives together, but he didn't believe Luc was telling the truth and had dismissed any reasons someone might want him dead as irrelevant because the threat was a lie in the first place.

Unless it wasn't... Were demons trying to permanently kill Luc?

Onyx didn't know how to feel about that. Half of him was sick to death of caring for a brother who treated him like trash. The other half ached at the possibility of Luc being scrubbed from the universe. No one deserved that fate. Onyx had stopped Dante from committing that crime against Luc, mostly to save Dante, but partially to save his brother.

"To trap everyone, Luc stole magic from me, Dante, and Ash, and created a seal around the Realm of the Damned. And what's more, those stolen pieces of magic apparently allow him to see through our invisibility illusions. We never knew that was possible. Luc kept that secret for a thousand years and must have seen us sneaking around countless times."

"But he told you he could see through your invisibility today?" Nico sounded surprised.

Onyx nodded, dread sending chills through his body.

Luc had given away two big advantages—that he could get past Onyx's protections and see him regardless of illusion— when he had no reason to. No reason except to prove he was on Onyx's side. Or to trick Onyx into believing he was on his side, more likely.

But then, Luc had thrown that potentially regained trust away by threatening Nico and attacking Onyx.

Admittedly, it had been a weak attack. Nothing bad had happened. Onyx hadn't been cursed or hurt like last time, only incapacitated for a second, allowing Luc to disappear.

Onyx took a second to assess himself with his demon sense, in case a latent curse had been laid. Everything seemed as it should be. He felt great. Better than usual. That wasn't the sign of an attack. He hadn't felt this good in so long, he'd forgotten this particular feeling of wholeness.

Onyx went rigid in Nico's arms.

"What is it?"

"He... Fuck. Luc gave me my magic back." Onyx scrambled from Nico's embrace and sat up, running a hand through his hair and along a horn. "My power is at full strength. My fire feels deeper. Complete. I haven't felt this way in a thousand years. What the fuck?"

Onyx stared at Nico as if he might be able to explain. Nico seemed baffled.

There was no mistaking it now that Onyx was paying attention. He'd gotten used to his missing magic. The hole had become part of him. But now that he had his power back, the difference was stark.

It had been agony when Luc first stole such an integral part of him.

Now he was whole.

"What the hell is he playing at?" Rage coursed through Onyx, more powerful than it had been in centuries. His fire flared.

Nico's mouth opened in awe at whatever he read on Onyx's face. He sat up, grabbing Onyx's hand. "What if Luc's not playing at anything? Wouldn't giving your magic back go a long way to proving he's sorry? What if he wasn't threatening me? You said Luc claimed he wouldn't hurt me. And he didn't."

"He hasn't yet," Onyx corrected. "I get what you're thinking, but I can't trust him. Not after everything. He has an agenda. He always does. Luc only looks after himself. Just because we can't see his game plan doesn't mean there isn't one."

Nico frowned, eyes disproportionately sad.

"I'm not risking it. I don't care how his actions seem." Onyx gripped Nico's hand tighter. "I'm not risking anything happening to you. Trusting the Devil is for fools."

You were never a fool.

Onyx nearly screamed to drown out his brother's words.

He couldn't do this. He needed Nico safe. As a witch, he'd go to the Realm of the Damned when he died and never reincarnate. Onyx didn't want that cursed afterlife for Nico, and he couldn't let Luc send him there early.

An idea struck.

Onyx let go of Nico's hand and grabbed his shoulder. "You're friends with a horde of vampires. Why are you still mortal? If you were thinking of joining their ranks, do it now. You'd be so much safer."

Nico's brows raised, forehead creasing. "I don't want to join Rowan."

He should. If Nico bound himself to the annoying vampire, then Onyx could keep him forever. Even if they weren't mates.

Dammit, he shouldn't think about mates. He longed for one more and more, even if he tried to deny it. "I won't hold joining Rowan against you."

"I appreciate that, but I'm serious." Nico rubbed the back of his neck. "The vampire bond isn't for me. Rowan and I are close, but I don't want to be one of his children. I don't want to be so...connected. And I don't want to live forever."

Nico didn't want to live forever. Was this confirmation that he wasn't Onyx's mate? Surely fate wouldn't grant him a mate that rejected immortality and chose not to bond. It would be cruel.

Facing the possibility that he was wrong turned Onyx's desire for Nico into something desperate. It was like a sickness growing inside him. There was no denying it, and Onyx couldn't shake the feeling that the evolving intensity of his attraction meant something.

If they were fated, would Nico change his mind about immortality?

"I don't blame you for not wanting to be bound to Rowan. I should have known you had better judgment." Onyx forced a haughty, approving look, unable to face sharing his suspicions. Not yet. "I'll get the others to protect your house and keep you safe that way."

Nico pulled Onyx close and pressed him into the mattress, looming over him. "Good. I like you keeping me safe." He smiled with so much warmth it cracked Onyx's soul.

Onyx closed his eyes. He couldn't take it.

Hope was the worst. It always ruined him. First with Luc, hoping he'd stay, hoping he wouldn't leave him behind. With Ash, hoping he'd see him and love him for who he was. For hoping things would get better after they fell. For clinging to the chance that Luc might change.

And now, hoping the man on top of him was his mate.

Onyx trembled, holding back until it was impossible not to give in. He couldn't fight his hope for Nico.

He wrapped his legs around Nico's hips and rubbed their groins together, smiling when Nico's cock hardened so fast it had to be some sort of record.

"I've been missing out, never having you on your back." Nico's fingers trailed over Onyx's chest and flicked his nipple.

Onyx forced his eyes open. "There are many ways you've

never had me. I heard there was a list. Missionary better not be the only thing on it, or I'll be disappointed."

Nico chuckled. "Brat." He tweaked Onyx's nipple, eliciting a gasp. Nico tugged the barbell piercing, and pleasure shot through Onyx's core.

Onyx's cock hardened and his tail trembled. "Get that big dick back inside me and let's tick off this position. Then, you can impress me with your next grand idea."

A full-on laugh burst from Nico. He seemed surprised with himself and shook his head. "I don't know if I want to. You make it sound like a chore."

"Fucking me is never a chore. Take it back or you'll find my legs permanently closed."

Nico pressed against Onyx, their foreheads knocking, Nico's big body shaking with more laughter. "Please don't. Once isn't enough. I've gotta make your needy purple hole mine."

Onyx's snark evaporated, and his face and tail flamed.

Nico's woodsy citrus scent washed over him in a refreshing wave, and Nico dropped kisses down Onyx's neck, giving his piercing a vicious twist.

"*Ugh*, go on then. Claim me, Nico. Fuck my blushing ass until I can't remember anything but being filled with your cum."

"Fuck, yeah. You've been so good today. Talking to me. Telling me what you want. Of course I'm going to give you another load." He kissed down Onyx's chest, then bit and sucked on his nipple, flicking it with his tongue.

A hand snaked between them, and Nico aligned his cock with Onyx's hole. A quick flare of magic renewed his slick, and Onyx bore down, opening for Nico as he pushed in.

Nico's cock stretched Onyx just right. Though honestly, sex with Nico would be perfect no matter his size or shape, or how they came together. It wasn't about parts or bodies. Fitting with

Nico was bigger, mushy and soul-altering, like Onyx had never cared to be with past lovers.

"That's it. You're taking me like I already claimed this sweet hole." Nico filled him until their bodies met, slick leaking between them. "You're so messy. So filthy and dripping for me, little butterfly. I'm going to pin you down and never let you go. Keep you stuffed tight."

Nico pulled back and thrust. Onyx arched beneath him, hips undulating, matching Nico's rhythm with loud smacks of wet skin.

"You say the sweetest things," Onyx panted, head thrown back and horns digging into Nico's pillow.

Rocking back on his knees, Nico hitched Onyx's legs over his arms, changing their angle. "How's this?" He thrust, hitting Onyx's prostate.

Pleasure shot through him, and his tail shook, squirming against the mattress. "*Mmm*, perfect. More."

Nico pounded into him, face flushed and eyes hooded with lust. "Play with your nipples. I want to see."

Onyx obeyed, taking a nipple in each hand, pinching his skin and tugging on his piercings. Nico's scent filled the room, and Onyx didn't hold back a single moan. This was bliss. He'd stay in bed with Nico for the rest of time.

Couldn't he have this one thing? Didn't he deserve Nico?

Nico's desire seemed like it would never run out. Not when it was fixated on Onyx like that. Pleasure was like a living, breathing thing between them, a beast feeding on the seed of hope planted inside Onyx.

"So pretty," Nico praised, hips snapping. "I want to watch you get off. Put on a show for me. Blush so deep that your colors never fade. And your eyes, fuck Onyx, don't look away. I need those fiery eyes on me."

Onyx tried to do it all for Nico. Fixed his burning gaze on

him, played with his nipples for him, let Nico pound his hole. His fangs itched to pierce Nico's skin, and lengthened. Nico's scent was so strong, tangy and mouthwatering. His blood must taste amazing.

Would Nico let Onyx bite him?

Nico's focus seemed to zero in on his fangs, and he swore. He thrust so hard, Onyx jolted up the bed. Nico's mouth dropped open on a moan and he filled Onyx's ass.

It set Onyx off, and his pleasure spilled over his stomach, hole clenching and tail vibrating. The air seemed to pulse between them, and something tugged deep in Onyx's chest.

A magnet.

A string, pulling tight.

His addiction to Nico like a drug.

Or something more.

A feral animal was born between them, clawing them together as it gorged on their growing connection.

Nico crashed down on top of Onyx, melding their bodies together like the force between them was as real as gravity binding the Earth to the sun.

Panting breaths and musky citrus overwhelmed Onyx. Nico wrapped his arms around him and squeezed.

Onyx's heart burst, the useless organ giving out.

This was it. It had to be.

His mate.

19

———

NICO

A KNOCK on the front door jolted Nico out of his drowsy half-sleep. Thanking his past self for cleaning up before flopping back into bed, he rose and pulled on jeans and a T-shirt.

"Who's that?" Onyx whined, rolling over and burying his face in the pillows.

Nico's attention fell to Onyx's exposed ass.

As disappointed as he was that all evidence of his spanking had healed, he couldn't complain as he stared at Onyx's tail. He'd left his demon features out much longer than Nico expected after releasing them unintentionally.

The lavender blush had faded, leaving behind translucent blue skin that seemed to shimmer, and a spiderweb of delicate veins encompassing his tail's sensitive base.

Nico tore himself away. "I'll go see who's here. My guess is the neighbor from across the hall."

A quick glance in the mirror confirmed he was presentable, and he hurried from the room, shutting the door.

The whole day had a dreamlike quality to it. Nico needed time to think and regain his bearings. At least Onyx hadn't left.

He'd expected the demon to disappear after they'd washed up the second time.

What did him staying mean?

Butterflies swarmed Nico's insides.

He tamped them down, checked the peephole, and opened the door. "Lucia." Nico smiled at her and the foil-covered tray she'd brought.

"I figured I'd drop these off before I head out." Lucia walked in, rounded the entryway corner, and made a beeline for the kitchen, where she set the tray on the counter. "Are you coming to Emilio's with me tonight?"

"Who's Emilio?"

Nico whipped around.

Onyx stood in the bedroom doorway, his hair tousled and demon features tucked away. He wore Nico's clothes—a T-shirt and a pair of shorts—and damn, he looked well fucked. Positively scrumptious. There was no mistaking the ill-fitting outfit for anything other than borrowed.

Insides flaming, Nico became painfully aware that their clothes from earlier were all over the living room. Anyone with eyes would know what they'd been up to.

"Hello!" Lucia's brows rose, and she clapped her hands in delight. "I'm so sorry for intruding. I guess that's what I get for walking in like I own the place." She swatted Nico's arm. "You should have told me to go away."

Nico's face and neck burned. "I'd never send you away. Especially not after you've made me dinner."

Onyx crossed the room and peeked under the foil. "Empanadas? These smell amazing." He replaced the foil. "I'm Onyx, by the way."

"Lucia." She held out her hand, and Onyx shook it. "Since it seems Nico's not jumping to explain, Emilio is my son. I go to his place for dinner every Sunday. You're welcome to join us.

That might actually get Nico to come along. We're trying to suck him into the family," she added in a stage whisper.

Onyx nodded, playing along. "Well, I won't stop you. Unless... Emilio isn't single, is he?"

Nico choked.

"Not at all. Married with kids," Lucia said proudly. "I'm sure you two have a more exciting evening planned than tagging along with me, so I won't feel bad if you don't come." She beamed at Nico. "I'll get out of your hair."

All Nico could do was nod and walk her to the door.

"He is stunning," Lucia whispered, actually keeping her voice down, and squeezed Nico's hand. "Hope I see him around more." With that, she left.

Nico shut the door and pressed his forehead to it.

Onyx cackled. "She thinks I'm stunning. What a wonderful woman."

Eavesdropping must be another demon trick.

Nico stalked back to the kitchen, where Onyx was eating an empanada. "She's a good friend, but I didn't need her knowing I spent the day in bed."

"And on the couch." Onyx pointed to their clothes.

"Don't remind me."

Onyx's eyes narrowed. "Why does everyone get so embarrassed by the existence of sex around older people? She knows what's what. And don't forget, I'm somewhere around three and a half thousand years old. By your logic, you should have been too scandalized to say a quarter of the dirty things you crooned in my ancient ear."

"Good point. But I don't generally share details of my sex life with Lucia, or anyone."

Onyx's gleeful expression faded, his face closing off. "Did I fuck up? If you wanted me to stay hidden, you should have said."

"You didn't fuck up. No, nothing like that."

How did Nico explain that he didn't want Lucia knowing because now she'd be asking about *the stunning man named Onyx* until the end of time, or until Nico and Onyx announced something official? Normally, her encouragement didn't bother Nico, but in this case, he wanted to be Onyx's partner even more desperately than Lucia wanted to see him in a committed relationship.

It would be so much harder to brush off her questions. So much more heartbreaking to tell her Onyx had moved on.

Unless Nico was Onyx's mate. Then everything would work out.

Nico's heart leapt.

Harper had said Lucifer might think Nico and Onyx were mates if he caught wind of them together. That had to be why Lucifer mentioned him to Onyx. Why else would the Devil notice him? Harper had to be right.

Then why hadn't Onyx said that when he'd explained?

Fuck, maybe Nico was seeing what he wanted to see. Even with his distrust of the mating bond, he couldn't help wanting to belong to Onyx. Apparently, he'd throw his scruples to the side for him.

That was terrifying, but after the day they'd shared, doubts were on the back burner. Nico wanted to be Onyx's fated mate. It had become that simple.

If only wanting made it true. Maybe Onyx hadn't told Nico that Lucifer believed they were mates because Lucifer was wrong.

"I'm glad I didn't fuck up." Onyx finished off the empanada and wiped his hands. "Wouldn't want to overstep and mess with your friendships. Unless Lucia was setting you up with her son, then there'd be an issue."

"Oh?" Nico smiled slyly. That hint of possessiveness had to mean something.

"I'd say I don't share"—Onyx frowned—"but that's not true. I like to share. Just not with your neighbor's son."

Nico bit his lip so he wouldn't grin like an absolute dork. Was Onyx saying what Nico thought he was saying? "I'm not opposed to sharing either, but why don't we lay out some boundaries since it seems we'll be doing this again?"

Onyx went stock-still, his eyes flickering as his face reddened. "Doing this again? What makes you think I'm still interested?"

Oh, please. It was like Onyx couldn't help trying to hide his feelings even when he'd already given them away. "You're staking your claim. That's why you came out here, and why you keep asking about Emilio."

Onyx lifted his chin and made a sniffing sound. "Is that so? Guess I'm more transparent than air."

Nico would have laughed if he hadn't been tamping down dangerous levels of excitement. "Don't feel bad. Nothing gets by me."

Onyx grumbled unintelligibly.

A laugh slipped out, and Nico cleared his throat. "I've got no issue with you claiming me, or that you like to share. I can be non-monogamous."

"Really?" Onyx's brow creased. "If Lucia had set you up with her son, would you have expected to be exclusive with him?"

An odd question. Nico scratched his chin. "It's irrelevant since we were never set up, and I was never interested. But how about I answer what you're really asking, *hmm?*"

Onyx glared but didn't object.

"I've had monogamous relationships, but that's not the only

way I operate, and being non-monogamous doesn't mean I'm any less serious about someone."

Onyx took a small step forward, seemingly without realizing, his glare losing its intensity. "Do you have a preference?"

Nico's chest swelled. Onyx was finally comfortable being direct. "I prefer having a romantic relationship with one person, and exploring sexual relationships with others, usually together as a couple, but not always. How about you?"

Onyx stilled as if stunned. Or perhaps spooked.

Was letting the phrase *romantic relationship* out into the open too much? Nico might be pushing his luck, but Onyx had started it. He couldn't act like he cared who Nico was involved with and then run from this conversation.

But he didn't run.

Onyx planted his hands on his hips and his eyes raked over Nico as if inspecting him for the first time. "My preferences seem to align with yours. So, while we're doing this, there's no one else unless we're in it together or discuss it beforehand."

"Sounds perfect to me." Hope surged through Nico. Everything seemed to fit as if they were made for each other. Could this be a sign that they were mates?

In one fluid motion, Onyx stripped off his borrowed T-shirt.

Nico's cock came to attention like it had never been touched in his life. "What are you doing?"

"I'm leaving." Onyx dropped the borrowed shorts, picked up his discarded underwear, and put them on, followed by his pants.

Nico deflated in more ways than one. He should ask Onyx to say. He should ask about mates.

But Onyx had already opened up more than Nico expected. He had to be at his limit. Unless this was one of those times Nico was supposed to push. He was usually more sure of the right move.

Dammit. He was nervous in a way he hadn't been before.

He couldn't let it stop him. "You don't have to go. I was hoping you'd stick around and play *World's End* or something."

Onyx ran a hand through his blue hair, combing away the freshly fucked look. "I'm aware I don't have to go. But I need to round up Dante and Ash to protect this place. Are you okay with them having your address?"

"Sure." Suddenly, Onyx leaving didn't feel like it was putting distance between them.

"Good. Otherwise, I'd have to get mad at you." Onyx threw Nico a sweet, lopsided grin and climbed out the window. "Don't miss me too much."

In a flash of blue wings, he was gone.

To Nico's disappointment, Onyx didn't stop by his window after the demons cast their protections. He texted, saying they were going to The Herb Emporium to prevent Lucifer from sneaking in there, and Nico hadn't heard anything further.

Which was probably a good thing. Onyx had to be ready to talk the next time they saw each other. So did Nico.

The more Nico ruminated on it, the more being Onyx's mate seemed like a real possibility. He'd never felt this way before, had never fallen so quickly for someone, or had this burning desire to know them and be there for them in every possible way.

The next day, Nico was preoccupied with memories of Onyx, laid out for him, naked and blushing, as he walked to work. The images pulled on his consciousness. He couldn't have gotten Onyx out of his head if he'd wanted to.

Nico paused at the corner as the light turned red, resolving to talk to Harper about mates, when someone knocked into his shoulder.

"Hey, watch—" Nico stiffened at the sight of Michael.

The witch cursed, fumbling with a small object in his hand.

"What are you doing here?" Nico called on his magic, wary of all the humans around.

Michael dropped a glistening item, and it rolled into the street. A car went by, and the shiny thing disappeared, either crushed or knocked into the nearby drain.

"You've been in my house," Nico accused. "Are you stalking me?"

Michael's wide eyes darted from the street to Nico, then back. He turned and ran.

"Shit." Nico took off after him.

People glared as they ducked out of the way. Michael was already half a block ahead. He pulled open the door of a parked car and climbed in. The car took off.

Nico stopped and took a breath. Had Michael been trying to get a sample of his blood or hair? The object he'd dropped could have been a small vial.

Turning back the way he came, Nico pulled out his phone to text Rowan, but he already had a message.

ROWAN:

Had some trouble at the club last night.
Reminded me of the Orlov business. You had
any word they're back in town?

NICO:

No, I haven't heard anything about the Orlovs.
Can confirm Michael is back for sure. Seen him
around my apartment twice now.

ROWAN:

Need me to send someone over?

Nico wasn't sure. He tucked his phone away and headed toward The Herb Emporium.

Nico could handle Michael, especially if he was inclined to run at the smallest provocation. Rowan had his hands full. The possibility of the Orlovs returning was a much more serious problem. Not to mention the bounty on the demons. Rowan had said he'd try to figure out who'd set it.

It wasn't like Michael could get to Nico at home. If he'd been trying to grab a blood sample to break past Nico's protections, he was barking up the wrong tree. It might have helped if Nico had hired a security witch, but that wouldn't do a thing against the demons' spells.

At The Herb Emporium, Nico unlocked the grate and opened the shop. As he turned on the coffee machine, he texted Rowan back.

NICO:

Na. All good.

I promised Michael's ex I'd tell her if I spotted him, so she might want someone around her place.

ROWAN:

No problem. Let me know what she needs.

Nico poured his coffee and called Evelyn. As they talked, Harper appeared and made himself a coffee before retreating to the main shop area. Luckily, Evelyn hadn't seen Michael around her place. She lived on the other side of the city but asked for one of the Valeros to come by that evening around the time she'd be returning from work. Just in case.

Once all that was coordinated, Nico topped off his coffee and joined Harper out front.

"How was the concert the other night?" Nico asked.

Harper lit up. "Amazing. I wasn't familiar with the band, but it was so fun."

"I'm glad."

"How about you, good weekend?"

Nico sipped his coffee. He'd never imagined he'd come to the younger man for advice, but here he was, hoping Harper had answers.

"My weekend was good. I hung out with Onyx yesterday."

Harper set his mug aside, shifting closer. "Ash mentioned that when he went over to protect your place. So you and Onyx are..." He gave Nico the politest, yet most curious look imaginable.

Nico resisted the urge to fidget. Going by Harper's knowing look, he suspected Nico and Onyx had done more than hang out.

"We're getting to know each other. I like him," Nico admitted.

Harper bit his lip, thankfully too polite to press.

Nico soldiered on. "Can I ask you something, between us?"

Harper's eager expression turned serious. "Sure."

Nico's cheeks heated. Now that he was about to say it out loud, being Onyx's mate seemed a hell of a lot more ridiculous. He cleared his throat. "What was it like being Ash's mate before you knew about the bond? Could you tell something was happening?"

If Harper was surprised, he hid it well. More likely, he'd seen this coming. "Yeah, I could tell. I was overly attached to Ash, no matter how much I told myself I shouldn't be." Harper's cheeks stained red, and he adjusted his glasses. "We had a one-night stand, and I couldn't get over him. Then, when we reconnected, I had this urge to trust him even though I didn't know him."

Harper was one of the least trusting people Nico knew. It had to have been an effect of the mating bond.

Nico trusted Onyx, but that made sense after getting to know him, so it was harder to be sure if it was a sign. "Before, you said Ash was drawn to you. Do you think it went both ways?"

Harper's face split into a wide grin. "Yeah. Ollie said that when he first met Dante, it was like something was pulling them together. I felt that too. Especially being physically close to Ash." His cheeks darkened.

"Was being intimate with Ash different than other people?" Sex with Onyx was like nothing Nico had experienced, and it wasn't about his demon features or magic slick, even if those things blew Nico's mind. It wasn't even about Onyx's attractiveness or their perfectly aligned kinks. Their connection went beyond physical.

That second time in his bed, Nico swore something came alive between them.

Harper averted his gaze. "I can't really say. Um. I wasn't super experienced before Ash."

Nico cursed himself internally for making Harper uncomfortable. "Sorry. I shouldn't have asked. It wasn't appropriate."

Harper's attention snapped back to him. "What? No. I want to be able to talk to you. We're friends, not just coworkers. I don't have much experience talking about my, um, sex life. It makes me awkward. That's all. Sometimes it feels like I don't have experience with anything. It's like my life didn't start until I left my coven."

Nico opened his mouth.

"Do not apologize for not helping me more than you did. We've been over this." Harper pointed an accusing finger at Nico, who clamped his mouth shut.

He took a second to finish his coffee.

Nico had been intrigued by Onyx from the start, had this desire to figure him out and not let him get away. If that wasn't being drawn, then what was? Being mates fit, but without knowing Onyx's feelings, there was no way to be sure.

Nico wanted Onyx so much, he was at risk of seeing things that weren't there. He needed an outside opinion at the very least.

"Don't laugh, but I think I'm Onyx's mate."

Harper squealed in a pitch so high, Nico winced. He flung himself on Nico and crushed him into a hug. "*Oh, Satan*, I'm so happy for you. I totally called it."

Nico's heart pounded, and nerves rocketed through him. "You called it?"

"You two have been spending a lot of time together. It makes sense. Tell me how it feels." Harper pulled back and inspected Nico.

"It feels like I don't want to live without him."

It was intense but true. Nico couldn't lose Onyx, couldn't watch Onyx move on and leave him behind. They could grow together, bring others in to join them, but Onyx and Nico were the beginning of a core, a foundation. They had to be a part of each other's lives from here on out.

This had to be what the mating bond felt like.

Harper bounced up and down. "Aww."

Nico laughed. "I didn't think you'd be this happy."

"Why not? I want everyone to have a mate. You deserve a fated love. I have to tell Ash. He might actually be right."

"Ash thinks I'm Onyx's mate?"

"Not exactly. He had a theory. Since Ollie was Dante's mate and I was the one to bring Ollie into our group, Ash wondered if I'd found Onyx's mate too. Except he guessed Dex, and that was wrong. You being the third mate actually fits better. It's *all* fate. There's no way it was random chance that I rented a room with Ollie and got a job with you, and we're all demons' mates."

"The odds do seem slim."

"Not slim, one in a million. Maybe even less likely. The demons have been searching for thousands of years, and then, boom, three mates all connected to each other? It's about fated connections. Who says they only form between mates? Why not among families? The brothers have each other. It follows that as their mates, we'd have our own bond."

When put that way, Nico's doubts began to fade.

He was scared of wanting this and being wrong, but the intensity with which he longed for Onyx wasn't usual. Instead of seeing it as a sign he'd be heartbroken, it could be a sign he was right.

"Can I tell Ash?" Harper pulled out his phone.

"Not yet." Nico grabbed Harper's hand. "I need to talk to Onyx. He hasn't even hinted that we could be mates. I need to figure out how he feels before anyone else gets wind of what I'm thinking."

Onyx wanted some form of relationship with him, but was he as all in as Nico? Was fear holding him back?

Harper put his phone away. "Okay, yeah. I won't tell anyone we talked. But I need to come up with something to tell Ash."

"Why?"

"He's going to ask what got me so excited, and passing it off as a reaction to a super successful brew seems unlikely."

"He'll know you got excited?" Nico's heart skipped. He'd heard there was a telepathic element to the mating bond, but not exactly how it worked.

What would being that in tune with Onyx's state of mind be like? His gut reaction was distrust. Being a mate was more intense than the sire bond between vampires and their children

—a bond Nico had never wanted, partly due to its invasive nature.

But Nico had never loved Rowan. Never wanted more with him.

He wanted everything with Onyx, and bonded, Nico would be closer to Onyx than any other soul. A connection like that was beautiful. Not frightening.

"Don't worry." Harper put a reassuring hand on Nico's forearm. "You don't have to share your emotions all the time if you don't want to. Ollie and Dante don't. And you aren't mated yet. You can always wait to complete the bond, if you want."

"Why do you sound skeptical?"

"It's not that I'm skeptical. The connection will grow naturally between you, now that it's started. You'll feel it more and more. And you're not like Ollie, you're familiar with magic, and even mates. It's hard to imagine wanting to wait when it's all right there in front of you."

All that potential, ready for Nico and Onyx to seize. Nico had never been more excited about anything in his life.

20

—————

ONYX

"We don't need to protect my place," Onyx said for what had to be the hundredth time as he, Ash, and Dante headed down a narrow street behind the waterfront, on their way to Ren's apartment.

Ash grabbed his arm. "Luc broke into the gallery. He'll break into your house."

Onyx pulled from his grasp. "Then I'll stay at work or with Nico."

"Stay with Nico? Seriously? Why do you have to keep where you live secret?"

Onyx spluttered. "Yes, seriously. Why are you so angry that I won't tell you?"

"Because it's illogical," Ash growled, cinnamon-spiced smoke tinging the air.

"Illogical? Big word for you. To be honest, at this point I'm keeping it secret to piss you off." It wasn't true. Onyx needed at least one piece of his human life to remain untouched.

"Fuck. Fine." Ash threw up his hands. "I don't care. I bet your house sucks. It's probably over the top. Ugly. I bet you live in the suburbs."

Onyx cracked up. He should have fumed, but Ash was unintentionally hilarious. It reminded Onyx why he wanted to like the oaf.

If only Ash had apologized instead of acting like he hadn't called Onyx a traitor.

"Would you really stay with Nico?" Dante asked.

Fuck, Onyx hoped they'd gloss over that. "If Luc is after Nico, I should keep an eye on him."

Ash's steps faltered. "Luc thinks he's your mate, doesn't he?"

Onyx had left that part out when he'd told his brothers about the Devil's visit to Gallery Four. "Who cares what Luc thinks. He didn't think Harper was your mate and was wrong. Are you going to start taking Luc's word for anything? Even you're smarter than that, Ash."

Dante grabbed both their arms and pulled them into the alley beside Ren's building. "What happened at the gallery, Onyx? You said Luc broke in and threatened Nico, but I want the details."

It had been a relief that Dante and Ash hadn't pressed for more information earlier. They'd jumped into action to ensure Luc wasn't getting into Nico's building or the apothecary without a fight. Seemed Onyx's luck had run out.

He explained, more or less, exactly what happened.

"He gave you your magic back?" Ash gaped at him. "How'd you forget to tell us *that*?"

Onyx bristled. "I didn't forget. It took me a while to realize that's what he'd done."

Dante stared at him unblinking. "And he said he wouldn't hurt Nico?"

Ash grabbed Dante. "Who cares. We can't believe him."

Dante shook himself. "No. We can't, but..."

Unease churned in Onyx's gut. The suspicion that Luc wasn't up to his usual trickery wouldn't go away. He'd let Luc burrow too deep inside his head. "Fool us once, shame on him. Fool us—what are we up to now? Well past twice. We can't trust him, Dante."

"No, we can't." Dante gave a tired sigh. "But we have to figure out if demons are trying to kill Luc. If that's confirmed, then it calls everything else into question."

"You think he broke into the gallery to genuinely tell Onyx he wouldn't hurt Nico?" Ash's lip curled. "Please."

"Why else give Onyx his magic back? Why tell us he can see through our invisibility illusions? *After a thousand years of keeping that tidbit to himself.* He could be trying to gain our trust because he needs us to save him."

"Or to trick us into getting close so he can betray our trust again." Onyx had told himself he'd never give Luc an inch, and here he was, considering it. What a nightmare.

"Let's talk to Ren." Dante ushered them out of the alley. "With the bounty on us, it's not unreasonable to think someone's hunting Luc too."

Ash snorted derisively. "The bounty is for information leading to our capture, not deaths. If the same demons are looking to capture Luc, fine. They're welcome to hunt him down and imprison him. It'll save us the trouble."

Onyx wanted to agree. Luc's claims had to be a trap, even if there happened to be a kernel of truth in there somewhere.

But if it wasn't a trap, and Luc's permanent death was a real threat, what then? Luc didn't deserve their help after everything.

Too bad what someone deserved never seemed to matter.

Dante knocked, and Ren let them in, showing them into the apartment where she'd been living since first sneaking out of Hell.

She perched in an armchair and folded her hands in her lap. "I was wondering when you'd be back."

Ash remained standing as Onyx and Dante settled on the couch. He crossed his arms and loomed. "We wanted to check in on our alliance."

Ren seemed unruffled by his unfriendly demeanor. "Unless you're here to tell me otherwise, our alliance remains unchanged. I appreciate the *text message* telling me everyone was released from Hell, by the way. I can't imagine what you're here to tell me if that wasn't in-person news."

She was growing on Onyx. Prickliness was a respectable trait.

Dante leaned forward. "Have you caught up with many demons since the exodus?"

"I prefer to keep to myself." Ren examined her nails. "But a few found the magic I left around the city and tracked me down. I might have to move."

Onyx frowned. "Did they threaten you?"

"No, they asked a bunch of prying questions. I pretended I'd just gotten here. Didn't want anyone aware that I snuck out early. And don't worry, I didn't mention you three."

"Good." Dante glanced at Onyx like he was expecting something.

Onyx made a confused face.

Ash cleared his throat. "Have you heard any rumors?"

"Rumors about what?"

"The three of us? Lucifer? What demons are doing in Shearwater Landing other than tracking you down?"

Ren's posture straightened. "You and Lucifer didn't come up. No one advertised what they were up to, and I didn't pry, but I can give you a list of who found me before I scrubbed my magic from the city."

It didn't seem like she'd heard of the bounty, and if she was keeping to herself, that made sense. Even if Ren's visitors were the demons looking for Onyx and his brothers, they wouldn't have said that outright without a clear read on Ren's loyalties.

Dante got to his feet like he was ready to leave. "Someone's looking for us, and we'd rather they not learn anything useful. Can we still trust you not to sell us out?"

"Nothing's changed. I'd like to stay as far away from whatever's brewing as possible." Ren stood as well, and gestured to the door. "If you need to see me again, I'll probably have a new place, so text first."

Dante agreed, and they all left.

"Maybe we should have kept in touch with Pamala," Ash muttered as the door shut behind them. "She might have better information."

Dante pulled out his phone. "Pamala's still in the city."

Ash sniffed. "Didn't you tell her to stay away from your mate?"

"Yes, and she has, but apparently, she's dating Ollie's coworker Ellie, and Ellie has been telling him all about it."

Onyx had missed the drama with Pamala thanks to Luc's curse knocking him unconscious. Apparently, she'd tried to kidnap Ollie to blackmail Dante into freeing her friends from Hell.

"You aren't worried about her hanging around?" Ash asked.

Dante grimaced. "Ollie doesn't seem bothered. Pamala hasn't come near the salon, and we don't have the right to tell her not to date Ollie's friend."

Ash looked displeased. At least Dante was more reasonable.

"I'll ask Ollie where we can find Pamala. We can see if she's heard anything about the bounty or demons hunting Luc."

Onyx sighed as if he'd had the most trying day of his life. "You do that. I'm going to go."

"Wait, I was hoping you'd go see Pamala."

Why him? Onyx dropped his head back. "Come on, Dante. Leave me alone. I don't want to talk to her."

Ash's brow quirked. "Have you got something better to do, like look after Nico?"

Onyx opened his mouth to snap at him, then realized Ash wasn't teasing. There was no sneer to his tone, no hint of mocking in his face. He seemed genuinely interested.

Onyx couldn't find words. Why was Ash looking at him so tenderly? Like he was happy.

"I can talk to Pamala if you need to go to The Herb Emporium," Ash offered.

What the fuck was happening?

"No. I don't need to go to The Herb Emporium," Onyx snapped at last. "Why would I? It's protected against Luc."

Ash scowled. "Don't you want to be close to Nico?"

He did, but how had Ash guessed? Oh, hell. Did Ash believe Luc and think Nico was his mate? Why did that send a wave of panic coursing through him?

"Pamala works at a boutique in the Arts District called Jaune," Dante said, looking at his phone, seemingly oblivious to what Ash was saying.

Relief coursed through Onyx. "Ash can't go to Jaune. They won't let him in the door."

Today, Ash wore scuffed jeans and a wrinkled T-shirt that he'd probably bought in a pack of three from a chain store. Not that there was anything wrong with that, but he'd stick out like a sore thumb in that quarter of the Arts District, and for once, no one would be starting because of his hulking form.

"I'll have to go," Onyx concluded.

Dante and Ash looked at him in shock.

"What? I'm not actually busy this afternoon. The gallery is closed." And he didn't want them aware of his longing to lurk on The Herb Emporium roof.

Onyx wasn't ready for his brothers to know he'd found his mate. *Hoped* he'd found his mate. Onyx couldn't face the reality himself. He needed Nico more than life itself. It fucking scared him, and he had to work it out with Nico before he let his bumbling brothers in on what was happening.

Nothing could touch him and Nico. Not yet. Not while their bond remained fragile. Onyx could hardly let himself believe it. He kept reminding himself that nothing was confirmed. Not with one hundred percent certainty.

When Onyx was sure this thing between him and Nico wouldn't break and destroy his life, then he'd admit it was real.

From the outside, Jaune looked about the same as it had the last time Onyx stopped in, despite that being close to a year ago.

He opened the yellow door and breathed in the subtly perfumed air. A sheer blouse on a nearby rack caught his eye, and he trailed his fingers along the fabric.

"Welcome to Juane, I'm Pamala," said a tall, immaculately put-together woman. "Is there anything I can help you with today?"

Onyx glanced around the shop. If anyone else was here, they must be in the changing rooms.

"I may have been passed out the last time we were in the same alley, but don't you remember me?"

Pamala's eyes widened, her composure otherwise intact. "You're looking much better. For what do I owe the pleasure of your company?"

Onyx snorted. "Relax. I'm not here to bother you."

"Are you here to shop?" she asked hopefully.

"Not exactly."

Another worker appeared at the counter in the back, along with a customer.

Onyx grabbed the blouse. "But why don't you help me style this, and we can chat along the way?"

"Good idea. My boss is human," Pamala whispered, taking the top and leading Onyx to a rack of pants and skirts. "Do you have a preference?"

Onyx cocked his head. It had been a while since he'd played around with his clothes. For all he liked dressing up, his day-to-day wardrobe had gotten monotonous with all his designer shirts and jeans.

"How about a pair of shorts?"

"Good call." Pamala led him to another display. "Is Dante going to ask me to leave the city?"

Onyx cringed at the pain in her voice. "No." He shook his head at the first pair of shorts Pamala presented. "I've got ones in that color already. Dante didn't send me here. At least not about Ollie."

"But Dante knows I'm seeing Ellie?"

"Not really Dante's business, but it sounds like Ellie's been keeping everyone at work updated."

"Yes, she wants me to go out for drinks with them. But if Ollie's there..." Pamala gave her head a tiny shake. "Anyway. Why are you here?" She selected a pair of tiny leather shorts and held them out.

Onyx took them. They were perfect. The only leather shorts he owned had a zip down the ass. Not exactly the kind of thing he wore to the gallery.

"We wanted to ask if you've heard much from the other demons in town. Are you in touch with anyone?"

Pamala's expression tightened. "Lillian and Maxwell share a house with me. But that's not what you're asking, is it?" She glanced over her shoulder. "Would you like to look at shoes or accessories?"

"Sure." He handed the shorts to Pamala and followed her farther from the woman at the register.

"Maxwell ran into a few demons one night and asked me to meet them at a bar," Pamala whispered as she sorted through necklaces. "They were going on about the Hounds and Lucifer. I said you didn't support Lucifer, and Maxwell backed me up. They asked how we knew, but I had a bad feeling, so I didn't say we'd spoken to you. Max kept quiet too, for once."

She offered two necklaces, and Onyx selected the silver choker.

"One of the demons—his name might have been Ambrose, but don't quote me on that—went on about his friend who believed the Hounds and Lucifer should all die for imprisoning us. I argued with them, but they didn't seem serious, more big-headed than anything, talking about some sort of bounty. But how would they have set that up? Discussing permanent death in a bar with relative strangers couldn't be anything more than spouting off."

Onyx's heart sank, dropping into a pit that seemed to have no bottom. "Maybe freedom emboldened them."

Pamala looked at him more closely, frozen for a second. "You think they were serious?"

"It's not the first time I've heard something like this."

Maybe Luc was telling the truth. Onyx could have burned the boutique to the ground. The only thing worse than falling for one of Luc's lies was finding out he was telling the truth and being tempted to believe everything else.

And what? These demons meant to permanently kill all four of them? He and his brothers were slated to die because they'd stood at Luc's side several millennia ago? It was out of hand.

This wasn't the same as Dante flying into a rage after Luc almost murdered Ollie. All he'd needed was a moment to see reason. Did these demons plan to give Onyx, Dante, and Ash a chance to explain, or had their minds already been made up? They seemed to have decided on Luc's sentence.

Even if he was the Devil, this wasn't the answer.

Onyx had truly believed none of his fellow demons would stoop so low. It didn't matter how long they'd been locked out of the Eternal Realm. Some rules could not be broken.

But did that mean helping Luc?

Onyx couldn't leave his brother to die.

21

———

NICO

RIGHT AS HE was meant to close the shop, Nico got caught up chatting with a long-time customer. By the time he got around to shutting down, Harper was long gone. Staying late wasn't a problem, or a rare occurrence, but usually he'd at least remember to post the closed sign.

The bell rang. Nico sighed and tried not to begrudge the extra business.

He pulled back the curtain and reentered the main shop. "How can I help?"

Recognition stirred as Nico took in the customer approaching the counter. A tall, hollow-faced vampire named Emmett, who he'd hoped he'd never see again.

"Out." Nico pointed to the door, finding a woman blocking it. She was one of the people he'd seen with Michael outside his building.

What the fuck was this?

Emmett was an Orlov, and had left Shearwater Landing with the remainder of his coven. Were all the surviving members back? He should have asked Rowan for more details.

Nico averted his eyes and called on his magic, weaving a

shield to prevent the vampire's illusions from enthralling him. His hands flashed, hidden behind the counter.

"I'm not sure why you're here, but I don't want any trouble." Nico's pulse raced, but he stayed firm.

Emmett stalked closer, posture relaxed. "You shouldn't have gotten involved with scum if you didn't want trouble."

He was one to talk. Nico had hardly been involved in the Orlov mess. The most he'd done was help rescue the humans that the vile coven had been attempting to traffic. Rowan and the rest of the Valeros had taken out the trash.

"You and I don't have any conflict as long as you're not hurting people again." Nico's shield against hypnosis was complete. All he had to do was keep things from escalating and get these two out of the shop.

Onyx and the demons had only protected The Herb Emporium against Lucifer. It made sense given the shop was open to the public, and Nico hadn't even considered extra security when Michael was the only one on his radar. Going up against another witch wasn't an issue.

Had the witch joined the vampires? Was he even still a witch, or had he been granted immortality?

Emmett reached the counter. "You don't get to tell us what to do. There's a new game in town. Rowan's time's up. I'm here to send a message."

Nico's pounding heart skipped. Fuck. He raised his hands, casting a spell to rupture a blood vessel in the vampire's brain. Killing them temporarily was the only way to incapacitate a vampire.

The spell was halfway past Nico's lips. Emmett's hand flashed, and something wet hit Nico's face.

He sneezed and faltered, rubbing at his eyes before he could stop himself. Dizziness hit, and he grabbed the counter, slumping to the side.

Nico blinked, finding Emmett right beside him. He grabbed Nico's jaw and wrenched his mouth open, pouring the rest of the contents of the vial inside. Nico tried to spit it out, but it was no use. The substance absorbed into his tongue and gums, burning like acid.

"You've got enough time left to pass on our message. Rowan needs to fall in line, or this is what's waiting for every one of his little soldiers. Don't bother wasting time trying to get help. Nightbrush kills in less than an hour, and there's no antidote. But you'd know that." Emmett gestured around the shop. "Expert in herbs and potions as you are."

He turned and strode out of the shop, the woman slamming the door behind them.

Nico swayed and sank to the floor. He blinked, and his vision blurred. *No.* He had to do something. But Emmett was right, nightbrush was as lethal as it was rare.

He was dead, and his body would catch up to that fact soon.

Heart skittering, Nico pulled out his phone. His hand shook, and he almost dropped it. Onyx. He needed to talk to Onyx. Nico had to tell him how he felt.

It took three tries to unlock his phone. Finally, he found Onyx's contact and hit call. The phone rang and went to voicemail.

Tears slid down Nico's cheeks. There wasn't time for Onyx's games. He needed Onyx. He had to tell him he was falling in love. Nico couldn't leave this life with his feelings trapped inside him.

He called again, and again. His head swam, and his body went cold. He couldn't feel his toes.

"Hello, Nico. What's so urgent? I'm busy shopping." Onyx's voice hit Nico like a jolt of electricity, almost enough to bring him back. But not quite.

"Onyx." Nico gasped for air like he'd been running. "*Onyx.*"

His voice sharpened. "What's wrong?"

"I want to be your mate. I'm f-falling f-for you." Nico closed his eyes, head pounding. He couldn't focus on the blurry shop and talk at the same time.

"Nico. Where are you? Why are you slurring like that?" Onyx sounded frantic, but he hadn't acknowledged what Nico had said.

They must not be mates after all.

Nico's heart cracked, and it hurt worse than the poison slithering through his veins.

"Nico, where are you!"

The shout jolted him. Nico tried to rise and couldn't. His head lolled. He almost dropped the phone.

"Th-the sh-shop," he slurred. "Bad. Nightbrush. Gotta message."

A loud whooshing filled his ear. Nico winced. Had Onyx hung up?

"Nico, talk to me. I'm coming."

Nico clutched the phone, but words were impossible. Onyx was still there. He smiled. That was nice. At least he wouldn't die alone.

22

ONYX

Onyx tore through the sky so fast, the city blurred.

"Nico!" he shouted into the phone. There was no response.

If Nico was at the shop, it couldn't be Luc. He'd said night-brush. The damn herb was deadly to any mortal. It killed humans in minutes. A witch had a little longer due to the magic in their blood, but not long enough.

Onyx's chest constricted, pain radiating through his body.

Nico couldn't die.

I want to be your mate.

Oh, hellfire. Flying at superhuman speed wasn't the only reason the world blurred. Onyx's tears whipped in the wind.

Why hadn't he gone to lurk on The Herb Emporium roof? If Nico died because Onyx was more concerned about spiting Ash and not giving away a single one of his feelings than caring for Nico, Onyx would never forgive himself.

He'd follow Nico to the Realm of the Damned of course. But his mate deserved better than to spend eternity in that wretched place.

Even if they bonded, Onyx didn't think he'd be able to bring Nico back to the Human Realm. That wasn't how mortal souls worked. Nothing could bring a witch back to Earth once the magic in their blood robbed them of the ability to reincarnate.

Onyx had to save Nico.

His mate.

He was a fool for being afraid and denying them both the chance to embrace the truth.

Onyx landed on the sidewalk in front of The Herb Emporium with a crash, cracking the pavement under his shoes. He tore the door open and burst inside, knocking over a table full of candles.

Nico wasn't here.

"Nico!" Onyx raced through the shop, wings catching on the shelves until he retracted them. "Nico!"

Onyx rounded the counter and saw his mate slumped on the floor, his phone lying beside him, hand outstretched.

Onyx dropped to his knees. Nico's skin was ashen, his eyes closed. Onyx grabbed his hand, finding it clammy and cold.

"Nico, I'm here. I'll save you."

Nico's fingers twitched, and he moaned.

Oh shit. Oh shit. What if he was too late?

Onyx scrambled, his heart beating such a frantic rhythm that it was bound to burst. He brought Nico's wrist to his lips and bit down, fangs extended.

Sucking the poison from Nico's blood was the only way to stop the nightbrush. The herb couldn't hurt Onyx. He'd metabolize the poison, but he had to get it all out to save his mate.

Nico's blood was thick and bitter. Onyx pressed a hand to Nico's chest, using magic to call the poison toward him and away from Nico's vital organs. What if it had spread too far already? Did they have enough time to perform the mating spell before Nico died?

As he drank down gulps of poisoned blood, Onyx cut his

wrist and pressed it to Nico's mouth. His blood would help Nico heal and give them more time.

Onyx trembled. It wasn't enough. Nico was limp and cold, but Onyx couldn't speak the ancient binding words to mate them while he drank Nico's ruined blood. He'd have to give up on the poison and put all his hope in mating and the magic of the bond saving Nico.

He couldn't bring himself to tear his lips from Nico's wrist.

Nico jolted beneath him. Fuck, he was convulsing. It was too late! Onyx closed his eyes against a fresh wave of tears. His heart burst into flames and crumbled to ash. He had to pull back and perform the mating spell, praying it worked in time.

A hand closed around Onyx's wrist. Onyx opened his eyes. Nico clutched the hand feeding him, his throat working as he drank Onyx's blood.

Nico's eyelids fluttered.

Onyx could have collapsed with relief. Nico was healing. Poison filled Onyx's mouth, but Onyx's blood gave Nico strength with every passing second. Onyx called more poison toward him, and his throat burned with it, but it was no match for his demon healing.

Nico met Onyx's stare, his eyes bloodshot and hazy.

My mate. I'm sorry.

Onyx would have shouted the apology if he dared pull his lips from Nico's wrist.

Seconds seemed to drag by, taking an eternity. This was longer than the thousand years Onyx had spent in Hell. He gripped Nico's wrist tight enough to bruise, not allowing his mate to slip away. Nico's hold tightened in turn, eyes not leaving Onyx as tears fell down his already damp cheeks.

At last, Nico's blood began to clear. His citrus scent flared, and the earthy taste of orange burst on Onyx's tongue.

As if he felt the last of the poison leave, Nico pulled Onyx's wrist from his mouth. "Onyx, I..." He choked on a sob. "I'm not dead."

Onyx's eyes flashed. One more swallow of Nico's clear-tasting blood, and he withdrew his fangs. "You're not allowed to die."

Nico smiled. Still clutching Onyx's wrist, he brought Onyx's hand to his cheek and nuzzled his palm.

Onyx's chest burst with sizzling energy, filling like a balloon. He stroked Nico's rough jaw, his body's renewed warmth the best feeling in all the realms.

"Tell me who I have to kill." Onyx should have led with something sweet, but his fire burned, not dampened in the slightest. He understood Dante's rage after Ollie's attack like he never had before.

Nico rubbed his cheek against Onyx's hand and muttered, "Emmett Orlov."

Who the ever-loving fuck was that? How dare some random nobody attempt to take Nico away. "What's going on, Nico? Why did Emmett poison you?"

"To send a message to Rowan."

Onyx tasted smoke. Seemed the vampire had made his shit list after all.

"Onyx, please." Nico kissed his hand. "Can I explain later?"

He sounded exhausted. Of course revenge wasn't immediately important, but it was easier than facing what had almost happened.

Emotion clogged Onyx's throat. This had been too close, and it wasn't even Luc. Onyx pulled Nico against him, burying Nico's face in the crook of his neck and hooking his chin over Nico's head.

"Don't suffocate me," Nico murmured, even though his arms wrapped tightly around Onyx.

Onyx swallowed, and his voice still came out thick. "Shut

up. I'll do whatever I want. You scared the hell out of me, Nico. I'm so sorry I wasn't here. You—" His voice broke. "You said you wouldn't leave me."

Nico whined and clutched Onyx tighter. "I won't. I'm sorry."

Shit, Onyx sucked. "No, don't be sorry. I shouldn't make this about me, but I need you. If I'd accepted that, this never would have happened. Please forgive me." Onyx trembled, and it turned into a shiver, racing through his body. Once it started, he couldn't seem to stop.

Nico pulled back and looked up. "Forgive you for what? I knew you needed me, and I was happy to wait to hear you say it. Telling me wouldn't have stopped this."

Onyx choked on a half-laugh, half-sob, and Nico smiled. "I wanted to be here today, but I wouldn't let myself come." Damnation, it sounded so petty now. So juvenile.

"You wanted to be here?" The hope in Nico's eyes broke Onyx's soul in two.

I want to be your mate. The desperate words rang in Onyx's ears, so full of regret and longing. Nico's dying wish.

And Onyx could grant it.

"I always want to be with you. You're mine, Nico—my mate—and that scares the living daylights out of me. I'm not brave, and I almost lost you because of it. I'm sorry. I let everything else get in the way."

Nico tangled a hand in Onyx's hair. "I'm your mate? You're sure?" It was like he hadn't heard anything else. His eyes shone bright with tender hope.

"Yes, Nico. You're my mate."

Nico tightened his hold on Onyx's hair and pulled Onyx down to meet him. Onyx fell into it like it was the only real thing he'd ever done in his life.

Their lips brushed, Nico's soft yet firm. He took command

of the kiss, stubble scraping Onyx's cheeks. Onyx's mouth fell open, and he breathed in Nico's deep citrus scent. Nico's tongue delved into his mouth, bringing with it a sense of possession, of security.

They'd never kissed before. Not on the lips. Why the hell hadn't they?

Kissing pushed Onyx off a cliff he hadn't realized he was on the edge of. He fell, and it was like flying above the clouds in the Eternal Realm. Only better. He soared, his soul vibrating in tune with Nico, who flew alongside him.

Their lips danced, and the connection between them bloomed.

Their bond knitted together, thrumming and writhing. Onyx's skin tingled. He had his mate. He had Nico.

23

NICO

Nico's hands shook as he cupped Onyx's smooth cheeks, the tremors no longer an effect of the poison. It was as if the foul substance had never touched him. There was so much life bursting out of him, he might combust.

Onyx's lips were as sweet as a dessert wine, rich and layered. Nico would happily drink nothing else for the rest of his life. If he didn't know better, he'd think they were lying in a field of orchids. The flower's fragrance hung heavy in the air, and the very space around them seemed alive. The beast that Nico swore had begun to grow between them was even stronger now, more consuming, like it fed off their kisses.

Nico would never have to give up this prickly demon. He was Onyx's mate.

His mind swam with relief. He was alive. He'd been brought back from the despair of thinking Onyx wasn't his.

Onyx broke the kiss, out of breath, his eyes burning deep blue. "Why haven't we been doing that the whole time?"

Nico sucked in a deep breath, the taste of Onyx lingering on his tongue. "I wasn't sure if you wanted me to kiss you."

A small frown pinched Onyx's kiss-red lips. "You read me

well. I've never been big on kissing. Mouths are better used else-where." He trailed a delicate finger over Nico's lower lip. "But not yours."

"Oh, I don't know. My mouth is pretty talented anywhere I use it."

An evil grin lit Onyx's face. "I have no doubt, and I'll hold you to that. But this is something else." He bent and recaptured Nico's lips.

Boy, was it ever. Nico could forget himself, drown in Onyx's lips. He planned to do exactly that, however, the floor of his shop was far from an ideal location to kiss until time ceased to exist.

What if Emmett returned?

Fear strangled Nico's gut even with Onyx wrapped around him.

"What's wrong?" Onyx whipped his head back, panic lining his face.

"Nothing. Let's get out of here." Nico disentangled from Onyx's hold and stood.

Onyx followed, his sharp attention unwavering. "Don't say it's nothing. You almost died. There's no way you're fine. What happened just now?"

Nico ran a hand through his hair. "It crossed my mind that the vampires might come back. We should lock up and leave."

A low growl erupted from Onyx, and the hair on the back of Nico's neck stood.

"Let the vampires come. I'll burn them to ash."

Nico hauled Onyx close and buried his face in his hair, a foreign, floaty feeling filling him. "Let's go. Fuck, I have to call Rowan."

Onyx went rigid and pulled from Nico's grasp. "Screw Rowan. I'll burn him too if this was his fault."

"Hey." Nico met Onyx's flaming eyes. "It wasn't his fault."

"Then what the hell happened?"

Nico hesitated. He had to tell Onyx. Why was it so hard?

"I've been having trouble with this witch that the Valeros and I ran out of town a while back. He abused his girlfriend and was trying to set up some criminal shit, but we took care of it."

"What's that got to do with vampires poisoning you?"

"I have no idea. Michael broke into my place and has been lurking around. This morning, Rowan said a vampire coven he'd destroyed was back and causing trouble for him, but that had nothing to do with Michael. Then, Emmett showed up with a woman I'd seen Michael with outside my apartment and..." He gestured to the floor.

Fuck, had Michael been trying to poison him that morning, not merely get his blood to break into the apartment?

Onyx's cheeks flushed, and Nico swore he smelled smoke. "Why didn't you tell me someone broke into your apartment?"

"It didn't seem like a big deal. I had it under control."

Onyx's eyes flared. "Under control? Did you tell Rowan someone broke in?"

"No. I passed on that Michael was in town, but Rowan's busy enough. Besides, you protected my apartment. No one could get in."

The break-in still didn't make sense. If they'd planned on poisoning him, why not do it then?

"They couldn't get to you at home, so they attacked you here." Onyx cupped Nico's cheeks, giving him a hard look. "Why didn't you ask for help from me or Rowan, or anyone?"

"I didn't need it." Nico's gut twisted. "I've always managed on my own."

Ever since his dad died, Nico had taken on his own problems. He'd needed to be there for his mom, for his friends. Taking care of himself was a strength and made him feel secure.

The fury faded from Onyx's face. "I'm sure you can manage

on your own, but you don't have to. I'm your mate. I want to be there for you." His voice faded to a whisper, and his gaze dropped. "But you didn't know that. I never acted like someone you could turn to. I'm sorry."

"Hey." Nico covered Onyx's hands with his. "You were here when it mattered. We both thought we had plenty of time to open up and figure out what was going on between us."

Onyx's next words were strangled. "Please let me apologize for pushing you away."

Nico kissed him. "Apology accepted. Come on. I need to get out of here."

Onyx reluctantly let go and followed him through the shop. Nico left the upended table and battered shelves as they were, locking the door and pulling down the grate. Maybe he'd text Harper and close the shop for a few days. Give them both some time off.

As he turned to walk toward home, Onyx caught his hand.

"Let's go to my place. I'll fly us."

Nico's heart leapt. "All right."

Onyx led Nico around the back of the building. He was already shirtless, and released his wings, his usual cocky attitude nowhere in sight. Onyx seemed more and more shaken as time passed. That wouldn't do.

There was no reason for Onyx to feel guilty. Nico wouldn't change anything about how they'd come together. He was falling in love with the feisty brat. Onyx didn't need to be anyone other than himself, or be instantly comfortable with Nico being his mate.

But behind the apothecary by the trash cans wasn't the place to discuss the big stuff.

Nico crossed his arms. "Are you going to carry me?"

"Yes." Onyx bristled, as Nico had hoped, his familiar indignation warming Nico's soul. "I'm a hell of a lot stronger than you. Now get over here."

Nico obeyed. Onyx scooped him up like he weighed nothing, enveloping him in his invisibility illusion.

Nico wrapped his arms around Onyx's neck. "I don't think anyone's held me like this since I was a toddler." It was strangely soothing, even though he hardly fit.

Onyx squeezed him tight. "Take it as a reminder that I'm here to care for you."

Before Nico could respond, Onyx launched into the air. They cleared the buildings, and Onyx pumped his wings, taking off toward the river. He picked up speed and soon everything was a blur.

Nico closed his eyes. Onyx's secure hold didn't prevent him from being all too aware of his bulk and awkwardly cramped limbs. He wasn't scared of falling, however, his instincts couldn't help sending his pulse racing.

Before long, Onyx landed and set Nico down on a deserted flat roof surrounded by similar industrial buildings.

"Welcome to my loft." Onyx marched to a service door and held it open.

Nico entered a stairwell and headed down, Onyx beside him. "Did Ash and Dante protect this building for you like they did with my place?"

Onyx's steps faltered, but he didn't answer right away. They continued to the ground floor, where Onyx led them along a short hallway.

He paused in front of a set of metal double doors. "No, they didn't. I haven't shared my home with my brothers."

"You aren't worried about Lucifer after what happened at the gallery?"

Onyx seemed to wilt. He sighed, opened the door, and ushered Nico inside.

Nico forgot his concern as he stepped through. He stood in a huge open space nearly the size of the entire building, the lofted ceiling high above their heads.

The wall to the right was a floor-to-ceiling window, with many panes, some frosted, others clear, all buzzing with a strong privacy spell, and looking out on the South Banks. The building sat on a hill overlooking the river, and gave Nico a view of the neighborhood that he hadn't seen in a long time.

Couches and cushions were nestled in front of the view, set atop an array of colorful rugs. In front of Nico, a ladder led to a catwalk and a platform that seemed to hold a small library. There was no kitchen visible, and only one door in the far corner.

A ridiculously large bed with four tall posts, an ornate headboard, and a canopy of wispy rainbow cloth was situated to the left of the room's center, surrounded by shaggy carpets and a sturdy trunk.

Art lined the walls, and a second seating area was nestled in the back corner, surrounded by books. Delicate wire sculptures hung from the ceiling by thin cables, and a large statue stood near the door.

"Damn, this is amazing."

Onyx shut the door with a tentative smile. "I'm glad you like it. You're only the second person I've let in here."

"Second? Don't break my heart."

Onyx tipped his head back and laughed. "Sorry. It would have been a crime not to share my private art collection with Scott. If it makes you feel better, you're the only lover I've let in here. The only mate."

Shit, yeah, that'd do it. "I can live with that."

"What a relief." Onyx surveyed his space, turning serious again. "To answer your question, I'm not as worried about Luc as I was." He snorted, like he couldn't believe he'd said that.

"Luc isn't lying about demons wanting to kill him. I found out they want to kill all four of us. I think Luc was telling the truth when he asked for my help. Fuck, he might even be telling the truth about not hurting you."

Onyx met Nico's gaze like he was looking for reassurance.

Nico moved closer. "I think you're right. You have every reason to be wary of Luc, but he gave your magic back. How can that be anything other than an olive branch?"

Onyx closed his eyes like he was in pain. "I hate him for tempting me to trust him again—but I can't ignore it. I can't lock him out when part of me longs to speak to him. I want to listen even if I feel like a fool for it."

"Wanting to help your brother doesn't make you a fool."

"In the case of the Devil, it does." Onyx gazed at Nico with a pained expression. "I can't trust him again. It hurts too much. I don't want him killed, but I can't give him any more of me."

Nico's heart clenched. "What did he do to you, little butterfly?"

Onyx's lashes fluttered, his voice breaking. "He left me."

Nico cupped the back of Onyx's neck securely, squeezing and stroking his thumb through the hair at Onyx's nape. "I'm sorry."

Onyx seemed to find strength in the touch. Vulnerability shone in his eyes, but he didn't back down. "Luc was going to leave me behind in the Eternal Realm, even though I begged him not to go to Earth. I couldn't stand how much it hurt, so I followed him. But he didn't care. None of them cared. They still don't."

Onyx's naked pain tore Nico to bits. "That's why you fell?" To not be left behind.

"Yes. I was so fucking stupid. The biggest fool. I didn't care about mates. I never even requested mine like the others did. I figured I'd want one eventually, but a mate wasn't everything. I needed my brothers, and they were going to leave me."

Onyx swallowed, blinking away the moisture gathering in his eyes. "Luc never acknowledged that I'd fallen for him. Nothing ever changed. He never cared. All he did was use my love for him to take advantage of me and get what he wanted. And I hate him. I hate how much I want him to care about me. I don't want him dead, but I can't trust him. He doesn't get another chance. He's wasted them all."

Nico pulled Onyx close, his slight body trembling. Onyx's hurt was so devastatingly simple. So understandable.

What would thousands of years of rejection do to someone? Make them guarded. Push them to test everyone. Show them they could never count on anyone to put them first. Sharpen all their edges into defensive spines.

"I'm not going anywhere," Nico murmured into Onyx's silk-soft hair.

Onyx's breath caught and he gripped Nico's T-shirt like he couldn't help clinging.

"I'm not leaving you behind, and you can't push me away."

"That scares me. I don't know why. I want you to stay but it freaks me out that you might. I can't explain it."

"You don't have to explain. All you have to do is tell me how you feel."

"Is that all?" A laugh ghosted past Onyx's lips. "Even when it's not logical? Like how I want to be taken care of. Me, an immortal. Deep down all I want is someone to protect me, but from what? It's silly. Is that what you want me to tell you?"

"Yes. You can tell me anything. It doesn't matter if it make sense. Everyone wants to be cared for. Have their heart protected. And I've got you, Onyx. I'm here. You can be scared of that and it won't change a thing."

Onyx's cheeks flushed red, then lavender. His horns

appeared, blooming with color. "Can you force me to feel it? Make me believe?"

Tenderness flooded Nico. "I sure can. Want to tell me how you'd like me to do that, or do you want me to decide?"

Onyx bit his lip. "Tie me down and force me to stay. Tell me I can't run. That you won't..."

"I won't leave you."

Onyx whimpered and his sweet scent filled the air.

"Do you have restraints or do I need to get creative?"

Onyx's breathing shallowed. "I've got anything you could possibly imagine."

"Then strip and get on the bed. On your hands and knees."

Onyx crossed the room, seeming unsteady on his feet. Nico paused, watching him go, the heaviness in his chest making this moment monumental. Onyx was giving him everything, trusting him when it didn't come easy.

Nico was so proud of him.

His mate reached the enormous bed, which was at least three times as wide as a king and twice as long, and stripped off his pants and underwear, freeing his tail.

Nico slowly stalked forward. Onyx glanced over his shoulder, fangs extended and eyes burning. Then, Onyx released his wings, blue feathers spreading wide.

Nico could have fallen to his knees. "That'll never stop taking my breath away. On the bed, little butterfly."

Onyx shuddered, feathers rustling, and climbed onto the bed. He faced the carved wooden headboard and draped a wing over each side, the bed large enough to support his wingspan. He knelt forward, tail flicking back and forth, and stuck his ass in the air, spine arched and head resting on his hands.

"Everything you need is in the trunk," he breathed, sounding half gone already.

"Perfect. You're being such a good boy. Keep it up and be patient while I get ready."

Onyx moaned in response.

Nico stripped off his clothes, cock already erect. He stooped to open the trunk and found it packed full. "Damn. I thought you didn't bring lovers here."

There was a whole array of cuffs, paddles, and toys, including gags and blindfolds, and that was just what Nico could see at a glance.

"I don't bring lovers here. All that's... It's what I use when I play by myself."

Fuck. Nico's mind filled with obscene image after obscene image. "You enchant these things to pleasure you?"

"Come on, Nico, we've covered magic. Stop acting like a human. I don't need a partner to get tied up and spanked into oblivion."

Nico chuckled. "An all-powerful demon, and what do you do? Fuck yourself."

"What's magic good for if I can't do that? Stop making me wait or I'll take back everything I said and see to myself."

"No you fucking won't, brat. Don't get smart with me."

Onyx *humphed*, his ass wiggling, and Nico smiled, warmth blooming in his chest. Damn, it was good to have his prickly demon back.

"Seems like doing what I tell you already has you feeling better."

There was a beat of silence. Onyx repositioned, bracing on his elbows, and glanced over his shoulder, eyes hooded. "Yes. But please hurry. I need you."

Nico shivered. He liked his demon desperate. "Not very patient, are you?"

Onyx whined.

Nico crossed his arms. "You can manage. Waiting will make you feel even better. Promise."

Onyx nodded, giving in and trusting Nico yet again.

Not intending to torture his mate, Nico bent down and quickly sorted through the cuffs, selecting leather ones for Onyx's wrists and ankles, along with attachable chains, and brought them to the bed.

Onyx watched him with avid attention. "You can anchor those to the posts or the bedframe."

Nico inspected the bedframe and found the perfect place to attach the chains on either side, leaving Onyx on his knees at the center. The chains turned out to be the perfect length to prevent him from closing his legs.

Climbing onto the bed, Nico attached the leather cuffs to Onyx's ankles, tightening the buckles, then secured them to the chains, making sure nothing was too tight.

He came to rest behind Onyx. His mate held his body still, his feathers ruffling slightly and that pretty tail twitching back and forth. Nico caressed Onyx's legs, kissing his calf muscles and inner thighs. Onyx's tail flicked vigorously, flushing lavender, as he let out soft panting breaths.

Nico ran a hand along Onyx's arched spine to caress his shoulders, exploring the place where Onyx's wings sprouted from his back, the feathers almost as pale as his skin.

"My pretty little butterfly."

Onyx dropped his head forward and moaned, horns hitting the mattress.

If he'd have survived the prolonged anticipation, Nico might have drawn this out. However, they had the rest of time to tease. Being with Onyx felt so right, he couldn't deny either of them.

Their growing connection begged to be nurtured.

Climbing off the bed, Nico moved around Onyx's wings to

the head. He knelt in front of Onyx and dropped a pair of leather handcuffs.

Onyx inspected the restraints hungrily. "Please, Nico." He tipped his head back and hit Nico with a brilliant stare.

As if Nico was being pulled into the sun's orbit, he leaned down and kissed his demon's pouty lips.

Onyx responded like he was starved. "My mate. *Nico*. It doesn't seem real that you're mine."

Nico hummed. "But it is. I'm all yours. Forever. You're stuck with me."

He pulled back, finding pure happiness lighting Onyx's lavender flushed face. Nico stroked his cheek and positioned the cuffs around Onyx's wrists, not that leather or even the chains were any match for a demon, but that wasn't the point.

Onyx's eyes fluttered closed as Nico secured his wrists together. He seemed relaxed, almost blissful.

Nico caressed his face and ran gentle fingers up one of his horns. They were more similar to leather than skin, yet looked so delicate, a spiderweb of veins peeking from beneath the surface. A bloom of crimson followed Nico's touch, fading to lavender.

"I'm enchanted by you, Onyx. I wasn't lying about wanting to see all of you. I want you so stripped bare that there's nothing between us. I want you angry and petty and spiteful, and I want you soft and pliant. All of it."

Onyx spoke so quietly, it was hard to hear. "I want that too. All of you, Nico."

Nico kissed Onyx, unable to pull away.

"Your lips are my new addiction," Onyx murmured, seeming dazed.

"Likewise." Nico forced their mouths apart. He'd planned to retrieve one of the leather paddles from the trunk, but the sight of Onyx, open-mouthed and at his mercy, wasn't one he could turn away from.

Nico grasped one of Onyx's horns, stroking it, and guided Onyx from his elbows higher, onto his cuffed hands. Inching forward on his knees, Nico pushed his cock into Onyx's mouth.

Onyx moaned around him and sucked eagerly.

"*Mmm.* That's it. Your mouth belongs around my cock." Nico thrust his hips. "Suck me so the next time I kiss those pretty lips, they taste like my cum."

Onyx hollowed his cheeks obediently, and Nico thrust deep.

"You feel like you're mine yet?" Nico groaned as he hit the back of Onyx's throat. "You're trapped. I'll never let you slip away now. You're my mate and I'm keeping you right here, where you belong."

Onyx whined and shuddered, his lashes fluttering.

"Mine, Onyx." Nico thrust and his body flashed hot. It was as if he could feel Onyx begging for more without words, that living, breathing beast that thrived between them tipping back its head and roaring.

More.

"Shit. Oh fuck." Nico's spine stiffened and he came down Onyx's throat.

Onyx sucked him like his life depended on it. Even as Nico pulled out, Onyx tried to push forward and latch on to his retreating cock, the chains holding him back.

Nico ran a hand through Onyx's hair. "Greedy little butterfly. Pinned you down so I can keep you forever."

24

ONYX

Y ES. *Keep me. Please.*

Onyx couldn't get the words out. His tongue didn't work. Nico had him exactly where he needed to be.

Nico wiped spit from Onyx's lips. "Do you feel like you're mine yet? Like I'm not going to walk away?"

Onyx blinked. "Yes. No. I don't know."

Why was thinking so hard? He believed Nico, but wasn't done being told. He needed more. To feel like Nico would never uncuff him. It was ridiculous. Or was it? Onyx was always cast aside. Being locked up was the only cure.

"That's okay. You don't have to know. You're being so good. You want this so much. I'll always reassure you. Is that what you need to hear?"

Onyx nodded.

Nico hauled him up, his hands leaving the bed, and kissed him, licking into his mouth, lips and teeth attacking with bruising force. Nico sucked on Onyx's bottom lip and held the back of his neck so tight that Onyx believed there was no escape.

Nico pulled back, breathless, his deep brown eyes lit with

excitement. He dropped Onyx roughly onto the mattress and climbed off the bed.

Onyx struggled to his elbows and looked over his shoulder. Nico climbed up the foot of the bed and crawled forward on his hands and knees, cock swinging limp between his thighs.

He looked like a panther stalking prey.

Onyx's feathers ruffled, electricity zipping down his spine.

Nico reached Onyx, planting two possessive hands on Onyx's ass. "I'm going to take you apart and see everything hidden inside this beautifully lethal body."

"Everything?" Onyx whimpered.

"*Mmm.*" Nico's eyes darkened, and his grip tightened. "Then I'm going to hold you and never let go."

Onyx's skin tingled like it'd transformed into pure energy. He longed to run, to hide, to throw Nico off and fly away. "You won't let me go, no matter what you see?"

"No matter what I see. I want all of you." Nico brought a hand down on Onyx's ass, the smack echoing through the cavernous room.

Onyx lurched forward, head down, and the urgent need to flee slipped away.

He expected Nico to spank him again, but his palm didn't reconnect with Onyx's stinging ass. Nico caressed his tail, sending a violent shudder of pleasure through him.

Nico draped Onyx's tail over his back and kissed the arching base, wet lips and stubble teasing the sensitive flesh. Onyx cried out, squirming away from the intense pleasure, chains clanking.

"There's nowhere to go." Nico kissed him again, licking around his tail. "Isn't this where you want to be?"

"Yes," Onyx panted as Nico ran his tongue up and down his tail. Fuck it was as good as a blowjob, no, better. Onyx's cock leaked between his legs and the tip of his tail twitched wildly back and forth.

Nico gripped the globes of Onyx's ass and spread him open. His lips traveled from Onyx's tail to his hole, kissing Onyx's entrance as punishingly as he'd kissed his mouth.

"Fuck, Nico." Onyx pushed back onto Nico's face.

A hand wrapped around his tail. "Slick yourself," Nico ordered.

"W-what?" Onyx couldn't think past the pleasure. Nico's grip was unfaltering, his touch setting Onyx's fire raging. And his mouth. Oh, his mouth.

Nico rumbled against his hole before saying, "I want you wet so I can taste you."

Onyx's face flamed. He shut his eyes, and his chest expanded. Magic flared, and he slicked his entrance and inner channel.

Nico groaned and pressed his tongue inside Onyx's hole. They moaned as if they were one, fused together by their pleasure.

Nico attacked Onyx with a renewed fervor, pulling his cheeks apart and claiming him. He licked around Onyx's tail, then delved back into his core. Onyx's legs shook. He couldn't stop himself from thrusting, his cock bouncing, hitting nothing but air.

"So desperate and so fucking sweet, just like your blood."

"*Uhh*," Onyx whimpered.

"Don't even think about touching yourself." Nico impaled him with his tongue. "I'm taking care of you."

"Yes." Onyx's pulse raced, his magic crackling.

Something sparked back.

Was that Nico's magic?

Yes. The connection between them transformed into a completely new creature. Onyx swore he could feel Nico's hunger, his burning desire to possess Onyx, to own him, and keep him close.

Their magics melded together. Onyx's fear and pain—all the baggage he carried—came out into the open. Nico's power sucked it up as readily as he sucked Onyx's slick hole, shooting Onyx full of warmth. Every comforting flare of Nico's power that Onyx accepted made their bond sing with pleasure.

Onyx gripped the bedspread, writhing against Nico's mouth. "Nico, please. I can't... I'm gonna come."

Nico growled and pressed forward like he was trying to crawl inside Onyx. It was too much. Onyx came, his tail quivering in Nico's grip, hole clenching, wings straining as he fought the urge to fly. Onyx's pleasure spilled between his legs, and Nico didn't relent.

Onyx was wrung dry. Nico bit his ass and thighs, then his mouth disappeared and his cock pressed against Onyx's hole.

"You're mine, Onyx." Nico snapped his hips forward and filled Onyx so fast his breath caught. "I'm. Never. Leaving. You. Behind." He punctuated each word with a thrust.

"Y-yes," Onyx whined, his eyes watering.

Nico grabbed Onyx by the shoulder, his other arm around Onyx's waist, and hauled him back. Onyx fluttered his wings, helping Nico lift him from the bed. He nestled his back against Nico's chest, coming to rest on Nico's lap, impaled on his cock.

Nico crooned in his ear. "That's it. See how deep inside I am? Does it feel like you're mine now, little butterfly?"

"*Yes*," Onyx sobbed. "Yes, Nico."

"What am I?"

"You're my mate."

"*Mmhmm*. That's right. And you're my mate. Mine."

"Yes," Onyx whispered. He squeezed his eyes closed. Being Nico's was divine, even if it scared him. Fuck, maybe fear added to it. Made it real.

Nico thrust into Onyx, fingers digging into his hips. Onyx let his body go limp, his wings draped to the sides. He didn't move except for the jolts Nico's thrusts forced through him, bouncing him on his cock, Onyx's cuffed hands flopping against his groin as his spent dick hardened.

Nico snaked a hand up Onyx's chest and gripped his neck, thumb and forefinger digging in beneath his jaw. "Hard again already?"

Onyx nodded, a whimper slipping past his lips.

Nico held him tight enough that there was no ignoring his hand, but not enough to restrict his air. Onyx was completely trapped. Possessed.

It was perfect.

Nico thrust his hips, cock dragging along Onyx's oversensitive bundle of nerves. "Touch that needy dick. Let me see you spurt all over yourself."

Onyx gasped and wrapped a hand around his length. Nico drilled into him, his groin rubbing Onyx's tail, their magic like electricity in the air, as Onyx jerked himself without mercy.

Nico held him tighter, growling as he stiffened beneath Onyx and erupted, filling Onyx's ass. Onyx's cuffed hands knocked together, and his pleasure spilled over them.

He was completely owned. Nico wasn't going anywhere.

25

———

NICO

Nico's chest heaved. Onyx's full-winged weight had every one of his muscles straining, but he never wanted to move. He held his demon tight, fingers digging into his hips, palm resting against Onyx's bobbing Adam's apple.

They caught their breath. With a tickle of magic, Onyx retracted his wings, the soft, warm feathers against Nico's chest disappearing. Nico wrapped him in a tight embrace around the middle, clasping Onyx's sticky cuffed hands.

"Whose are you?" Nico whispered in Onyx's ear.

"Yours."

Nico hummed. "Good boy."

They stayed like that until Nico began to slip out of Onyx. He kissed Onyx's neck, then gently dropped him forward.

Nico leaned down and massaged Onyx's tattooed back, finding him loose and relaxed. "I'm going to uncuff you now."

"Okay." Onyx sounded floaty, if a little disappointed.

"I'm releasing you so I can hold you better. Not to let you go. That's what I said I'd do. Remember?"

Onyx made a soft sound of assent.

Nico quickly undid the ankle restraints and pushed the

chains out of the way before massaging each of Onyx's ankles, giving him the attention he deserved regardless of his demon endurance or healing.

Onyx's tail remained flushed a deep lavender. Nico spread his ass cheeks to inspect his messy hole. Fuck, the tight skin of his pucker was lavender too.

If Nico was hard, he'd slip right back inside. He pressed two fingers in, and Onyx moaned, his tail arching out of the way in invitation.

"You'll never be satisfied, will you?"

Onyx tilted his hips up. "Do I need to be?"

"No." Nico withdrew his fingers, an idea hitting him. "Don't move."

He climbed off the bed and pulled a plug from the trunk. Back behind Onyx, he aligned it with Onyx's pretty purple hole and slid it inside, the pink jewel at the plug's base perfectly complementing Onyx's complexion.

Onyx squirmed and made a throaty sound, like a purr. Nico's heart fluttered. He flipped Onyx onto his back and uncuffed his hands, then arranged them on a clean section of the bed so he could massage each of Onyx's wrists.

Onyx curled against him, nestling into the crook of Nico's neck. Nico held him firmly, their legs tangled, and that deep throaty sound started up again.

Nico was right, Onyx was purring like a cat. He hadn't been aware demons did that.

What a sound.

Moisture tickled the corners of Nico's eyes. His mate was safe and happy and purring. The connection growing between them was as alive as ever, sated rather than raging, but not dormant. Nico had never belonged to someone like this, or been so in sync with anyone.

It was like coming home.

Nico drifted, basking in Onyx's purring contentment, as soothed as his mate. Relaxed down to his bones.

"Thank you," Onyx murmured after a while.

Nico squeezed him. "My pleasure."

Onyx snorted. "It damn well better be."

"How are you feeling?"

Onyx wiggled around to look at Nico. "Calm. Safe. Really fucking good."

Nico's face split into a grin.

"Smug bastard." Onyx shoved Nico's shoulder. "Don't get cocky. I'll probably turn around and freak out about the next thing in record time."

"Bring it on. You don't have to be perfect. In fact, you better not be, or I'll feel like the weak link in the bond."

Onyx narrowed his eyes. "Neither of us is weak."

"No. We're not." Nico's stomach flipped. "So...what happens now?" He understood what Harper meant when he'd said he couldn't imagine waiting to mate. Nico was ready.

Onyx hesitated. "Do you mean now that we've admitted we're mates?"

Nico nodded, holding his breath.

"Mates..." Onyx bit his lip. "My anger over what the quest for mates did to my relationship with Luc and the others was the reason I never wanted one. But all that feels irrelevant. Finding you is about *us*, nothing else. That baggage can't touch our bond. I want you more than anything."

The hairs on the back of Nico's neck stood, tingles racing down his spine. "I want you too."

Onyx's brow furrowed. "Are you sure? You said you didn't want immortality."

"I didn't." Nico didn't see this as choosing immortality. He tried to explain. "Like you said, it's about us. I'm choosing *you*. I want you however I can have you. For as long as I can have you. I never wanted to be a vampire, living forever bound to a sire, and eternal life itself had no appeal, but that's not what this is."

"You're right, it's not. You'll be bound to me far more tightly than you would have been to any vampire."

"That's not a drawback. I want to *see* you Onyx. I know what I'm getting into. The bond's already there. I can feel it. Can't you?"

Onyx's eyes sparked, and he gave a tiny nod.

Nico's heart stuttered. "I want more, not less. No less than *all of you.*"

It finally seemed to sink in. Onyx's eyes turned shiny, his lips parting. "Me too. You've been calling to me since we met, I just couldn't see it for what it was."

Nico pulled Onyx tight against him. "Same, and I don't want to hold back. You don't have to be ready, but I'm all in. Whenever you want to mate, tell me, and we'll do it."

Emotions twisted Onyx's face. "I want to mate you now. I never imagined going from indifferent to craving the bond so fast, but I guess that's the nature of the beast. I need to claim you, Nico. To mark my territory. Make sure you can't get away. And keep you safe."

Nico's stomach dropped. He'd come too close to death, and he hated that he still had to deal with the fallout. "I want you to keep me safe, too. I was terrified, and fucking heartbroken when it seemed like I wasn't your mate after all."

Onyx cupped Nico's cheek. "I can't have you heartbroken. Let me put your mind at ease, *hmm?*"

The sinking feeling fled. Nico's chest was full and warm, as if Onyx's demon fire had found its way into his heart. "Yes, mate me, Onyx. I'm yours."

Onyx pulled him into a kiss, licking into Nico's mouth. Nico opened, savoring the sweet taste of Onyx's tongue and the lingering hint of sex. He ran a hand through Onyx's hair, and Onyx's fingers flexed against his jaw.

Their kisses were languid and sloppy, neither of them in a hurry. Yes. This was what Nico needed. Warm panting breaths, orchids and sweet wine, his mate's warm skin rubbing him everywhere.

Onyx tipped his head back, and his fangs lengthened. He purred and scraped them along Nico's jaw. Nico's pulse pounded in his ears, begging for Onyx's bite.

He didn't know the process for mating, but had a hunch.

"Bite me, little butterfly."

Onyx rumbled, purring until it turned into a growl. He pushed Nico flat on his back, tilted Nico's head to the side, and kissed his exposed neck. "I'm going to keep you forever."

"Yes." Nico arched beneath him, and Onyx bit down.

Pleasure bloomed in Nico's blood. He gasped and hugged Onyx close. Their hips rocked together, bodies connecting in a sweet rhythm, dancing in time with Nico's pounding pulse.

Onyx drank, purring deeper than ever, his hands tight in Nico's thick hair.

Nico was breathless. Onyx called to him, pulling him closer, their magic twisting together.

Onyx withdrew his fangs on a moan, his head tilting back as he licked the last of Nico's blood from his lips.

Nico rolled them, positioning himself on top. Onyx's eyes burned, and his face bloomed in a beautiful patchwork of color. He tilted his head to the side and ran a sharp nail along his skin, drawing blood. Nico leaned in and licked, then sucked.

It was more intimate than tonguing Onyx's ass. More intimate than drinking his blood in The Herb Emporium. Their souls connected, and Nico felt Onyx's delicate joy echo his own.

Onyx began to chant, the language as melodic as a song. Nico's whole body came alive. How had he ever doubted belonging to Onyx? As their connection solidified, it became hard to remember his doubt.

Nothing in Nico's life had given the impression it was meant to be, yet this moment rang with the magic of something that had been coming for a long, long time.

He pulled back as Onyx finished the incantation, and their lips were drawn back together. Nico tasted citrus on Onyx's tongue, and fizzles of joy coursed through his blood—through Onyx's blood—against their skin, and deep within them.

They were bound together.

Onyx's tender kernel of happiness tickled Nico along the bond. Onyx's lingering fear and worry prickled, and all the trepidation he had about letting Nico in swelled between them.

Nico loved every single feeling with all his heart.

"I feel you," Onyx gasped between kisses.

"Then you know that I love you, little butterfly."

A swell of deep affection—Onyx's emotions—drowned out all other sensations and enveloped them like a tidal wave.

"I love you too, Nico."

26

———

ONYX

IDEALLY, Onyx would never leave the loft again. He'd keep Nico prisoner. Though he preferred to be tied up, so his plan needed work.

His phone buzzed somewhere on the floor, and he groaned.

Nico stood naked by the window, finishing a phone conversation with Rowan. Onyx had texted Dante as he'd left Jaune—before he'd answered Nico's call—and figured he had a slew of missed calls by now.

He crawled from the bed. There were better things to do than talk to his brothers now that he and Nico were mated. Like address the plug in his ass.

Even with that alternative, Onyx wasn't as grumpy as he might have been, fishing his phone from the pocket of his discarded pants.

Who knew having a mate would make dealing with his brothers more tolerable?

He'd never had anyone of his own, and now he had Nico. No matter how talking to Ash and Dante went, Nico would be there. Onyx had someone on his side. Someone to vent to.

Someone to look out for him. Someone who wouldn't walk away like Onyx was nothing, even if everyone else did.

Onyx accepted the call. "What, Dante?"

"*What?* You said we were at risk of permanent death and then disappeared off the face of the Earth."

Onyx brought the phone back to bed, frustration lighting his internal fire. "Nico almost died, so your freak-out wasn't a priority."

"Wait, what?" Dante's panicked tone was gratifying, even as it turned to a snarl. "Was it Luc?"

A growl sounded in the background, likely Ash.

Despite himself, the support mollified Onyx. "No, it wasn't Luc. Calm down. It was some witch-vampire nonsense to do with Nico helping Rowan kick dodgy covens out of the city."

Onyx had listened in on Nico's conversation with Rowan, and even though he'd learned the context around the Orlovs and Michael's clash with the Valeros, he didn't see why either of them would purposely stir up trouble now that they'd returned. Wouldn't it be better to sneak into Shearwater Landing and strengthen their foothold before anyone caught wind?

He pulled his focus back to Dante. "Vampires poisoned Nico to send a message to the Valeros. I'm waiting for Rowan to get over himself and admit he's got no control over the situation, so I can kill the problem."

Nico appeared beside Onyx, apparently done with his call, and slung an arm around Onyx's shoulders.

Dante huffed as if he were displeased. "Ash and I are in. Let us know when you go after these vampires, and if Nico needs extra protection, we're here."

Dante didn't even realize Nico was Onyx's mate and he'd offered to help. It was who Dante was. Nothing personal. And Ash would probably take the attack as a potential threat to

Harper, considering he worked at the apothecary and could have been caught in the crossfire.

But—in a complete one hundred and eighty degree flip from that morning—Onyx hated his brothers' ignorance of how much Nico meant to him. He'd hidden how much he'd cared, terrified Nico would walk away, afraid his feelings could be used against him, and he regretted it.

After denying to his brothers what Nico meant to him, and then almost losing him, Onyx would never do that again.

Stomach twisting almost like he was nervous, Onyx cleared his throat. "Thanks for the offer to protect him, but Nico is my mate. We're fully bonded now. He can't get poisoned again."

"*Onyx, oh my gosh.*" Dante sounded so tender, it hurt. "I'm overjoyed for you. We hoped Nico was yours. This is beyond my wildest dreams."

"I was part of your wildest dreams?"

"Of course." Dante seemed confused, like that should have been obvious. "I wish Nico hadn't been hurt. Did you have to mate to save him, like I did with Ollie?"

"Nearly. I was able to suck the toxin out in time."

"Good. At least you got to choose to cement your bond." Dante sounded immensely relieved. "Where are you?"

Onyx squirmed. He'd usually have found something to snap at by now. "We're at my house."

"Not the shop? We need to protect your place so Luc can't get in. Please, Onyx."

He rubbed his brow, and Nico massaged his back, responding to the tension Onyx sent down their bond. "No. Fuck, Luc isn't our biggest threat right now. We've got to hunt down the demons who set the bounty and end this."

"All right. Come to my house, and bring Nico. Ash is tracking every demon in the city. We'll take them by surprise, one by one, until we uncover our enemies."

Onyx cut a look at Nico. He was near enough to hear what Dante was saying.

"It's not a bad idea. Rowan can help with backup if we tell him where we're headed."

Onyx didn't want to. He'd rather stay cooped up in the loft exploring their solidified bond. "*Ugh*. Fine, we're in. See you soon."

Dante said goodbye, and they hung up.

"Do we have time for a quickie before we go? We're already naked." Onyx didn't wait for an answer and climbed onto Nico's lap. He wrapped his tail around his mate's waist and rolled his hips.

Nico gasped. "We shouldn't."

"So? I'm not a fan of denying myself."

"No surprise there." Nico gripped Onyx's hips, stilling him. His hooded expression told a very different story. One Onyx chose to play into.

"I'm slick and ready, pull out the plug and slide in." Onyx canted his hips in invitation.

Struggle twisted Nico's features, and Onyx grinned, showing fang. The exact moment Nico gave in, his lust tore down the bond. He pulled the plug from Onyx, tossing it away, and Onyx sank onto his mate's rigid cock.

They came together fast and hard, every sensation shared through their bond. Onyx burned with pure pleasure, pulse racing, and magic whirling around them like a tornado. They came as one, eyes locked, panted breaths mingling.

"Fuck, it's going to be a lot harder to leave now." Nico buried his face in Onyx's hair and huffed him like he was trying to get high.

How had either of Onyx's brothers maintained a balanced life when they could have been in bed with their mates twenty-four-seven? He might have to ask.

If the threat looming had been less serious, Onyx wouldn't have bothered doing the right thing. "You're right, but we have to go. Otherwise, Ash might make good on his threat to track me."

Nico chuckled. "We can't have that." He patted Onyx's ass, and Onyx rose from his lap.

Showering wouldn't lead to anywhere but more orgasms, so they tidied quickly with the help of a little magic and got dressed.

"I'm not planning to keep my hands off you," Onyx warned as they climbed the stairs to the roof.

Nico chuckled. "I can feel how horny you are thought the bond. At this rate, we aren't going to be much help."

"It'll be fine. We can hang out in a guest bedroom until Ash finds our first targets. Then we'll be good to go."

All in all, it wasn't a terrible way to spend the night. Onyx pushed open the door to the roof, looking forward to filling Dante's large house with the moans of his and Nico's mating.

The night was as dark as it got in the city, late enough for relative quiet if you didn't count the distant sounds of traffic. There was so much for Onyx and Nico to explore, and the city seemed to stretch out before them, twinkling in invitation.

Nico followed Onyx outside, his own lust heating the bond. "I'd normally say no to hiding away and fucking while everyone else does the work, but I can tell how much you want me. It's like your desire has become mine. This bond is wild, and I can't resist."

Onyx's insides heated. He might as well be floating. Nico's knowledge of every one of his needy desires freed him in a way he hadn't thought possible.

He turned, facing Nico, smiling wide, when pain flared in his back, sharp and consuming. Onyx jolted, frozen as his heart stopped. *What the fuck?*

Nico's happy expression transformed into shock, fear shooting down the bond. "Onyx!" Nico lurched forward, arms outstretched. There was a flash of light, and Nico jolted, lightning striking his chest. His eyes rolled back, and agony overwhelmed the bond.

Onyx struggled to scream, to move. Pain radiated from his back as he was struck again.

He never should have trusted Luc. His guard had been so low, he hadn't even seen him lurking on the roof.

Nico crumbled to the ground, killed temporarily by the lightning strike. Magic swelled, electrifying their connection as Nico's body began to heal, but not as rapidly as Onyx's.

Still, Onyx's heart healed too slowly for him to regain control of his body. A bag slid over his head, enveloping him in complete darkness. Another shock rattled his bones as something pricked his arm, strong hands holding him tight.

His bicep burned like he'd been stung. Onyx's mind fogged. Fuck, it must be a potion. He stumbled, only then realizing he could move again.

Onyx fell against a firm chest, and someone grabbed him around the middle. It wasn't Nico. Onyx could sense the healing magic working, but with Nico unconscious, their bond was quiet. Why couldn't it heal his mate as quickly as it healed him?

Onyx opened his mouth, but no words came. All sensation faded, and he forgot what he'd been about to snarl. The blackness of the hood consumed him, and he knew no more.

27

———

ONYX

Onyx sucked in a sharp breath, choking on cloth. Something covered his face. Where was he?

He remembered the rooftop.

Nico!

Onyx ripped the sack from his head, his surroundings so dark he almost couldn't tell the difference. A cold stone floor lay beneath him. After a second, his eyes adjusted to the faint light outlining a door, barely illuminating the small, bare room.

Nico wasn't there.

Had Luc kidnapped him and separated him from Nico? Was this what Onyx got for being tempted to trust his brother?

Anger swelled inside him, and tears threatened. He pushed them back. Nico would be all right. Thank Onyx's damned eternal life that they'd bonded.

Onyx reached for their connection. Yes, Nico was there. Onyx pulled his mate's soul closer, but Nico didn't come, so to speak. His presence seemed faint, like he was far away. Distance shouldn't affect a mated pair's ability to share emotion. Something was hindering their connection.

At least Nico was alive and seemingly conscious. Faint hints of fear and panic reached Onyx through the bond, strangling his heart. His mate was hurting.

Onyx scrambled to his feet and lunged for the door. Nico could be in another cell. Onyx had to get to him. His head swam as he stood, and he stumbled, falling forward. Onyx's knees hit the stone, his head pounding.

What the hell? He had the coordination of a drunk man.

After a few tries, he made it to the door and braced a palm against it, out of breath. Vision tunneling, Onyx sank to the floor. He grabbed the handle on the way down, but it slipped from his grasp.

He blinked, confused. Where was he?

He inspected the empty cell and remembered what happened on the roof. *Nico!* He had to find Nico. They'd been attacked.

Struggling to his feet, Onyx touched the door. His vision went black, and he awoke on the floor. What happened?

Onyx had no idea how many times he went through the motions before an intense sense of déjà vu had him wondering if he'd messed with the door before.

He hesitated, pulling his hand back. Was touching the door knocking him out and stealing his short-term memory? It was a clever trap. No witch could pull off an illusion like that, but Lucifer could.

Sounds outside caught his attention.

Onyx straightened, trying to gather his wits. His head swam like he'd downed a whole glass of intoxicating potion.

The door swung outward, light spilling into the cell. A figure stepped into the doorframe, and Onyx hastily gathered his power, releasing a bolt of lightning. The spell exploded, filling the doorway with electricity without reaching its target. A shield must cover the opening. Dammit.

Onyx's eyes adjusted to the glare. The figure was tall but too wide to be Lucifer. Was this another illusion? Had the cell addled his brain?

The demon, Valac, stood before him. A guy Onyx vaguely recognized from their time in the Realm of the Damned.

Onyx steadied himself. "What the fuck do you want?"

"Your head on a plate." Valac bared his fangs, eyes flashing bright.

At least there was no misunderstanding his intention.

Valac's huge white wings extended beyond sight of the doorway. His looming posture was reminiscent of Ash. So was his smirk. "Where are the other Hounds?"

"As if I'd tell you. Let me out of here. There's no quarrel between us. You're free. Dante, Ash, and I never wanted to trap you in Hell."

"Please. You stood by Lucifer until the moment you decided to escape and leave everyone behind. Now, it's time for all of you to pay."

Onyx's head pounded. Valac must have set the bounty. Was he close to finding his brothers? Something had given Onyx away, and it better not have been Rowan's coven. "How did you find me?"

His captor shrugged. "I got a tip from a man who joined my cause."

Onyx willed his brain to work faster. Whatever he'd been injected with must have been potent. Unless this was the disorienting illusion addling his mind. "What cause?"

"To rid Shearwater Landing of oppressive scum, and allow the magic community to flourish freely."

So fucking noble, but anything could be spun to sound good. "My brothers and I have let the magic community flourish freely. I'm not even involved with the damn community. Cut the crap and admit you're after vengeance."

"It's hardly crap. Like you aren't twisting your words, saying you're not a part of the magic community. What about your witch friend?"

Onyx reached for Nico's presence, and Nico reached back, the bond thrumming. He was still there, but as Onyx tried to get a sense of Nico's physical location, he slipped away. Something was blocking him.

Valac continued, apparently displeased by Onyx's silence. "Even if that witch was your friend, he isn't anymore. Seeing as I stopped the guy's heart."

Onyx dropped his fangs, eyes flaming. He clung to Nico's presence within his soul.

Nico wasn't dead.

But Valac assumed he'd killed Nico. He didn't seem to know he and Onyx were mated. That was good. Maybe Onyx could use that. Hopefully, it meant Nico was safely back in the South Banks and not in another cell.

Onyx snarled. "Killing random witches isn't conducive to letting the magic community flourish. Sounds like you're full of shit."

Valac's attention shifted down the hall. "I've got a better friend for you. Why don't you two reconnect while I round up the rest of the dogs? Then we can put the whole pack down together, and be free."

"No, wait! You are free. We aren't enemies!" Onyx surged forward, hitting the shield blocking the doorway. His teeth clenched as electricity shot through him, stopping his heart.

Valac sneered as Onyx stumbled back. The big demon shifted out of the doorway, allowing two other demons to thrust a limp figure past the protective shield.

A man crumpled to the floor, and the door slammed shut.

Recognition shook Onyx's healed heart. "Luc?" He staggered back. Was this a trick?

Luc stirred and rolled onto his back with a pained moan.

Blood marred his almost unrecognizable face, his jaw dislocated and cheekbones smashed.

Onyx's heart skipped, and his chest seized. Seeing Luc hurt shouldn't matter. Onyx had spared no feeling when Dante had ripped the Devil's throat out in retaliation for hurting Ollie. But then, permanent death hadn't been on the table.

Despite everything, Onyx still cared for his brother. It was his greatest weakness.

Luc groaned as his face healed, features popping back into place. His swollen eyes opened, glowing red in the darkness.

"Onyx." Luc spat blood and pushed himself to a seated position. "Fuck, they got you too." He sounded heartbroken.

Lies! Onyx's better judgment screamed, but all he'd ever wanted was his brother's love. For Luc to care. To speak to him with that much emotion.

He shoved that longing down. "How did they manage to capture you? Aren't you an expert at sneaking around under everyone's nose?"

Luc laughed. It turned into a wet cough, as if his internal injuries weren't healed. "I thought so. Guess I got cocky. Careless." He shook his head and wiped a hand over his face, clearing some of the blood. "They found me on your roof."

"*My roof?* What the fuck?"

Onyx had left his loft unprotected so Luc could reach out, but the idea he had indeed been lurking—maybe not for the first time—sent shivers down Onyx's spine.

Luc straightened, and a flare of magic cleaned the remaining blood and grime away, leaving him camera-ready and nearly relaxed in appearance. "I was waiting for you. You hadn't been home since the gallery. Then, you finally showed up carrying your mate—"

"Do not talk about Nico," Onyx snarled.

Luc raised his hands. "Sorry. You went inside, and I wasn't

sure if you'd take me barging in when you had company as an attack, so I was waiting until you were alone. I needed to talk to you, but Valac and his chums showed up."

"How'd they find my loft? Almost no one knows where I live."

Luc's eyes narrowed. "I don't know. I didn't see them coming, obviously. They must have detected my invisibility spell once they arrived, and attacked me."

It sounded plausible. Luc might be telling the truth. Had Valac detected Onyx's invisibility and followed him home? But how had he figured out where to look? Scanning all of Shearwater Landing for invisibility illusions simultaneously wasn't possible.

"Valac seems to be leading the hunt for me," Luc went on. "He's gotten progressively more vocal in opposing me since you left the Realm of the Damned. Though never extreme in his rebellions. Until now. It appears I was right in assuming the reason demons never attempted to assassinate me was fear that, with me gone, they'd be trapped in Hell forever. Now that they're free, there's no reason to spare me."

A chill ran down Onyx's spine at how calmly Lucifer referred to his own demise. Why had he freed everyone if confinement was the only thing holding his enemies back?

There wasn't time to dwell on it. They had to escape. "How many does Valac have on his side?"

Luc stood, stretching his back with an audible click. "I'm not sure. At least half a dozen hung around him in Hell. He had me in a cell like this, and I saw three others when I arrived."

Even if there were only four, they were still outnumbered. Not great odds. Onyx and Luc would need backup.

Wait. Was Onyx trusting his traitor brother just because he'd been beaten up and tossed in a cell with him? How fucking foolish. The bounty and threats of permanent death could be a ruse, with Valac working for Lucifer.

But it didn't feel like a ruse. The hollow way Luc spoke of his death rang sharply of the truth. If he were lying, he'd lay it on thick with the self-pity.

Onyx shifted his stance, ready to strike at the first sign he had this wrong. "Why didn't you tell me all four of us were on Valac's hit list?"

Luc jolted as if he'd been shocked with lightning. "What?"

Was that genuine surprise? Obviously, Valac was after more than Lucifer, given Onyx was in a damn cell. "He's hunting me, Dante, and Ash too, asshole. We're all slated for permanent death. Why the fuck do you think I'm here with you?"

Luc's face twisted, a mix of bereft and agonized. "I—I had no idea."

Onyx's anger flared, and for a brief flash, he couldn't think or see. "Stop acting like you care! You treated us like shit for over a thousand years, and before that, you used us. Fuck you, Lucifer. You don't get to act like we're on the same side."

Even if they worked together to get out, they weren't allies. They would never be.

Luc cast his attention to the floor. "I do care, Onyx."

He snorted. "Because now you need me. You have no one, and you're grasping at straws."

"No." Luc lunged forward and grabbed Onyx by the shoulders. Onyx struggled to throw him off, and Luc's grip tightened. "I do care. I love you."

With all his inhuman strength, Onyx wrenched from Luc's hold and slapped him across the face. "You've got some way of showing it. You stole my magic. The most integral piece of who I am. You kept me prisoner. That's not love."

"I'm sorry. I had to do something. I couldn't let things get worse. It all got out of hand."

"So what if your plan to find mates on Earth didn't work out? That's no excuse to treat us the way you did."

"You're right. Fear seemed like the only way to bring demons in line once magic infected Earth. But I was wrong."

Onyx shoved Luc in the chest. "You were the one to infect humanity with magic and damn us all in the first place!"

Luc's eyes flared, red flames dancing dangerously. "I wasn't. I never fathered a half-human child. I only said I did."

"Bullshit." Why would he claim to be the one to damn them if it was a lie?

"It's not bullshit. It's the truth. The Eternal Realm was bound to retaliate for the creation of witches. I was responsible for the fall, therefore, I was responsible for anything that happened by default, even if the child wasn't mine. What would throwing the rightful father to the wolves have accomplished?"

Onyx's mind reeled. Could that be true? There was no way. Luc didn't put anyone before himself. He wouldn't claim to be the father of the first magical human to protect some other demon from the Eternal Realm's scorn. Being the one that led them to Earth wasn't the same as being responsible for destroying the balance of magic and mortality in the universe.

Fuck, it hardly mattered now. Onyx's resolve hardened. "Maybe I'd believe you were that selfless if you'd acted like it even once in the last millennia. Attacking Ash and Dante's mates the first chance you got tells a different story. Your words are empty."

Luc scrubbed a hand over his face. "I'm not proud of hurting them. I let anger rule me."

Onyx scoffed. "Oh, you're not proud? That makes it all right."

"What do you want?" Luc advanced, grabbing Onyx once more. "What can I do to prove that I've changed and that I'm ashamed? I was wrong. How can I atone for my mistakes?"

Onyx's pulse thudded in his ears, his breaths uneven. He should pull away, but didn't. "It's not my job to tell you how to make up for everything you've ruined."

Luc gripped him harder, smoke tinging the air. "Fine. Then what can I do to earn your forgiveness? Tell me that. I can't die like this."

"Like what? Reaping what you sowed?"

Luc released him like he'd been burned. "No. Alone. I can't die alone."

Onyx staggered into the wall behind him. Luc's words cut so deep it was a wonder Onyx didn't bleed. "*Alone?* You're upset you have no one? You drove everyone away!"

Luc winced, but Onyx didn't stop, his shouts bouncing off the stone walls. "You're the one who left *me* behind. You took everyone! You had the love of hundreds and pissed it all away, and you have the audacity to tell me you have no one?"

Luc's brow furrowed, frown lines cutting his sharp features. "I didn't leave you behind. I didn't take anyone from you."

Onyx screamed, eyes clamped shut. His fire raged, coating his skin as his demonic features sprang forth, wings hitting the walls. There was so much fury inside him, he might never burn out.

Hands clasped his upper arms, pushing through his burning blue fire.

Onyx choked, and his eyes popped open against his will.

Luc held his stare, no sign of the pain he must feel as Onyx burned him. "How could I have left you? You're here with me."

Onyx shook his head, fire snuffing out. Luc's grip tightened. "I asked you to stay with me in the Eternal Realm. Begged you. You chose searching for your mate over me."

"I didn't choose my mate over you. We all longed for our fated loves. We couldn't stay in the Eternal Realm. It wasn't an option. Falling to Earth never meant leaving you behind. You wanted your mate too. You were coming with me."

"No, I wasn't. I didn't need a mate. All I needed was you, Ash, and Dante. I fell because you were leaving regardless. If I hadn't come, I'd never have seen you again."

"What do you mean you didn't need your mate? You're saying you didn't want to leave at all, even if it meant never being granted your partner?"

Onyx's eyes burned, and he willed himself not to cry. Luc's expression softened, and Onyx couldn't take it. "That's exactly what I'm saying. It's what I said back then. I told you all this."

"I thought you were putting on a brave face by saying you only needed your brothers and not a mate."

Onyx trembled. "See? You didn't listen. I couldn't stand losing you. Come on, Luc. It's not as if you'd have stayed in the Eternal Realm if I hadn't given in and followed."

Luc seemed to mull this over seriously. "True. I fear nothing could have held me back once the idea to fall took root. But I never wanted to leave you behind. It was always the four of us going."

But it wasn't. Fuck, why bother arguing? Luc left. Onyx followed, and the gesture was completely lost on his brother. Luc's disregard ran so deep he hadn't realized what was happening in front of him, too blinded by his own narrative to see Onyx as someone with differing goals and desires. Even when he voiced them out loud.

Luc pulled Onyx into a tight embrace, and Onyx stiffened in shock. "Let me find a way to put things right. I'm sorry you gave up so much for me, and then I...I failed you in every way. But I'm glad you followed. I'd be heartbroken to never see you again."

Onyx should've recoiled from his brother's touch. It had no

right to soothe something inside him. He didn't trust Luc's words, but he longed for them to be true more than anything.

The desire pulled him apart.

Was this soul-destroying yearning for another's love how Luc felt about mates? Onyx could understand the agony driving him to recklessness. To fall from the Eternal Realm. To destroy everything he loved.

Onyx couldn't help clinging to the possibility that Luc told the truth—loved him deep down—no matter what it cost him.

Luc pulled Onyx closer. "I won't let you die here. I'll get you out, little brother, and if I survive, I'll never take you for granted again."

28

___

NICO

Nico blinked awake, a chill coursing through his body. He lay face down on something hard. Shit. He scrambled to his feet and glanced around the deserted roof.

Where was Onyx?

Nico reached within, searching for their bond, but couldn't find it. He was empty. No. That wasn't possible.

What had happened? Nico hadn't seen a thing except Onyx freezing like he'd been stunned. Then, Nico had been engulfed in pain and blacked out. What if Onyx had been worse than stunned?

Nico's heart raced. Onyx couldn't have been permanently killed. Could he? Nico shoved a shaking hand into his pocket and pulled out his phone, calling Dante.

"Nico?" The demon's confused voice cut through the still night air. "Are you on your way over?"

Words spilled from Nico in a rush. "Onyx is gone! We were attacked on his roof. I was knocked out, and I can't feel him."

"Shit! What roof? Where are you?"

"At his loft. We flew here. Fuck, what's the street address?"

Nico brought up a map on his phone, searching for his location's address and rattled it off to Dante.

"We're coming. Were the protections breached?"

"I don't think so. We were outside. I didn't even see who attacked us."

"That's all right. Go inside. We won't be long."

Everything in Nico screamed to look for Onyx. He couldn't hide in the loft. He needed to act.

He could track Onyx with a spell if he had a personal item, so he raced down to the loft. Witches needed something physical to build the tracking spell around—blood was best— but Nico wasn't experienced in those kinds of surveillance spells.

A better idea struck. "Can Ash track Onyx?" he asked into the phone.

"He's already on it."

Onyx's presence in Nico's soul was nowhere to be found. It was like a hole had opened up inside him.

Bursting into the loft, Nico grabbed a small, beaded box from the sitting area. Maybe tracking Onyx would help him grasp their connection.

Calling on his magic, Nico recited the spell, but couldn't concentrate. He kept slipping up, forgetting the words. He tried again.

Minutes ticked by, and Onyx's presence was still nothing but a gaping chasm in his chest.

Dante's voice emanated from the phone. "We're about to land."

Nico hardly realized he was still on the line. Giving up for now, he grabbed the box and fled the apartment, racing back up the stairs.

Dante and Ash met him on the first landing.

"Why can't I feel him?" Nico gasped.

Dante steadied him, grabbing his elbow. "Onyx could be unconscious."

"Not dead?"

Dante and Ash shared a look. Ash cleared his throat. "Now that you're bonded, if Onyx died permanently, I don't think you'd still be here."

"I'd be erased from the universe, too?" Nico's chest seized.

"I can't be certain, but you'd probably end up in the Realm of the Damned like any other deceased witch soul. It's good that you're still on Earth. It means we have time."

Nico nodded. Fuck, he was panting as if he'd run for miles. "How long does your tracking take?"

Ash grimaced. "Not long if I'm close to the demon, like I am with Onyx, but I can't get a direction. He could be somewhere guarded by anti-tracking protections."

"Shit."

"I'll keep trying."

Dante patted Nico's shoulder. "You should, too. Keep reaching for the mate connection."

Nico closed his eyes as if that would help, and let every cell in his body yearn for Onyx. As the emptiness threatened to overwhelm him, something flickered.

"There!" He clutched his chest. "He's there! Onyx feels confused. He's really faint, but he's there."

Dante let out a long breath. "Good."

"I still have nothing," Ash grumbled.

"Can you use me?" Nico clutched the little box, more helpless than he'd ever been in his adult life. "Can you track Onyx through our connection rather than his magic?"

Ash's eyes widened. "Let me try. If you were a demon, you'd be able to find Onyx regardless of anti-tracking spells. Witch magic isn't as strong, even with the mating bond. But if I can tap into your connection, maybe we can combine the two."

Nico reached for Ash, and they clasped hands. "We have to hurry. If he's been captured by the demons hunting you, they could kill him at any moment!" Nico didn't fear dying. He feared a universe without his mate.

They'd only just found each other.

"We'll rescue him in time," Dante promised, even as fear lined his face.

Sweat broke out on Nico's brow. He couldn't lose Onyx, and wouldn't let him down. Nico concentrated on his mate's presence, on Onyx's fear and anger jolting painfully down the bond.

Ash's magic warmed Nico's hand, the heat radiating up his arm.

How far away could Onyx have been taken? Nico wasn't sure how long he'd lain on the roof. What if he, Ash, and Dante were outnumbered when they finally found Onyx? There were too many ways for this to go wrong.

Nico clung to Onyx's presence as Ash's magic flared. They'd find him in time, even if they had no idea what they were walking into. They had to.

29

ONYX

Onyx pulled from Luc's embrace, retracting his wings. He couldn't let hope distract him. There'd be time to figure out if Luc was genuine later.

He cleared his throat, uncomfortable under Luc's gaze. "How are we going to get out of here? They'll sense us unpicking the spells trapping us."

"True. They'll come running and we'll have to overpower them."

"That's the plan?"

"Got a better one? I'm not waiting for them to return, giving them enough time to prepare for whatever they're planning to do next."

Onyx crossed his arms. "We need to destroy the shield covering the doorway, or there won't be any chance of overpowering them." But there was no way they could destroy the shield before their captors sensed what they were doing.

Luc inspected the wall to his right, pressing a palm to the stone. "We could smash through here. I don't feel a shield in the stone."

Onyx inspected the wall with his demon sense. Luc was right. "We might end up in another cell."

"Or in a room with Valac. But the longer we do nothing, the longer we give them to come back and kill us."

A chill shot down Onyx's spine. "Valac said they were going to capture Dante and Ash first."

"And you believe that? It would be smarter to get our executions out of the way."

"Hey. Whose side are you on?"

Luc's lip curled. "I'm just pointing out the obvious. Don't act like I've ever plotted a permanent death."

"Whatever. Let's get out of here."

Luc grabbed Onyx's wrist. "Wait. Let me protect you."

Onyx snatched his hand away. "I can protect myself."

"I still have Ash and Dante's power. I can protect you better than your power alone."

Onyx's mouth dropped open. "I'm not letting you use stolen power on me."

Luc growled. "Fuck, Onyx. They'd want you to be safe. Of all the things I've done with what I stole, let me do this."

Onyx hesitated. "You actually want me to get out of here alive."

Luc gritted his teeth, his eyes flashing. "I said I'd get you out. Now, stop fighting me."

Fighting Luc was all Onyx had known for millennia. Breaking the habit went against everything in him. The Devil could turn around and betray Onyx as soon as they were free, but Onyx believed Luc didn't want him dead.

Wasn't Luc's care and protection what he craved? He could give in until Valac was dealt with.

"Hurry up," Onyx snapped.

Luc's lips curved in a tentative smile, and power enveloped Onyx.

While shields were usually constructed of immortal fire, this was invisible, the magic familiar. Ash and Dante surrounded Onyx—so did Lucifer—in a snug, soothing embrace that wound around him from head to toe.

To top it off, Onyx sheathed himself in protective fire, and Luc did the same. Turning toward the wall, Onyx concentrated on the grouting between the stones and transformed it to dust. He pushed a stone through the wall, and it fell to the floor on the other side.

They quickly made a hole big enough to accommodate a person. Onyx crawled through and stood, stepping over the discarded stones.

"Another cell. Great."

Luc appeared at his elbow. "Don't bother with the door. It's humming with magic."

"How long did the hallway look when you were out there?"

"I didn't see. My eyes were too busy healing."

Onyx wrinkled his nose. "Let's try the back wall. We need to get out of the cells, away from the protective shields before they come looking."

Luc nodded, and Onyx de-grouted the back wall of the second cell. Luc carefully pulled out the first stone and peered through the hole. "We're good. No one's there."

Onyx helped pull the wall apart and crawled through after Luc. They didn't seem to be in a cell. The space was larger but still had no windows, and only one door.

A shout came from behind them, and Onyx whirled around. "Shit. Sounds like they're in our cell."

Luc blasted through the wall in front of him, opposite the door, apparently no longer worried about being quiet. Dust rained down, and Luc's fiery red form disappeared into the next room.

Onyx hurried after, pausing to throw up a hasty magic barrier over the gaping hole.

Luc grabbed his arm. "Come on." He dragged Onyx through an open door.

A shout came from ahead, and Luc sent lightning down the corridor. A blast hit Onyx's shield, causing his fire to flare. They ran away from the shouting and banged through a door into a stairwell.

"Think one of these walls leads outside?" Onyx shouted as they ran.

"Let's find out." Luc blasted through the wood and plaster. It seemed they'd left the stone behind.

Night air greeted them, and Onyx leapt outside, Luc at his back. Onyx freed his wings, correcting his fall and soaring upward.

His head smacked into a solid barrier, pain flaring. "*Argh!*" He rocked back. Nothing was in his way. Demon sense flaring, he found a powerful spell spanning the open air.

"The whole courtyard is sealed off," Valac called.

Onyx whirled around, seeing Valac and two other demons holding Lucifer in mid-air as a third wrestled a rune-covered collar around Luc's neck.

Fuck. How was Onyx supposed to free them both on his own? "We aren't your enemies," he pleaded.

Valac remained unmoved. "There's no guarantee you won't turn around and imprison us again. Sounds like enemies to me."

Luc went limp in his captors' arms. Was it the collar, or was he playing it up? "Let Onyx go. Please. I'm the one who held you captive. He had no part in it."

Valac rounded on the Devil. "Do you think I'm stupid? Your inner circle always had your back."

"Because I forced them to," Luc snarled.

Onyx's pulse raced. Luc had never admitted his Hounds were leashed to anyone. He clung to the illusion that they were still a family above almost everything else.

Valac's brows raised. "A likely story, but I'll keep both of you, just to be safe."

Onyx's heart plummeted. Valac would never listen.

"Don't wait for me," Luc shouted, runes on the collar flaring bright red, likely absorbing any power he tried to use.

Without hesitation, Onyx darted to the other side of the courtyard, shooting lightning at Valac, who dodged expertly. This side wasn't any better. There was no way out. Onyx flew, evading shots but getting nowhere.

Another lightning strike narrowly missed him. At least the shield of his, Ash, Dante, and Luc's power hadn't faltered. Was Luc using the little strength not drained by the collar to protect him? Onyx's heart clenched. He couldn't leave Luc behind.

Onyx would never let Luc die. Even if Luc had thrown Onyx to Valac to save himself. But he hadn't done that. Luc was trying to spare him, and Onyx burned with hope.

Two more demons flew out of the building and zoomed toward Onyx. He darted away, scrambling to undo the spell caging the courtyard. He couldn't help Luc if he was recaptured.

A bolt of lightning hit his shield. If they stunned him, he was toast. How long until they broke through his protection?

Onyx kept as much magic as he could spare, blocking their shots as he countered the containment spell, flying back and forth like a trapped fly, praying no one would catch him.

The mate bond tugged on his heart. Nico's presence flared bright, sending an anxious determination down their connection. Onyx's heart skipped, but he couldn't think about Nico. He had to get out.

A boom sounded from the other side of the building. He was running out of time.

Valac swore and sped off toward the sound. The protective magic around Onyx flickered. He circled the courtyard, catching a glimpse of Luc, weak in his captors' hold, his eyes half closed, but the other demons seemed distracted.

Onyx raced to undo the containment spell. The two demons not occupied with Luc seemed less worried about the noise and shot lightning toward him simultaneously. A hit found its mark, and Onyx's shields faltered. Another blast struck, and every one of Onyx's muscles froze.

He plummeted from the sky, crashing onto dry, packed earth.

"Stop!" bellowed someone who sounded a hell of a lot like Ash.

Onyx's heart would have leapt if it hadn't been healing.

"Put your lightning away and come have a conversation like civilized beings."

Ash was so full of himself. No one would listen. Onyx would've rolled his eyes if he could have.

At last, Onyx regained control of his body and leapt to his feet. Burning with protective fire, Ash and Dante stood in the middle of the courtyard, Valac held between them.

Nico stood beside Ash, his gaze boring into Onyx, filled with love and fierce protection. His mate had come for him, facing demons without a shred of fear. Onyx had never felt so loved.

All around, everyone seemed frozen and unsure of what to do with Valac captured. The mating bond sparked, and a magnet seemed to pull Onyx toward his mate. Onyx forced himself not to give in and run to Nico. It could be a mistake to betray how much Nico meant to him. The last thing he needed was someone taking Nico hostage.

Nico might be here to save him, but Onyx had to protect his mate, too.

Footsteps thundered, and Onyx tensed, calling on his magic as more demons ran out of the building. Valac's supporters snarled as Ren, Pamala, Lillian, and Maxwell joined Ash and Dante.

Onyx smiled and silently thanked Dante and Ash for calling backup.

"No one else is inside," Ren announced, her silver eyes glowing with satisfaction.

Ash pushed Valac to his knees. "You're outnumbered. Release Onyx now."

"No one's holding him," Valac sneered.

Onyx crossed the courtyard, and Nico stepped forward, his presence instantly soothing as he clasped Onyx's hand.

He wanted to fall into Nico's embrace and never leave. Soon. He cleared the lump in his throat. "You have to release Lucifer, too."

"You said you weren't on his side. Such a liar." Valac spat into the dirt. The demons holding Luc landed, but didn't relinquish him. Valac strained under Ash's hold. "What are you going to do to us? Send us to a new prison?"

Onyx caught Nico's eye. They couldn't do that. They had to resolve this, not act like the enemies Valac accused them of being. Nico's understanding radiated through their connection, even though they couldn't share precise thoughts. He seemed determined to see an end to this, too.

Before Onyx could speak, Luc shouted, "They won't imprison you. That's what I've been trying to say."

Everyone's attention zeroed in on the Devil. Luc's spine straightened, and his captors jostled him into a tighter hold.

"Onyx, Ash, and Dante never wanted to imprison anyone. They didn't believe banning demons from Earth served any purpose. I forced them to go along with my plan by stealing pieces of their magic."

"What?" Maxwell staggered back, eyes wide.

Pamala covered her mouth, her yellow wings ruffling. "Stealing magic is unheard of."

Luc grimaced. "I used our combined power to create the seal around the Realm of the Damned. I couldn't have done it on my own, but I had no voluntary supporters."

"So what?" Valac snarled. "You still did it, and now you'll pay."

The two holding Luc rumbled their agreement, eyes glowing.

Onyx lunged toward Luc, pulling Nico with him. "Not with his life. Please."

Valac clenched his fists. "Why not? He's admitted to violating you—his most loyal friends—and stealing pieces of your very being. Why do you care what happens to him?"

How could Onyx not care? His soul cracked. Compassion flooded the bond, and Nico squeezed his hand. How could he get Valac to understand?

"It's a crime to kill an Eternal being," Dante reminded everyone. "You risk the council's wrath if you go through with this, and they are never forgiving."

The first shadow of doubt crossed Valac's face. "They've washed their hands of us."

"Have they?" Dante cocked his head. "I wouldn't bet my life on it, though I've been tempted. I know what it's like to want to kill Lucifer. But nothing is worth forfeiting my own existence."

Valac blinked in surprise. "You were going to kill Lucifer?"

"Yes. In a fit of rage, before Onyx reminded me of the reality."

Valac hesitated.

Counting on the council's retaliation wasn't enough. They had to resolve this between themselves, or one day, they might find themselves back here again.

Onyx fixed Valac with a fiery stare. "Luc gave me my magic back."

"So?" he sneered.

Onyx narrowed his eyes. "So, genius, how can he reimprison anyone in Hell without it?"

Valac opened his mouth and faltered. "Th-there isn't enough power without yours?"

"Onyx is right," Luc said desperately, "and what's more, I'll give Ash and Dante their magic back too. Take this collar off, and I'll do it now, in front of you as witnesses. It will be impossible to reimprison anyone in Hell once their power is restored. You'll be utterly free. Forever."

Lucifer's captors' grips slackened, and he broke free, stumbling forward.

The air grew tense. Onyx pulled Nico close. He never dreamed Luc would give away such an advantage. Fuck, he may have changed after all.

"You could be lying," Valac countered. "Without the collar, you might attack. Maybe giving Onyx's power back still leaves you with enough to rebuild."

Luc clenched his teeth, his lip curling. "I'm not lying. How can I ever prove it's the truth if I'm not given the chance?"

"You've had an awful lot of chances," Ren pointed out. Fuck, she was fierce. Onyx liked her more each time he saw her.

Luc glared at her. "I won't attack. I'll give the remainder of the stolen magic back, and I will never be able to re-steal it. This will end here and now."

Nico huffed. "How can we be sure you won't go back on your word?"

Luc turned toward Onyx's mate, and a growl ripped from Onyx's throat.

"To steal my brothers' magic, I had to be close to them. And I don't mean in proximity. You can't take magic with a spell. Magic is part of who we are, our essence. To even touch their magic, I had to be held within their hearts. I don't harbor any delusions that I'll ever be that close to them, or anyone, ever again."

Heavy silence fell on the courtyard. The raw devastation in Luc's words scraped over Onyx's skin and sent shivers coursing through him.

Luc's admission was heartbreaking, and the fact that his loss was self-inflicted came as no comfort.

Ash pulled Valac to his feet. "Undo the collar and let him give our magic back. You want guaranteed freedom? This is the only way to do it without tempting your own execution."

Valac ran a hand through his hair. "Fine." He gestured to his supporters, who removed the collar.

Luc ran a hand over his neck, his eyes fluttering closed. "Step forward."

Ash and Dante did so without hesitation.

Onyx gripped Nico tight. No longer able to hold his protective instincts back, he encased his mate in protective fire. No one seemed to notice, all eyes on Lucifer.

Luc raised his hands in front of him. Above the right, a ball of orange power appeared, and above the other, a ball of black shimmering power. Ash and Dante's essences. Both demons stood stock still, fixated on the glowing orbs.

With a murmur too quiet to hear, Luc sent the power forth, magic shooting toward its owners like lost dogs racing home.

Ash and Dante gasped as their magic collided with their chests. Luc fell to his knees, panting as if in pain. Ash staggered to the side, gasping. Dante caught him and they held each other tight.

No one else in the courtyard moved a muscle.

Dante sputtered, the sound turning into a strangled laugh. "It's back. My power. Fucking hell, Luc, you're not a total liar after all."

30

———

NICO

Ash and Dante embraced, and Onyx's desire to join them flared through the bond into Nico's chest.

"Go," Nico whispered in his ear.

Onyx shook his head. "We aren't in the clear yet. Stay ready."

Nico was primed for action, but they seemed past the worst. Onyx's hope surrounding his relationship with his brother was blinding. Nico had experienced nothing like it. His demon was so vulnerable, so scared of the thing he wanted most in the world.

No matter what happened, Nico would get Onyx through this. He'd protect his heart and take care of him.

"Can we agree to part on neutral terms?" Lucifer asked Valac.

The big, white-winged demon scowled. "I'm satisfied we can't be reimprisoned, and I'll hold no ill will toward Onyx, Ash, and Dante, but I will never be neutral toward you."

Luc's face closed off. "That's your right. Are you going to keep hunting me?"

Nico's heart sank. Would this conflict never end? Long memory was a serious drawback to immortality.

"No, I won't." Valac brushed dirt from his knees. "I'd rather ignore you and forget you exist. You're nothing now. But if I hear rumors of you scheming, I'll be the first to oppose you and knock you right back down."

"Fair enough." Luc shrugged as if he hadn't been threatened.

"Good. We'll be going." Valac beckoned to his supporters and turned toward the building.

"Wait!" Onyx pulled Nico forward. "While I appreciate that you finally believe we never wanted to imprison you, you still put a bounty on us."

Valac stilled. "Are you planning to retaliate?"

Onyx glanced at the sky as if resisting an eye roll. "No, I don't want to be enemies. How many times do I have to say it?"

"I'll call off the bounty. Happy?"

Ash snorted.

Onyx's frustration sparked down the bond. "Why don't you answer a few questions, like how you found me? There aren't many beings in the magic world who could've given me away."

Valac released a heavy breath. "I told you, I got a tip. A vampire coven—Orlov—contacted me after I set the bounty, and said they were interested in ridding the city of the ruling mob, and wanted to join forces. I said I'd consider it."

Nico's blood boiled. Coming across as the bad guy was the downside to Rowan's chosen image, but in this context, it was unacceptable. "Ruling mob? The Valeros protect the city from scum like the Orlovs. Their coven was destroyed because of their dealings in human trafficking."

Valac bared his teeth in a snarl. "They didn't tell me that. They said it was the other way around. I heard from one of them today, saying a demon had landed outside an apothecary shop, invisible, but cracked pavement betrayed their presence. I showed up to check it out."

Nico's neck prickled, Onyx's fiery anger spiking between them. "Was it Emmett who contacted you? He was at my shop trying to kill me for kicking his scummy coven out of the city."

Valac's cheeks stained red. "He left that detail out. It seems I was misled, too eager for any allies against the Devil and his Hounds. I'd never side with vampires who abuse humans."

"Are you forgetting that you tried to kill Nico?" Onyx snapped.

Valac did a double-take as if he hadn't recognized Nico until now. "Why aren't you dead?"

Onyx marched toward the hulking demon, nose in the air. "He's my mate."

Valac paled. "You're bonded? I—I didn't realize."

"No shit. Come near him again, and all this neutrality goes out the window."

Valac nodded, but Onyx didn't back down, his glare chilling. Valac held up his hands, now the one wanting to de-escalate the situation. "I'm sorry. I was blinded by my need to secure freedom. As a show of good faith, I can lead you to the Orlovs and help you get rid of them."

"That'd be a good start." Nico pulled out his phone and hesitated, not ready to relay all this to Rowan. "The Valeros will want in on wrapping things up with the Orlovs. It might be good for you to meet them, since they're the actual protectors of this city."

"All right. Text me." Valac rattled off a number—which Nico entered—before turning back to Onyx. "Will it be acceptable to come near your mate to end this vampire business?"

"That's up to Nico. If he agrees, I'll be watching you closely."

"Sounds like a plan. I hope that in time, there will be no

hard feelings between us. I'll cancel the bounty and remove the spells around here so you all can leave."

With that, Valac and his supporters disappeared into the building.

"We already destroyed the spells over the main entrance," a woman with light gray wings and silver eyes muttered to a yellow-winged woman. "How does he think we got in?"

The second demon rolled her glowing yellow eyes.

The group seemed to relax. Only Lucifer remained tense, standing apart from everyone. Was the Devil hoping they'd forget about him? Without his horns, wings, or tail, he looked more like a human model who'd wandered into the wrong court-yard than anything sinister.

"Surprised you haven't disappeared into thin air," Ash sneered. Seemed Nico wasn't the only one with eyes on the Devil.

Lucifer flicked his wrist dismissively. "I wanted to see if you still plan on imprisoning me."

Nico's chest tightened as Onyx's attention returned to his brother, the bond going haywire as a storm of emotion raged within him.

Ash crossed his arms and considered Lucifer. "Maybe we should. I don't trust you and probably never will. You can't tell me that you planned to give our magic back when you first followed us to Shearwater Landing."

"I didn't," Luc agreed, matter-of-fact. "I came to scope you out since my plan to release everyone from Hell was set and ready. I was never dragging you back down there, you know."

Onyx made a sound of disbelief, echoed by Ash and Dante.

"Accuse me of lying if you want. I can't stop you. All I can do is tell the truth and trust that one day, it will become clear."

"All you can do?" Ash stomped closer. "You tried to kill Harper. And Ollie."

"I got derailed," Luc admitted as if attempted murder was a minor distraction. "I'm not saying I'm good. Fuck knows I'm not perfect. I wasn't planning to give you your power back even after freeing everyone. My plans were still...calculated."

"And now?" Onyx's voice rang out, soft but unwavering.

Luc's face darkened. "Now... Realizing your mates were real changed everything. What I did to Ollie changed everything."

Regret lined his face and hollowed his words. Nico could believe his remorse was genuine, but he was a master deceiver.

Lucifer continued, "I'm not pretending I'm flawless or that I haven't fucked up. But I want to do better. If you don't imprison me, that's my aim."

Onyx, Dante, and Ash shared a look, and Onyx's hope blinded Nico. His mate's desire to see Luc redeemed was so fierce, it was agony, but his skepticism was almost as strong.

Onyx approached Luc like he was a wild animal. "What are you proposing, a truce?"

"Yes, and more. If anyone is willing to let me, I want to make amends."

"No." Dante shook his head, and Ash clapped him on the back in support. "A truce is all we'll consider. We aren't letting you back into our lives. I will never forgive you for what you did to Ollie."

Luc's red eyes dimmed. "Again, that's fair. I won't push it."

The Devil was the picture of conciliatory. It was hard to imagine this was the same being who'd done so much harm.

That, Nico supposed, was the danger.

"But we're agreeing to a truce?" Onyx turned to Ash and Dante, lines straining around his eyes as they shone with hope.

The other two remained guarded. Ash stroked his chin. "We can manage a truce. Lucifer is no longer more powerful than any of us individually. He'll never get his paws on our magic again, and I suppose giving our power back is a fair trade for sparing him from indefinite solitary confinement."

Dante rumbled in agreement. "Everyone hates him. He isn't a threat when he has no one to use."

Everyone but Nico seemed to miss Lucifer's pained wince. Did he really care that everyone hated him? What did he expect?

"I'm not holding my breath to see if you do *better*." Ash curled his lip at the Devil. "Leave us and our mates alone, and there won't be any problems."

"Fine. I'll take my leave." Luc bowed like someone out of another era, a shaking hand clenched at his side. He faced Onyx. "I'm sorry I didn't listen to you, brother. I owe you for not allowing me to leave you behind."

"*Luc.*" Onyx sounded strangled.

"I'll be here if you want me. I'll respect everyone's wishes for space, but I'm not leaving. You're not alone." Then, Luc disappeared.

Onyx blinked and wiped his eyes. Ash and Dante's gaze pinged back and forth between him and the place Luc had been.

"Fuck, this is better than TV," the demon with the gray wings said without a shred of shame.

One of the other women elbowed her, hissing, "*Ren.*"

"What? Seeing that was almost worth a thousand years in Hell. Bet he's off to lick his wounds. Didn't even need his tail out to see it was between his legs."

The other demons gaped at her.

Onyx laughed, all sadness gone as if it had never been. "You and I need to spend more time together."

Ren grinned evilly.

Nico looped an arm around Onyx and pulled him against his chest. "It's time to go home, mate."

Onyx melted against him. "Best idea I've heard all night."

31

———

ONYX

THE NEXT WEEK FLEW BY, one thing after another annoying Onyx to no end. Why couldn't the world leave him alone? He had a mate, and every minute he wasn't strapped to his bed at Nico's mercy was a waste.

Admittedly, the Orlovs had been dealt with, and that was worth taking the time away from bed to sort out. Rowan, Nico, and Valac had taken care of the brunt of it, with Onyx's supervision. Emmett hadn't been given the option to flee. Onyx had seen to that personally.

Michael, Nico's other problem, had been taken care of along with the vampires. Apparently, he'd come back to Shearwater Landing under the impression that Nico had taken up with his ex-girlfriend, and had broken into Nico's apartment looking for an item to use to track his ex down. After that hadn't worked, he'd joined the Orlovs, since Rowan and Nico were mutual enemies, and their plans had turned to poison.

Onyx hated that Nico hadn't come to him when he'd been in trouble, but he understood. That would never happen again. They had each other, and Nico didn't have to put on a brave face or spare Onyx his troubles.

Luc hadn't popped up. Onyx felt like a fool for believing his brother wanted to repair their destroyed relationship. Maybe everything he'd said had been to grease the wheels of his escape, garner a little sympathy, and avoid the prison Onyx, Ash, and Dante had built for him.

Nico said to give Luc time.

Onyx checked the mail as he entered his building, finding a letter. He'd been at the gallery, meeting with Jade, whose name was actually Fiona. With their initial meeting concluded and the gallery in Scott's care, and Harper and Ash looking after The Herb Emporium for a few days, Onyx hoped to have Nico and the loft to himself for at least forty-eight hours without interruption.

He carried the letter upstairs and threw it on the entryway table. "Where's my mate? I'm lonely."

Nico chuckled from a seat by the window. He had a book on his lap and a bourbon in his hand. "I'm right here, little butterfly."

"Good." Onyx hurried over, his heart fluttering.

He hadn't doubted Nico would be waiting as he'd promised. Nico was dependable and would reassure Onyx that he wasn't being abandoned whenever he needed.

"You do realize I'm going to have to return to work eventually. Having the shop closed after I got poisoned was necessary, and I need these next few days off, but I'm not ready to be a kept man."

Onyx perched on Nico's lap. "I should hope not. You'll have to stay occupied while I'm at the gallery. Scott hates having people underfoot."

Nico buried his face in Onyx's hair and inhaled. "We can't upset Scott."

"No, especially when he's lining up a cat adoption for me."

Nico pulled back. "What?"

Onyx pouted. "I'm getting a cat. You're very important, but I need someone else around when you're back at your apartment. As much as I hate to admit it, Dante might be onto something with animal companions."

Onyx wasn't actually keeping Nico prisoner as he'd fantasized, and they'd decided not to move in together yet.

Nico hummed. "I figured you'd lurk in my window while I was at home. Not get a cat to fill the void of my absence."

Onyx playfully nudged Nico's shoulder. "Dick. I've got a life. And soon, a very cute cat." He paused dramatically. "You aren't going to get scared on me, are you?"

"Brat," Nico growled, affection flooding the bond. "I should teach you not to tease me."

"Oh, no." Onyx raised a hand to his forehead. "Not a lesson. Don't spank me. My poor abused bottom can't take it."

They dissolved into laughter, Nico hugging Onyx close.

Fuck, this was it right here. Life didn't get any better.

Onyx caught his breath. "I love this. Being with you is so damn addicting. Is it horrible that I keep thinking something is going to ruin it?"

"No. It's scary to get what you want because it can be taken away. I get that. Why do you think it's so hard for me to ask for help? Before you, I was afraid to rely on someone only to lose them, so I made myself manage without."

Onyx cupped Nico's cheeks. "Are you worried I'll get taken from you?"

For a flash, concern lined Nico's eyes. "I was when you were captured by Valac. But that's behind us. He's spreading the word that Lucifer can't reimprison anyone in Hell, and that you never supported what Lucifer did. No one is coming after you again."

It was true. Ren, Pamala, and her companions were also getting the word out about what had happened in the courtyard, and demons seemed to believe the story when it came from varied sources.

Luc had been stripped of his power. The Hounds of Hell no longer existed. Soon, everyone would know they had never been loyal dogs. Onyx, Ash, and Dante were guilty of no more than trusting Luc in the initial fall, same as any of them.

"No one is coming after you either." Onyx poked Nico in the ribs. "Though none of your adversaries stand a chance against me. I'll turn anyone who crosses you into dust."

Nico didn't laugh as Onyx expected. His forehead wrinkled. "Killing vampires and witches and sending them to the Realm of the Damned isn't the same as permanent death, I know that, but it feels wrong leaving them alone in Hell."

The abandoned magical souls had crossed Onyx's mind, too. "It can't be helped as long as the Eternal Realm bans all magical human souls. Who knows, maybe they don't mind having the place to themselves. I could ask Luc if I ever see his miserable face again."

Nico squeezed him. "Patience, little butterfly. He might surprise you, and if not, I'm here for you. Always. But why would you ask him about the souls in Hell?"

"When he disappears like he did in the courtyard, he teleports back to the Realm of the Damned."

Nico's brows raised. "He goes back down there?"

"It's a good place to hide and not be bothered. None of us would willingly follow." Onyx would hate the emptiness more than he hated everyone being stuck there. Did Luc?

"Can't argue with that." Nico kissed down Onyx's neck, banishing his melancholy.

Onyx arched his spine. "That's more like it. Tell me to shut up about Luc more often. I need your mouth on me instead."

Nico reached under Onyx's shirt and tugged on his nipple piercing. "Tell me what else you need."

"Please don't!" a panicked voice groaned.

Onyx and Nico spun around. Ash, Dante, Harper, and Ollie stood in the open double doorway.

"Excuse me!" Onyx sputtered. What the hell were they doing here?

Harper's cheeks went bright red. "Sorry. Ash said he called."

"He called, and I ignored him."

Nico chuckled softly in Onyx's ear.

"We brought food." Ash held up several covered containers as if that meant anything.

Onyx set his fiery glare on him. "I didn't ask for food. Nico is about to eat *me*, so unless this is turning into an orgy, we're good. You can all leave."

Harper went even redder, and Ollie coughed. Ash and Dante remained unfazed.

You didn't hang around someone for three and a half thousand years without ending up a some of the same sex parties. Though Onyx would be the first to admit it had been forever since the three of them had been in a situation like that.

"Whatever you're thinking, I want details later," Nico muttered.

Oh, that wouldn't be a problem. Onyx couldn't wait to show Nico off in the right setting and have a little group fun. Not with these fools, but perhaps at the right club.

The bond told him Nico's feelings were similar.

"We've hardly seen you all week," Dante complained, coming closer rather than leaving.

The audacity!

"Can't you take a hint?" Onyx hissed.

Nico pinched him.

"What?"

Nico cocked a brow. "We talked about this."

Onyx sighed dramatically, dropping his head back. They had, and Onyx appreciated everyone coming to see him, even if the timing could have been better.

Ash waltzed over to the sitting area and made himself at home on a couch to unpack the food.

Harper perched next to him, turning to Onyx. "We can go if we're intruding."

Damn, the little witch was too sweet.

"You're never intruding. I like you."

Harper beamed, and Onyx went all fuzzy inside. Nico too. Seemed everyone had a soft spot for Harper.

Ollie joined Harper, squeezing onto the couch, and Dante gazed out the window. "Lovely view."

"*Pssh*. Whatever." It was nothing compared to Dante's view from the clifftop.

Dante turned around, sounding offended. "I'm serious."

Damn it, he was being kind. Of course, he was. This was Dante. Onyx swallowed his next remark, muttering, "Thanks," instead.

Dante perched on an ottoman and accepted a cupcake from Ash.

Looking around at them all in his sacred space was surprisingly soothing.

Nico had suggested to Onyx that, if he was willing to give Lucifer a chance, maybe his relationships with Ash and Dante could improve too. Onyx had agreed. They deserved the chance more than Luc.

Onyx prayed he wasn't opening himself up to more hurt, but in this moment, he could believe Ash and Dante were here because they wanted to be. Not because Onyx had forced himself on them, and no one appeared at risk of asking him a favor.

Ash cleared his throat. "I'm sorry for accusing you of

betraying us." He focused on a sandwich rather than Onyx, but sounded genuine as he picked at the crust. "You've never done anything to hurt me or Dante. You'd never choose your brother over us, and you always wanted the four of us to get along. I shouldn't have forgotten that."

"Yeah, well, it was naïve wanting the four of us to stick together all those years ago, and no better hoping anything will come of Luc's apology now. I'm surprised you're not telling me off for giving him a chance."

Ash scowled. "I'm trying to say I'm sorry, not tell you off. I was out of line before. You can give Luc a chance to change if you want. I'm not telling you what to do. You're allowed to do your own thing, and I can do mine without thinking what you're doing is wrong or taking it personally."

Well, damn. "Yeah, okay, I get that. I don't think you're wrong for wanting him out of your life." Onyx's attention strayed to Harper and Ollie.

Onyx wasn't sure if he'd ever move past Luc hurting the little mates. Any reconciliation with Luc could take centuries, and Luc would have to prove himself in ways Onyx feared might not be possible. Though it could all be a moot point if Onyx never heard from the bastard again.

"How do you feel about me not telling Luc to get the hell out of my life?" he asked the mates.

Ollie and Harper shared a look. "It's not about us," Harper said.

Onyx shifted. "It kind of is. What he did to each of you was despicable, and I'm not forgiving him for it. That's not my place. I don't want my desire to hear him out to come between us. You're more important to me. Being unable to let Luc go despite hating him isn't the same as wanting you two in my life."

"Good, because we want you in our lives, too." Ollie smiled softly, and Harper nodded. "Your history with Luc goes so far back that I can't even imagine it. That's not all going to disappear. Wanting to hear Luc out doesn't mean you're okay with what he did. I get that. You'd never condone his actions, and what you decide to do about your brother isn't going to affect your friendship with me."

"Me either," Harper agreed.

Onyx's heart almost gave out at the sheer compassion. "You two are better than any of us deserve."

"Hardly." Harper rolled his immaculately done-up eyes.

"No, you are. And you deserve my love. Unlike my brother."

"Luc doesn't deserve your love," Ash rumbled, setting his sandwich aside. "But he loved you, Onyx. I can't speak to any of his feelings now, but back in the Eternal Realm, I know he did. You don't really think he loved me more than you, do you?"

Onyx's pulse skipped. "What?"

Ash shrugged. "Isn't that why you can't stand me?"

Onyx stiffened in Nico's arms. "That's what you think?"

"You've said it before, and you always seemed jealous of me and Luc."

Onyx squirmed. "I was. His love for you was different. He chose you. But that's not what bothered me." Fuck this was hard. Onyx reached for Nico's reassuring presence and found nothing but encouragement radiating off his mate. "It wasn't all about Luc. I wanted you to like me, too."

"I do like you," Ash said automatically.

"Do you? If I wasn't Luc's little tag-along brother, would you have cared? We wouldn't have been friends at all."

Ash turned to Harper, a pleading glint in his eye, and Harper squeezed his knee. Ash swiped a hand over his face. "I disagree. I'll always have been Luc's friend first—we were born the same year, and I can't help that you're a few centuries younger—but I want you around. You don't see Luc here, do you? I came to *your* house to see *you*."

Onyx's insides cramped. "You did, and I appreciate that. Especially since it's the first time you've sought me out without an agenda in who knows how long. I want you and Dante to see me as something other than Luc's brother."

"We do," Dante said softly. "But I gather you never felt it. Maybe we did a poor job of showing it. You're one of us, Onyx. You always have been."

Was he? Why had he always seemed to be on the outskirts?

"I never wanted to come to Earth," Onyx admitted in a rush, covering his face with his hands.

Nico rubbed his back, making the stunned silence almost bearable.

"You didn't want to fall?" Harper asked.

If it were anyone else, Onyx might have stayed hidden. He lowered his hands. "I didn't have a choice. I couldn't let these assholes leave me behind."

Ash and Dante were wide-eyed. Ash shook his head. "Fuck, Onyx. I'm sorry. I can't imagine leaving you behind now, but back then, we were so set on our mates, you're right. We wouldn't have stayed for anything."

Dante placed his uneaten cupcake on the table. "We're glad you followed."

"More than glad," Ash agreed. "I'd have hated losing you. You begged us not to go. I'm sorry."

Onyx sniffed, and Harper handed him a tissue. "It's never felt like you wanted me here."

Dante made a pained sound. "I'm sorry, Onyx. We do want you here. We should have done better to remind you."

"I haven't made it easy for you," Onyx admitted. "But when you don't even think to tell me something big—like a witch finding out about us—it's hard to believe I'm part of the group."

"Yet every time we try to include you, you push us away. There's no excuse for not keeping you in the loop, and I get why that hurts so much, especially now, but you haven't acted like you wanted us around in a long time." Dante retrieved the cupcake and took a bite. "It seemed better to give you space."

"Fair." Onyx couldn't deny it. It was too petty to admit he'd been testing them. Some of the responsibility for their distance undoubtedly lay at his feet.

Yet, Nico had seen through him. He'd read Onyx's behavior like a book and responded to the needy desires driving him. He'd also encouraged Onyx to communicate. To ask directly when he needed support rather than lash out.

Nico would always be there for him. Maybe his brothers would too. Trust between Onyx, Ash, and Dante could be rebuilt.

"You're our brother, and it has nothing to do with Lucifer," Ash promised.

Onyx bit his lip. "I believe you, and I'll try to be more upfront."

Ash seemed pleased, leaning back and relaxing. "Good. So will we, and while we're on the subject, stop acting like I'm dumb."

Onyx's gut twisted. "Sorry. I didn't think you cared about my jokes."

"For the most part, I don't, but enough is enough. You know, I'd never tolerate your insults if I didn't love you. You should have figured that out."

Onyx choked on a laugh. "Seems I'm not as clever as I thought. I'm sorry. I'll stop. But you're still overly muscled, and if you're going to show off, I'm going to call you out."

Ash flexed. "Damn right about that."

They all laughed.

Harper threw an arm around Ash. "I like when you show off."

"I know you do, sweet." He planted a kiss on Harper's cheek.

"You guys are too cute." Ollie stood and repositioned on Dante's lap.

"Like you aren't," Harper taunted.

Onyx spun in Nico's lap and buried his face in Nico's neck. All of them together, mated, was too much. He never imagined this was possible. He had almost everyone he'd ever needed.

Nico cradled him close, soft, loving tingles wafting off him in soothing waves.

Onyx wasn't afraid to be this happy, this hopeful, and that was a first. Hope had always hurt. Not anymore.

"Are you ready to join the family?" he asked Nico.

"I'm already in it, little butterfly. There's no one I'd rather be surrounded by for the rest of time." He kissed Onyx's nose, brown eyes shining with affection.

"Aww, you two are cuter than me and Ash," Harper cooed.

"They so are," Ollie agreed.

Onyx reluctantly peeked from Nico's protective hold. "Don't be fooled, little mates. I'm still trouble."

"I'm counting on it." Harper grinned like he couldn't wait to see what trouble Onyx would bring into his life. He grabbed a container and held it out. "Sandwich?"

Onyx took one for Nico, then himself. "Not bad for a first family meal, but let me organize the next one."

Ash cleared his throat. "I've already claimed our next meal. With more time, I can cook a lot better than this."

"All right." Onyx waved him off. "But I've got the one after. Dante isn't allowed to plan family meals, or we'll be stuck eating candy. Ollie, you're in charge after me."

Dante pulled his mate close. "Ollie is more than aware he's the one in charge."

Ollie gave Dante a sly smile.

"No surprise there." Onyx caught Nico's eye. "Can you believe they thought Ollie's human friend Dex was my mate? He couldn't handle me."

"No, that's my job." Pleasure sparked down the bond.

Ollie frowned. "You and Dex wouldn't be compatible, but I really wish he had a mate. Maybe one of the other demons will claim him."

"Maybe." Onyx was curious if they'd all start pairing off. It hadn't seemed any more likely that demons would find their mates just because some of them had, but there was an interconnectedness to all this that he'd never anticipated.

Onyx hoped Dex found a mate for Ollie's sake. It would be hard for Ollie to lose his friend. Ollie deserved the world as much as any of them.

As they ate, Onyx remembered the letter he'd brought inside. There had been no postmark, and Scott usually texted. Curious, he sent the envelope flying over with a flick of his wrist.

"Who's that from?" Nico asked.

"Who knows?" Onyx ripped it open and unfolded the paper.

Luc's familiar script greeted him.

I'M HERE *for you if you'll have me, brother, but if you need time, I understand.*

THE NOTE WAS SIGNED with a stylized L and a phone number. Luc hadn't walked away.

"He really wants to try, doesn't he?"

"I think so," Nico said. "Putting the ball in your court makes me think he's genuine. If he had an agenda, he'd be pushing it, whatever it was."

"Perhaps. This also leaves the work to me. I have to risk reaching out."

"Isn't this him reaching out?"

Onyx refolded the note and set it aside. "I suppose." He still couldn't take anything Luc did at face value. He had hope, but no less doubt than ever.

Nico threaded their fingers together. "Take your time deciding what you want to do. There's no rush. No one's life is at risk. You don't have to give him anything you don't want to."

Onyx chose to lean into hope. "Maybe I don't have to, but I want everything. I want you, all three of my brothers mated, and everything between us healed. I've never let myself want so much. Finding you opened me up, and I can't close back off."

"Then don't. I'll be here for you every step of the way, guarding your heart and taking excellent care of you. There's nothing we can't face together."

Onyx closed his eyes and let himself imagine that future.

Nico was right. Together, there were no limits but the ones they set themselves.

EPILOGUE
NICO

Ten years later.

"Are you ready?" Nico called.

"Yes. Keep your panties on," Onyx shouted from the bathroom.

"I'm not the one wearing panties."

"Neither am I, but that can be arranged." Onyx threw open the bathroom door and leaned against the doorframe. "How do I look?"

Nico shamelessly raked his gaze over his mate. "Good enough to fuck."

Onyx stuck out his bottom lip in a pout. "But I'm always good enough to fuck."

Nico shook his head. "You look smoking hot, little butterfly. You'll turn heads."

Onyx wore skin-tight black leather shorts that hid his tail tattoo and—though Nico couldn't see from this angle—had a zip up the back. The rest of his outfit consisted of a leather collar and ring-shaped nipple piercings connected by a gold chain.

Onyx toyed with the chain between two fingers, metal glinting. "You look hot too, but you could lose the jacket."

Nico ran a hand through his hair. "I'll check it once we get there. We don't all have immortal fire to keep us warm."

"True. Shall I wear my faux fur to blend in on the street?"

"Floor length fur will never blend in, my love."

Onyx pushed off the wall and sauntered over to the clothing rack. "It's as blended in as I feel like being tonight."

The loft had undergone a few renovations since Nico had moved in. Their main wardrobes were arranged on racks like their very own boutique, and Nico had a substantial gaming set-up next to the library. Onyx had also installed a kitchen for him, though they ate out enough that Nico was saved from cooking most of the time.

Lucia still kept his freezer stocked. She visited The Herb Emporium regularly, always bringing him something, and he had dinner with her family once a month. It was unreal to see Emilio's kids in high school.

"Do you think Harper and Ash will come with us one of these nights?" Onyx asked as he slid on his faux fur coat.

"Harper's been asking you about the club, too?" Nico had an in-depth conversation with him about kink clubs the other day. "He's turned into one of the most outgoing people I've ever known. I don't doubt he'll bring Ash along at some point."

Onyx sighed wistfully, like a proud parent. "Our sweet little witch is all grown up. He'll try anything once, just like me."

Nico laughed. "I haven't found anything you're satisfied with trying only once."

"Can you blame me? Anything we do together is worth repeating." Onyx fluffed his coat. "I'm looking forward to tonight."

Nico and Onyx were making an appearance at the exclusive kink club that Onyx had belonged to for years. It was a human-run establishment, so no horns, biting, or other magical elements were allowed, but holding back around unsuspecting humans—even as their bond heightened every beautiful sensation—was its own kind of fun. And the second round, when the two of them got home, was never short of explosive.

There were few beings Onyx was intimate with in full demon form. On those rare instances when he let completely loose, Nico couldn't have been more full of love or felt closer to his mate.

Watching his demon open up over the years was a continuous joy. Onyx was less guarded these days and revealed his demonic features in non-sexual situations often, no longer afraid to show others his emotions or be honest when he was emotionally attached to someone.

Nico tipped Onyx's chin and planted a kiss on his lips. Onyx opened for him, and Nico slid his tongue inside, his hand coming to rest over the leather collar. Nico squeezed Onyx's throat, gentle but firm. His mate purred, and the bond between them vibrated like a violin string.

"Careful, or we won't make it out the door," Onyx warned.

Nico brushed Onyx's lower lip with his thumb. "Rowan and his mate will be sad they missed you."

The vampire was all loved up in a way that had shocked Nico at first. Even Onyx hadn't been able to resist liking Rowan after seeing his dedication to his chosen mate.

"We can't leave them as the only magical beings at the club," Onyx agreed. "I suppose I can wait until we get there."

"*Mmm.* That's my good boy." Nico swatted Onyx's ass, the sound muffled by the fur coat.

"Am I a good enough boy that you'll finally let me commission a portrait of you?"

Nico bit back a laugh. Leave it to his demon to try and sneak that into the conversation. "Depends. Is Fiona the artist you have in mind?"

Onyx pursed his lips. "Who else? All I want is a tasteful boudoir painting of my mate. Why is that so much to ask?"

"As I've said, you can have as many as you like, if you promise not to show them to Scott."

"But Scott appreciates art."

"He can appreciate art, not my ass."

"Why not? We're off to a club where you've done all manner of lewd things to me and others. With an audience. If you're lucky, tonight I'll let you finger me until I'm sobbing in a room full of people. How can you be so hung up on a little painting?"

Nico's face heated, and pleasure tightened in his core. "Let me? I'll do what I please with you. Think you can take that much teasing without your tail popping out?"

"If you do it right. I trust you to only give me what I can handle and save the rest until we're home."

"Fuck. I'll always do you right, little butterfly."

"That's the mate I love. Now, let's go. We'll discuss the painting later."

Would they ever. Nico loved how riled up Onyx got when he refused, but he had every intention of giving in soon, whether Scott checked out his painted ass or not.

They headed out of the loft and onto the street to wait for their ride. Nico pulled out his phone, and a text from Ash popped up.

Nico read it and turned to Onyx. "You're still free for the Center's community night next week, right?"

"Yes," Onyx hummed, bounding on the balls of his feet. "I already told Ash. He's so funny, fretting like either of us would miss it."

Nico bit back a grin and replied to Ash.

He'd become close with the grouchy demon through the process of helping Ash and Harper open the Center, a place for witches escaping abusive covens. Nico and Ash saw eye to eye on most things, and Nico was proud of what Ash and Harper had accomplished together.

He ran The Herb Emporium as always, though he had a full-time shop assistant these days, which freed him to volunteer at the Center. Rowan had gotten involved too, behind the scenes, of course, and Nico was busy liaising between the Valeros and the official staff.

All in all, the magic world had adjusted to the demons' return to Earth well enough. It hadn't been without some serious hiccups, but ten years on, things were starting to feel settled. Looking back, it hadn't gone as badly as Nico had initially feared.

Even Lucifer had surprised Nico. He'd always hoped the Devil would do right by Onyx, and it was a work in progress, but Luc had accomplished more than anyone had expected that day in the courtyard.

"You got the invite for lunch tomorrow, right? To find out about Ollie's new job," Onyx asked as the car pulled up.

Nico held the door open. "Yeah, Dante texted me the details."

"Good. I don't know why Ollie's worried. He's got the position in the bag. That man is a natural teacher. Knows when to give praise and when to give direction."

"You're about to crack a Dante joke, aren't you?"

Onyx swatted him. "I'd never. Dante is too soft and gooey to tease about his sex life. He's turned into a candy bar, and might melt if he gets embarrassed."

Nico cracked up.

"Ash, on the other hand, I can roast all day."

"You can, but be careful. I almost died of embarrassment when he threw it right back at you yesterday."

"You can take it. You're my mate. Ash can't out-snark me."

"That he can't." Nico took Onyx's hand as the car pulled into traffic.

Onyx and Ash's teasing was nothing but good-natured these days. They'd both done the work to close the gap between them, and Dante never failed to keep Onyx updated on everything, to the point that it had turned into a joke.

They were a family. Not perfect, bound to piss each other off—Ash and Onyx still got under each other's skins—but love sat at the center of everything, holding them together, and everyone was committed to putting things right if they got off track.

Nico couldn't have asked for more. He loved his mate to bits. Onyx was his rock, his confidant, someone he could rely on, no matter what, and their family was one that would stand the test of time.

The End

Looking for more Onyx and Nico? Don't miss *Eat Me*, a steamy bonus epilogue available for free to my newsletter subscribers. Join now and see newly mated Onyx and Nico join Ash and the others for family dinner before Nico whisks Onyx away for something private.

Will Lucifer find his happily ever after? Does he deserve one? Find out in *Lovers of the Damned Book Four: Devil's Mate*.

WONDERING ABOUT ROWAN'S MATE? *His Eternal Temptation: Bound in Blood Book One* is a chosen mates romance starting an all-new series about the Valero Coven.

WANT TO KEEP IN TOUCH? You can find me on Patreon for monthly bonus ficlets, weekly WIP chapters, and behind-the-scenes updates. Patreon is where you'll find even more of Onyx and Nico, as well as the other *Lovers of the Damned* couples. You can also find me in my reader group on Facebook, Colette Rivera's Coven.

THANK YOU FOR READING DEMON'S DESIRE

I hoped you enjoyed Onyx and Nico's story.

Reviews are invaluable to authors. Please consider leaving a review for *Demon's Desire* on your favorite review site or the site where you purchased this book to help others find magical books they'll love.

DEVIL'S MATE

Love's price is redemption.

Happiness isn't for Lucifer. He chose to be the villain and no matter his initial motivation, he embraced being bad. Now he can't even make amends. Luc will never have the life he fell to Earth to find.

Luc doesn't deserve his fated mate, and yet there he is, strolling into a bar.

Dex Colt's life has been on hold for years. It's time to move on, sell the home that feels like a tomb, and take back his life. Starting with the gorgeous guy asking to join him for a drink. Usually, Dex would say no to more than a quickie, but there's something special about Luc, and there's no harm in agreeing to a date. Right?

As it turns out, harm doesn't begin to cover it. Dex's best friend drops the bombshell that magic exists, and reveals that Luc isn't the sweet man he appears to be. He's the Devil.

It's no surprise Lucifer's mate is the best friend of the man he once tried to kill. A mate who hates him is the universe's retribution. But Dex inspires a better world. If Luc can mend all that he's destroyed, he could give Dex a gift even greater than his love. And if Dex will have him, together they might truly have it all.

Order Now

ACKNOWLEDGMENTS

Thank you so much for reading Nico and Onyx's story. This was one of my favorite books to write. Onyx, my little bratty demon who just needs a hug, has been on my mind for ages. Thank you to everyone who's been looking forward to his happily ever after.

Thank you to Laura from Hummingbird Editing for working on this book with me! It was so great to work with you at last. You have such keen insights and attention to detail, and I loved chatting about the story with you as we went.

Thank you to CJ Editing for proofreading and being an invaluable extra set of eyes. Your enthusiasm for this series has been amazing.

As always, thank you to TK for coming on these magical journeys with me, reading my books, and listening to me talk about demons and vampires while we're out on a Friday night.

ABOUT THE AUTHOR

Colette (she/they) is an author of queer paranormal romance novels living in New Zealand. Colette loves to write couples who take care of each other and show their soft sides in love, even when they're prickly in other facets of their lives. Sugar, spice, and magic are key ingredients in all of Colette's books.

Colette can be found on Instagram @colette_rivera and on Facebook under Colette Rivera Author. Colette can also be found on their website coletterivera.com where you can sign up to their newsletter for bonus epilogues and updates.

Lovers of The Damned

Demon's Mate

Demon's Heart

Demon's Desire

Devil's Mate

Moonlight Falls

The Fall of Elijah Gray

The Seduction of James Gray

The Cursed Sebastian Storm

The Heart of Moonlight Falls

Love & Magic

Give a Witch a Chance

Keep Your Witches Close

One Wicked Night

Witch Boyfriend Wanted

www.ingramcontent.com/pod-product-compliance
Lightning Source LLC
Chambersburg PA
CBHW031208310726

48969CB00001B/268